Praise for John Whittier Treat's

First Consonants

"A flame of rage burns at the core of Brian Moriarty, ignited
by a traumatic birth and fueled by a lifetime of debasement
and abuse because Brian stutters. The text of John Whittier
Treat's *First Consonants* is incendiary, placing the reader in the
furious heart of Brian's world. As we may decry his actions, we
cannot help but want a balm for him, a cool soothing of his
implacable ire, lest it consume and reduce him to ash."

—Terry Wolverton, the author of *Stealing Angel*

"A compelling, at times relentless novel that gives the term
antihero a brand-new spin."

—Felice Picano, author of *Like People in History*, *The Book of
Lies*, and *Onyx*

"Brian Moriarty intuits truths about his life he never expresses
in words, nor even in thoughts. *First Consonants* tells the story
of his long journey to confront those truths. Brian traverses
landscapes, internal and external, and grapples with the reality of violence, the complexity of family, the insidiousness of

faith. Thrumming beneath it all, John Whittier Treat's unrelentingly poignant prose grounds and belies the central theme: the aching unrealized potential of language."

—Ana Maria Spagna, author of *Uplake: Restless Essays of Coming and Going*

"*First Consonants* touches on the origins of violence, of love, and what it means to find one's way through the maze that is the world. Here is a story that is engrossing, vulnerable and wise in a way that few books are these days."

—Jim Krusoe, author of *The Sleep Garden*

"This remarkable and moving novel of a boy and a man struggling to overcome the violence the world inflicts on him due to his stutter made me rethink so many of my assumptions about language and the body. Written in ludic, kinetic prose, at turns beautiful and harrowing, it has an expansiveness and ethical import that is rare."

—Alistair McCartney, author of *The Disintegrations*

FIRST
CONSONANTS

John Whittier Treat

 JADED IBIS PRESS

Published by Jaded Ibis Press
A nonprofit, feminist press publishing socially engaged literature
jadedibispress.com

Cover design by Crystal J. Hairston

Trade Paperback ISBN: 978-1-938841-86-6
eBook ISBN: 978-1-938841-85-9

First Edition: 2022. Printed and bound in the United States of America.

"Unlike most stuttering, mine began violently."

—Frederick Pemberton Murray, *A Stutterer's Story*

FIRST
CONSONANTS

Chapter One

Brian's problem became the whole town's one rainy morning.

He was a little late. His wet rubber boots made squishy sounds as he walked down the wide hallway of the new cinder-block school building. The green paint on the walls still smelled fresh. The too-bright fluorescent lights hummed in unison. His teacher, Mrs. Roland, was standing by the shiny red metal door to assist children as they arrived at her first-grade classroom. She peered down at Brian when he stopped in front of her. He didn't want to ask for help, but he had to.

"Can you help me take off . . . my. . . *buh-buh*-boots?"

Later, Brian would overhear Mrs. Roland explain to the principal that she had giggled at Brian half out of embarrassment for him and half because boys his age are so cute when they stutter.

"Your *boots*, Brian?"

He did not let his eyes meet hers. He focused on the small puddle gathering between his boots.

"I'll help you with your *boots*, young man," she said.

"Here, sit down on the bench. Now say *boots* for me."

Brian did not sit. Nor did he say anything. Instead, he looked up at Mrs. Roland with a face crossed with hurt. He wailed while stamping his wet rubber boots up and down. Soon he was flailing his arms within his raincoat, warding off his teacher lest she dare bend over to help him. He resolved that the grown-up who had betrayed him with her laughter would not touch him. His wailing grew louder and attracted attention in the school hallway. He knew he had done something wrong by stuttering. Adults always chuckled. He had no choice but to make his slipup worse by shrieking. No one would laugh at that.

Mrs. Roland insisted Brian to stop. He ignored her. She took a step back, as if she foresaw he'd need more room for his performance. Classmates poked their heads into the hallway to see what was going on. Two boys, not his friends, snickered. The girl with the ribbons in her yellow hair started crying. Another teacher, the old, ugly one, popped out of her own classroom and scowled. Not at him, but at Mrs. Roland.

Mrs. Roland, thus cued, insisted he stop again, but she betrayed her own resolve by retreating another step. Brian did not stop. In fact, he was inspired. He was going to use this chance to get back at everyone. He would ruin their morning. He screeched louder. For a long while, he'd been mad at stuttering and madder at others for not stuttering. Now they'd all know it. He did not stammer when he yowled. He'd show them how good he could be at yowling. He kicked the other kids' rain boots, lined up neatly against the wall under their coats, in every direction. Some bounced against the opposite side of the hallway. A boot here, a pair of galoshes there. He was enjoying this but didn't let it show. He kicked more footwear, including Mrs. Roland's fancy ones with the fake red roses on them and her umbrella, too. They ricocheted and landed helter-skelter far from where they belonged. Some kid's little rainbow-striped umbrella, propelled by his kick, struck a third teacher's shin and made her cry out. Brian knew he was in trouble. He'd pay for it later. But for the time being, he was in charge of everything in this hallway. He meant to get the most out of the moment.

He wondered what to attack next. The old teacher, the one with her eyeglasses on a chain around her neck, stepped forward. Unfazed by any six-year-old, she grabbed Brian by the collar and yanked him toward her, hurting his shoulder. He stopped yelling but left his mouth open, a signal that he was ready to resume at any second. She clutched his jacket tighter and barked orders to the other teachers in the hallway to get their pupils back in their seats.

Order restored, the teacher left the scene with Brian in her fast grip and led him to the principal's office. A lady behind the counter made a call to his mother. "Please come and take your son home," she said. While waiting, Brian heard Mrs. Roland explain to the principal what had happened, an account he had to listen to again once his mother arrived. They instructed Mrs. Moriarty that her son could return to school in the afternoon, after lunch, if he had sufficiently calmed down. He did not calm down. His mother confined him to his room for the rest of the day, a square room with a square window looking out onto a square backyard. He sat up straight on the edge of his bed's calico spread, legs swinging in defiance, now with no audience to appreciate his performance. His legs soon got tired, but stopping would have been an admission of defeat.

He had all afternoon to think about what he had done. If he had limped down the school hallway, he could have explained to Mrs. Roland that he was out playing ball the day before. If his arm had been in a cast, he could have told her about falling off his bike. If he had a fever, he could have asked to be sent to the school nurse. But when you stutter, Brian thought, you can't tell anyone anything for sure. You don't know if you'll succeed or not. There's no excuse for it, anyway. You've always stuttered and there's no new accident or cold going around to blame. You might think you know why you stutter. Brian had an idea or two. But explanations don't help. You're encouraged to talk, to say what's on your mind. They laugh when you can't. All that's left, Brian realized, are your two arms and legs: Limbs powered by a body's muscles actually working in coordination. Arms and legs, like swords, sliced through the air and made boots and umbrellas fly against school corridor walls. They came down with a clatter that a mouth, willfully muted, chose not to enlighten with words.

He never told his mother what had set him off, in part because he wasn't sure. It wasn't just Mrs. Roland's titter. There was more to it than that, but just what he didn't know.

Mostly he didn't talk to his mother because he worried he'd stutter more and get angry all over again. Nor did she ask for his side of the story. It was 1953, and problems went away by not talking about them. Brian was excellent at not talking. For that, he and his mother were grateful.

*

In Brian's earliest memory, he was sitting in a high chair in his family's kitchen and banging a teething ring against the tray in front of him. He watched his father, in one of the two identical charcoal gray suits he wore to the plant, rush out of the house through the back door. The house door slammed; the car door followed with another slam a few seconds later. Brian's attention turned to the now empty kitchen. The walls were pale beige, the cabinets off-white. The floor was checkered with black and gray linoleum tiles. Over the roar of a vacuum cleaner running in another room, he heard a radio on the counter. It was tuned to a radio station on which a deep-voiced man was talking about something. Brian did not understand words yet.

An alternative first memory competed with this one. It came to him in dreams, sometimes waking ones. Inside Brian Horace Moriarty's mother there was no day or night. He would never learn the words to describe that place. Language had failed him all his life. He recalled bits and pieces of this intrauterine time when feeling exceptionally dumb in a garrulous world.

In this dream, his parents made a wish when they

conceived him. They prayed he'd be whole. They didn't know their son was already more than heart, spine, bones, skin and blood. He had those things, all the accessories he would need for any reasonable task in life: Powerful arms, stout legs, a worthy penis, an upright head. He was a perfect growing swell in a woman's body, the early start to a man who would wonder about this dream. Ripped out of his mother's body and dragged into desiccated air, Brian would spend the total of his allotted years trying to recapture its intensity and exchange it for eloquence. He was lifted with forceps into the sterile light of a delivery room. His soft skull would bear the tool's mark forever. For now, he floated in his mother and grew aware of another with him. He looked a lot like Brian. The same arms, legs, penis and head. But when Brian touched his own face, there was no opening where the other fetus had one. He *didn't* have all the things he'd need. Soon he realized this missing part was a mouth, and its absence would leave him bereft of a tongue as well. He and the other fetus exchanged no grunts or groans. Only once, when Brian was pulled out of their mother, did his fraternal fetus make room for him. He shrank as best he could against the wall of the womb before he lunged without warning and struck Brian hard in the face. He made a bloody slit where there was no mouth but should have been; and Brian knew violence, one moment before brutal forceps would teach it to him a second time. He would recall, or think he recalled, that his brother's blow instructed this: *I am the one who gave you this mouth, out of which one day you might speak words that redeem you, or the world.*

Chapter Two

The Moriarty family lived twenty miles east of Seattle in Tummus. Their town sat up against the foothills of the Cascades, mountains high enough to halt the clouds drifting in from the Pacific that made it rain in sheets. On the western slope, dense green forests; on the eastern, not much. The Sammamish Plateau ran along the northern edge, and more mountains lay to the south. No matter where you stood in town, mountains seemed close. When he was very young, Brian thought all towns had mountains surrounding them. At night he'd hear bobcats catching raccoons. On Sunday car rides after mass at St. Joseph's, he saw telephone poles that stood askew and a town dump spilling over into adjacent woods. But streets in Tummus were straight and laid out at right angles. The newer parts of town were small ranch homes built by Boeing employees for their young families. Eisenhower was president, Khrushchev was first party secretary, and the race was on. Boeing was hiring men by the thousands.

The Moriartys lived in one of these ranch homes. Brian's father had built it with the help of his brothers, borrowing plans from his boss at work. A one-story, one-car garage, one-bathroom ranch, just like everyone else's. It was boom times in postwar America, and everyone was building something. In time, when television arrived, homeowners mounted the same roof antenna. Every house on his street had the same picture window looking out onto the same lawn looking in at the same furniture. A few, such as the Moriartys, had basketball hoops in their driveways. Some had three bedrooms. The Moriarty family had two. Some men built backyard decks. Some, including Art Moriarty, did not. Instead, the Moriartys had a concrete birdbath with white bird droppings on its rim year-round. Otherwise, the Moriarty home resembled every family's, distinguished by variations in the pale earth tones of house paint chosen from a palette meant to contrast only slightly with the Northwest's leaden winter skies.

Inside the house, however, Brian thought his family was special. His mother, Eve, was beautiful and his father, Art, handsome. She had a fair Irish complexion and a good figure. Eve wore dresses that smelled like flowers. Art had broad shoulders, large hands and a firm chin. His father's scent reminded him of the men's department at Sears, where he and his mother would go buy the khakis and short-sleeved shirts Art wore on weekends. Brian was special because he was their son.

On the fireplace mantel stood framed black-and-white

pictures of Art and Eve's marriage. They were standing in front of St. Joseph's church. There were no grandparents in the picture. They had died already. Some people in the photographs were men in uniforms. His father explained to him the war had just ended. Dispatched to places flat and dry, he said, now they were back where everything was green, and tall mountains encircled them.

In this town everyone had to fit in. There was a hole in the Moriarty family to fill, and Brian filled it. His mother's pregnancy had been long, and he later learned there had been "complications," but after baby Brian arrived, he was all anyone could have wished for. The mood in the Moriarty household changed as neighborhood children chatted away with new words each day. New words came slowly to Brian. Early on he'd managed the expected *ma-ma* and *dah-dah*, and for a time a handful of other pseudo words: *Jeez* for *cheese*, *guu* for *good*, *mee* for *milk*. So gradually that no one noticed right away, he spoke less rather than more. Art and Eve didn't mind at first. Neither said anything to him. He heard them tell neighbors their child was a quiet one, as his father had been. A sign of manly reserve. He would grow up to be good with his hands, they said, like his uncles in the construction trades. No need to be a chatterbox, other mothers reassured Eve as Brian listened to everything they said from his bedroom. It took time for his parents to understand what he had sensed since infancy: What was lodged inside him, what stuck in his mouth like glue, were words he did not say and no one heard. There were words he wanted to say, but all he could handle were the most minimal and necessary. *Wah-wah. Wee-wee. Poo-poo.*

*

Dr. Stevens wore a large headband around his head with a mirror attached to it. The rest of his face was dry and pasty. Brian wasn't sure if the mirror looked funny or threatening. He sat on the edge of the examining table, wondering what was about to happen.

His stutter deteriorated from occasional to constant when he was five, at the same time his parents brought home another child, a younger brother, Bruce Aaron Moriarty, soon nicknamed Bam. They told him his baby brother looked just like he had at that age, minus the small gash the obstetrician's forceps had left on Brian's scalp. He did. The same little snout of a nose, the same big ears. The same blue eyes, although one of Bam's seemed askew. No Moriarty was going to perfect, Brian thought with relief. They could have been twins.

Peering over the top of the crib on tiptoe, Brian would steal glimpses of the new baby and study its gurgling mouth: No words, just like him. Brian's near-total stammer meant he was trying less to communicate. He heard his parents say it might be the presence, the competition, of a new baby that was making his speech less fluent. A phase, nothing to worry about. Whatever problems Brian might have, the happy cooing of a second Moriarty son trumped them. But a year later, someone, perhaps the school principal, worried enough about the tantrum he'd thrown outside Mrs. Roland's classroom to suggest professional help. He eavesdropped on his parents talking in the kitchen about this, too. "It's a process of elimination," Eve said to Art. "We've thought about every reason he might have trouble talking: Shyness, confusion, maybe a little retardation. Now we're down to this."

A week later, his mother took him to the family physician after school, leaving baby Bam in the care of a neighbor. Dr. Stevens ran his small practice out of a two-room addition he had added to his home in their neighborhood. On the town's newly poured sidewalk, Brian and his mother walked to the appointment.

"Hello, Brian," said Dr. Stevens.

Brian had been to Dr. Stevens many times when he was sick. He didn't feel sick today, and didn't know why his mother had brought him. "*Huh-huh*-hello," he mumbled. *H*s weren't as hard for him as *b*s, but they almost were. It was rare for him to try.

"Scoot up here on the edge of the examining table, would you, young man?"

The doctor asked him to open and close his mouth. His mother sat in a chair in one corner of the room, her knees pressed tight together, hands holding her purse in her lap. She played with its latch.

"Stay open now," the doctor instructed. Brian didn't like the way the doctor's fat, pink hands smelled. He used a small flashlight to look down his throat. I wonder what he'll see in there, Brian thought. The doctor must know that words, like pieces of food, get stuck in your throat and won't come out no matter what. There must be thousands of trapped words down there, Brian guessed, and the doctor could see them with the flashlight. The doctor would somehow get them out. He hoped he wouldn't get a shot, just pills or some liquid to swallow with a spoon. His open jaw hurt.

"Brian, tell me about your stammer. Has it happened to you before? Often?"

"*Stah-stah*-stammer?" he asked.

"When you have trouble saying a word. Like now."

His cheeks grew hot. Brian didn't want to say the wrong thing. He didn't want to stutter in front of his mother and embarrass her or be sent away by the doctor because of it. Or have to get a shot.

Brian thought harder. Before his voice tried to form them, he saw some words in the alphabet letters he was learning but couldn't read yet. Words paraded before him, visible yet unintelligible and unpronounceable. If he could see them, they were already impossible to say. Inside his head, syllables cracked open and exploded into sharp pieces that tumbled down his throat into his stomach. His tongue became this worm that filled his mouth. Words shattered, and the shards clogged up inside him. It might be easier if he were allowed to whisper, to move his lips near the doctor's ears and speak softly, but those ears were far away. So words formed sticky clumps.

The doctor waited for an answer that did not come.

"You can hop down now, Brian. Would you like a lollipop?"

The doctor unwrapped the candy and, as instructed, Brian walked out into the reception room to sit alone on the leather sofa while the doctor spoke with his mother. He licked the cherry lollipop as quietly as he could, hoping to catch what the adults on the other side of the door were saying. He worried they were making decisions for him. More than that, he worried his stutter meant worse things were going to happen to him later. He swung his legs back and forth to make a sound each time they hit the sofa, hoping the adults could hear it and would remember he was there.

His mother walked out of the examination room. She had a blank look on her face he did not know how to interpret. Was he in trouble? Would he be punished? "Let's go, Brian. We've got some grocery shopping to do. You can help."

By the time they walked home and he was in the car beside his mother, the lollipop was gone. Brian twirled the white paper stick in his mouth and stuck it in as far as he dared. His mother fumbled with her keys before she found the right one and inserted it in the ignition. The car jerked backwards, and the stick jabbed his throat. If the doctor hadn't been able to dislodge the words down there, he could do it himself. His mother kept her eyes fixed on the road ahead.

*

When Brian looked up at the mountains, he could see a clearing on the side of one of them. There had been a fire there before he was born, and the trees had yet to grow back.

16

It hadn't been a great fire, but still the worst in Tummus' history. Brian liked to imagine that the gash on his scalp was the same shape as the mountain's bald spot. He would use his finger to trace the contours where hair grew and where it did not and believed he had proof of a resemblance.

Two men died fighting the fire, one of his uncles said. One had been up there with nothing but his fire axe. Brian learned about it one Thanksgiving. "One smothered, the other burnt." Other Thanksgivings, he had heard stories about the war, but this time it was the fire. "The winds shifted direction." His father stopped refilling his uncle's whiskey glass as he grew more animated. "Your aunt told me later she'd gotten down on her knees to pray." Eve excused herself to see to dinner in the kitchen. "The sky was red in the middle of the day." Like any mountain fire, the first signs of it struck fear into everyone. "Church bells were ringing." Scores of men rushed up the slope in their vehicles or on foot. "Smoke reached the town's streets." Like most forest fires, it did not end until the rains came. For months people looked nervously at the slash on the mountain until those rains came. "Fallen trees blocked the railroad." After hearing his uncle's stories, he started looking at the clearing often and sometimes rubbed the weird spot on the side of his head while he did.

*

One day he asked his mother why his name was Brian. He wanted a name he didn't stumble over. They were sitting at the small chrome dinette set in the kitchen, where his mother and he would share a snack when he got home from school. He was seven now and in the second grade at Tummus Elementary School. He had a new teacher who wasn't Mrs. Roland.

"Why, dear, don't you like it? It was your uncle's name. The name of your father's brother. Who died in the war."

"I don't like it."

"You don't like it? Don't be silly! It's a wonderful name!"

His mother did the worst possible thing to a child who stutters. She laughed. An almost beast-like laugh that slithered up her throat. It was a laugh that swallowed him whole. It was impossible for him to hear anything else, anything his mother might think to add, correct, redo or, just then, anything in the world.

"I want another name." He pushed away the Ritz cracker with peanut butter on it. He was afraid she would laugh louder if he told her why.

"Oh, stop it, darling. Your name is Brian. Be proud of it!"

"*Kuh-kuh-kuh*-call me John."

For an instant, it seemed his mother was going to laugh again. She stopped herself and raised a finger to her lips, a gesture showing she had realized why her son was having this conversation with her. Brian thought: Don't you understand how different life is when you can't count on saying your name?

*

Brian was loitering in the playground after school. An older kid, a girl not in the second grade, came and stood close to him.

"I'm Susan. You live near me."

He stayed silent. He knew better than to talk.

"I said I'm Susan. What's your name?"

After a pause Brian responded, "John."

"No, it's not."

"Okay, it's *nuh*-not."

"So what is it? You're cute."

Lured into the trap, he said, "*Buh-buh-buh*-rian."

A wide grin crept across the girl's face, revealing two rows of horsey front teeth.

"I'm going to call you Ryan. I know your name is Brian but I'm making it Ryan. If you can't say Brian, why should I? Hah hah! Ryan Ryan Ryan!"

He covered his ears with his hands. The girl kept on teasing. Her laughter merged with the recent memory of his mother's, and he could not bear the taunting. It was bad enough when adults made fun of his stutter, but, if a kid did it, he could not find respite from the laughter anywhere. It was crueler. Other children would grow up mocking him. He lowered his arms to his side, leaned forward and charged the girl like a wounded bull. He rammed her midsection and sent her flying backwards until she fell flat on her back against the playground's asphalt with a dull thump. It looked as if she was going to get up again. He prepared for a second charge by leaning forward again. She fell back against the ground and screamed. Not for help, not for anything. Only a raw, high-pitched and omnidirectional scream. Brian screamed, too. She did not try to get up. He turned to run with his hands blocking his ears. He kept them there until he was home.

He lay atop his calico bedspread and thought about what he had done. He had been mad at people before who laughed at him, but he'd struck none of them. There was no talking back to this girl and winning, she'd made sure of that. He had to do something. Did he really? Couldn't he have just walked away? That's what his mother would have told him to do. Sticks and stones stuff. That was impossible for Brian. It wouldn't have been fair. Susan had to pay if their school playground was going to be even-Steven again. Brian was working out the rules for his own private game, and he didn't care if they weren't anyone else's. When he grew up, he'd stick to those rules. They'd have to be simple. He made a fist with his right hand and raised it above his head, then rotated it to study it from all angles. He had crossed a line today, he knew that. There was no going back.

That night, about two hours after he had dinner, his mother came into his bedroom. She whispered, careful not to disturb baby Bam asleep in the crib alongside one wall of the room.

"Mrs. Wentworth's been here. Susan's mother."

Brian stared straight up at the popcorn ceiling.

"Your father's home now. He wants to see you when he's done eating." She turned and tiptoed out.

Brian had been punished before. He was grounded for a week after they caught him sneaking a candy bar at the grocery store. He was grounded much longer after telling kids at Sunday school there was no God, something he had said because it would provoke them and the nuns. It did. He didn't really know if there was a God or not. He bit his lower lip hard and wondered what his punishment would be this time, and whether now, too, he'd decide it was worth it.

His bedroom door opened again. He saw his father's silhouette in the hallway light, some of which backlit the thinning hairs of his crewcut. Brian could see well enough to know his father's face was stern, even grim. He had taken his suit jacket and necktie off, but still wore his Boeing company badge clipped to his shirt pocket. Rolled-up sleeves revealed muscular forearms and the big watch on his left wrist. He stepped forward. The door swung open wider of its own accord. The overhead hall light now illuminated Brian sprawled atop the bedspread. Feeling exposed, he crawled underneath the covers.

"We'll keep our voices down, all right, Brian? We don't want to wake your brother."

He was sure his mother was standing in the hallway, out of sight but listening. His father came up to the edge of the bed and pulled the bedspread back.

"So, you like to beat up girls. Is that what you like to do?"

He looked at his father.

"Answer me, Son."

Brian had his answer at hand, and it was an honest one. "She made *fuh-fuh*-fun of me, Dad."

"You like to pick on girls? Is that it, Brian? What, are you a girl, too?" He sounded like gravel if gravel could talk. Brian felt his father's body heat. He had never seen his father so serious.

"She made fun of my . . . *nuh-nuh*-name, Dad."

"Fun of *Brian*? Just how do you make fun of *Brian*?" His father's voice dropped an octave. "How do you make fun of *Brian*? Maybe I'll make fun of your name, too, and you can try to beat me up and see how far you get."

Brian's hands raced to find the edge of the bedspread. At the same time, his mouth gulped air like a fish out of water.

"Tell me how!"

The backside of his father's left hand came down hard on the right side of his face. It stung hardest where his wedding ring had struck. Brian stopped himself from crying out.

"Tell me how, I asked you."

A second blow landed where the first had. This time, he cried out.

"Go ahead, bawl all you want. No one cares." After a pause, he added, "No one cares about you." Through the sharp pain, Brian thought he could hear a small gasp in the hallway.

"Art, stop it. That's enough."

His father turned away from him and moved toward the door. "Art," his mother whispered just loud enough to hear, "leave him be. You're waking the baby."

His father marched through the door and left it a crack open, so he and his mother could hear if Bam cried during the night. Brian crawled back underneath the bedsheets and plotted his revenge. He would get back at the girl for telling. He'd push her again, so hard she'd never get up. He would get back at his father for hitting him, and he would get back at his mother for caring more about Bam than she did him. His brother had been silent through all of this. He could knock his crib over and he'd die. *That would show them what I could do. I could smother him with his stinky little blanket.*

He settled on another plan. He climbed out of bed and walked to the crib. It was the same crib his parents had used when he was a baby. He looked at his brother and saw, next to his head, the same dinosaur toy they had given Brian years ago to play with. It was chewed to pieces. He tiptoed to reach over the top of the crib and grab it. *It would be so easy to put the dinosaur on top of my brother's face and push hard, so hard he couldn't breathe anymore.* The baby squirmed and kicked his feet. *I'll cover your whole face, Baby Bruce, little Bruce Aaron Moriarty. Mommy and Daddy's precious Bam. You go ahead and fight. Try all you want and see how far you get.*

Brian didn't do any such thing. A new rule in his private game didn't allow it: Thinking about killing was okay, but not actually doing it. Bam was innocent, and only the guilty had to pay under his older brother's current dos and don'ts. Brian watched Bam's tiny mouth gulping for air, as he just had in front of his father.

He threw the toy onto the floor and stomped on it. Satisfied that he had at least destroyed one thing, Brian crawled back underneath the covers in bed. He opened his mouth and imitated a fish out of water frantically gulping in its last moments of life. He moved his lips close together to chant lines that could have come from his own private nursery rhyme: *Buh-buh-buh*-rian, *Buh-buh-buh*-rian, *Buh-buh-buh-buh*-rian.

CHAPTER THREE

Mrs. Cosini had an announcement for her fourth-grade class. The principal had selected them to put on the annual Thanksgiving pageant for the entire school. They would tell the story of the Pilgrims coming to America. "This will take a lot of work, boys and girls. Everyone will have to contribute to make this a success. Everyone!" She clapped and smiled.

A low murmur traveled through the room. Even Brian, who, from his back-row perch, had perfected a male nine-year-old's look of indifference, felt a little excitement. He had never been in a play. The idea of going on stage frightened him. Still, he was eager to do what the other kids were doing. He felt more excited walking home that afternoon. After mulling it over, though, he thought he wouldn't get a part. He didn't mention the pageant when his mother asked about his day.

The following morning, Mrs. Cosini had more details. Some people would work on the sets, others on the costumes. A dozen kids would be the actors. A few girls squealed. For an instant Brian tried to imagine himself dressed up as a Pilgrim, in a plain black suit, shiny leather boots and a fancy hat. He had almost talked himself into trying out for one of those roles when he realized he might have to say something.

Mrs. Cosini explained there would be Indians as well. One would welcome the Pilgrims to Plymouth Rock. Her list of cast members included one called The Silent Indian. More than one—several. Brian now imagined himself dressed as an Indian. Buckskin pants and moccasins, a bare chest and a head topped with a feathered headband. He felt excitement again, this time at the thought of being someone other than who he really was.

Two days later, they had the tryouts in the school auditorium.

"Now, you're not auditioning today for any specific role, children," said the drama teacher in charge. "All of you will read the same passage from the script. It's an easy one, no need to worry!"

Brian hadn't expected this. He was already tense, damp under the collar, and now this. He wanted to tell the drama teacher he didn't need to read from the script because he wanted to be The Silent Indian. The role was perfect for a stutterer. He wanted to explain, but he knew he'd stammer if he tried.

His turn came. The teacher handed him the script.

"Read that same first paragraph, dear. Don't be nervous now. Everyone's doing just dandy today!"

Brian had never been more frightened. He jerked his

head and stamped his feet until he saw his entire class waiting for him to start. They knew he was a stutterer. They were hanging around just to watch this. They looked forward to a little entertainment. Out of the corner of his eye, he saw another teacher turn off the tape recorder she had been using during the tryouts. Mrs. Cosini must have warned her he was apt to stutter. Turning off the recorder only made him more anxious.

"Go ahead, Brian."

He stood on the stage and held the pages between his hands. He didn't look down at the lines. There was no point. He faced the teachers and his classmates and said nothing. He couldn't even grunt. At the same time, he felt light. He wasn't solid anymore, only ethereal, as if floating. The old dream came back to him. He was in his mother's womb again, aware but speechless. Except it wasn't dark as it had been before. Now bright stage lights illuminated him.

He drifted upward. If he felt anything lifting off the stage, it was a little fear. He was between two worlds, the real one of the auditorium and another one all his own. There might have been room for another person in this limbo, but Brian didn't see anyone up there above the stage with him. His feet returned to the flooring and with them his full, earthly weight.

"Ma'am?" he said from the stage. "I don't feel so *guh-guh*-good. Can I go see the school . . . *nah-nah*-nurse?"

"You go right ahead, Brian," the teacher said, giving the other teacher a quick glance. "I think she's still here. You go see if she's in."

The nurse allowed him to go home without returning to the auditorium. The next day Mrs. Cosini took him aside.

"Brian, I have something to tell you. The drama teacher says you'll be one of the Indians!"

"The one who doesn't talk?"

"Well, yes, darling, I think so!"

He had humiliated himself the day before on the stage. Now he felt some relief, even joy, that it hadn't been for naught. Two emotions, shame and absolution, distracted him for the rest of the day.

After school, the cast assembled in the auditorium to read through the entire script. Brian discovered his role as The Silent Indian was not, in fact, totally silent. He'd have to say something. There was a line for The Silent Indian followed by a colon and one word. He seized up when it came time to read it aloud.

"*Huh-huh-huh*-how."

Brian kept his eyes fixed on the script. Stage directions read to raise his arm and welcome the Pilgrims to America with an open palm. Just like in the movies. So Brian did raise his hand, although this was only a reading. Someone snickered. Brian's mind focused on the mechanics of *How*. *H*s were right behind *b*s as his particular curse.

He didn't have to invent an excuse. The teachers told him he could help with the props instead. They'd need a pumpkin, a fish, a basket of corn, a musket, colored leaves made of construction paper. Brian disliked his assignment.

28

It was girly. Then he found the pieces of the teepee that had to be erected on the stage, and he took charge. It had five wooden poles and a tan muslin covering soiled along its bottom seam from years of use. Figuring out how to assemble it was a challenge and took Brian some time. There weren't any written instructions. Once he had it up and had pulled the flap back to open the triangular entrance, he crawled inside. He sat there, legs crossed, looking out at the rows of empty auditorium seats. "How," he said, tapping his mouth as if making an Indian war cry. "How!" he said, louder. He didn't stutter on his *h*s either time.

The next day, he stood in the wings and watched his classmate who had taken over as The Silent Indian walk onto the stage. He said his one-word line. It was fine. Brian felt no resentment. Nothing suggested he was about to float in mid-air again. He escaped humiliation and didn't need to punish anyone for it. But he realized that he was nonetheless making a tight fist with his right hand. He could have dressed up as another Indian and just sat quietly in the teepee. If only someone had suggested it.

*

A few weeks later, the classroom door opened in the middle of language arts and the assistant principal walked in with a new boy beside him. The assistant principal whispered to the teacher, who motioned for the new student to take the empty seat in the second row.

"Boys and girls, this is Jim. He'll be joining us from

now on. Everyone say hello to Jim." Some of the girls waved. From the boys there was a low rumble of ambivalent welcome.

"Do you want to introduce yourself, Jim? No? Well, perhaps later."

Jim sat up straight in his chair and stared at the teacher. He didn't look around the room as any normal kid might. Brian sized him up. Something was not right about him. He was shy or something. He thought the kid's head was too big for his body. One of his shoulders drooped lower than the other.

"Jim, do you have the book in front of you? No, you don't. Why don't you look on with Sheryl? Next to you." Jim moved his chair toward Sheryl, the girl with the ribbons in her yellow hair, but not close enough to see her textbook.

"Jim, would you like to read from where Thomas stopped?" She walked over and pointed at the passage in the textbook.

From behind, Brian watched Jim squirm. The room was silent. He knew what was happening even though he couldn't see Jim's face. It would be twisted all out of shape. His mouth would be forming a circle, an oval, and then a circle again. His eyes wide with terror, the new kid in class would try to talk; those hopes abandoned, he would then just try for any sound. Jim didn't know yet to sit in the back row and be ignored. Brian's own face burned hot. He imagined what the new kid was going through. He was glad it was not him.

After school let out, he walked over to the new kid,

who was standing by himself on the playground.

"Hey, hello. Jim, right?" Brian's *h*s came out perfectly, surprising him. Jim just nodded and went *uh uh uh uh*. He's avoiding his *h*s, Brian realized, like me. This was the first time he had encountered another stutterer his age. He had heard cartoon characters stutter on TV, where it was funny. But it wasn't funny for him in real life, and it wasn't funny for this kid. Brian was both curious about another stutterer and repulsed by seeing himself in him. He moved closer to the smaller boy and leaned forward, knowing he was intimidating him. "What's your problem?" he asked. "Were you *buh-buh*-born this way, or did you get . . . *huh*-hit on the head? Did they *suh-suh*-send you to the doctor, too?" Jim looked down at the dirt on the playground.

Another student Brian hadn't seen before today, a girl, came up to them. "I'm Mary," she said. "This is my brother, Jim."

"I know he's Jim. He's in my . . . *kuh-kuh-kuh*-class." He was going to stutter badly now. Mary was pretty. She had curls in her hair and big eyes, like a Raggedy Ann doll. He was glad she had spoken first.

"We're twins. I was born first. So I'm older. Same grade, but they placed us in separate homerooms."

"*Wuh-wuh*-where *ah-ah*-are . . . *yu-yu*-you *fuh-fuh*-from?" He asked with his eyes cast downward, like her brother's. His stutter had roared back. It was thicker than ever. He was in front of a girl he thought he could like.

"Michigan." Brian wasn't sure where that was, but it

was easier to say than *Wah*-washington.

She smiled and took her brother's hand in hers. "Jim, let's go over to the swings," she said. She hoisted her brother onto one of the wooden seats and gave him slow pushes. Brian followed them. He stood at a distance.

"Do you . . . *stuh-stuh-stuh*-stutter, too?"

"No, just my brother. Girls don't stutter. Much. Well, I used to."

"I stutter. *Suh-suh*-sometimes. Lots."

"Like my brother."

"Yeah, I heard him today. In . . . *ruh-ruh-ruh*-reading class." His and Jim's eyes briefly met. Both knew he had said nothing in class.

"Let's form a club," Mary offered brightly. "You stutter, right? My brother stutters, too, right? So that means I'll be president of the club. I can do the talking for the three of us!"

*

One day, alone at home, Brian had an idea. He would give his stutter a name. A nickname, one that just he and his stutter would know. First, he considered naming it Godzilla. He changed his mind after going through some of his old Batman comic books. He'd call his stutter the Joker. *J*s aren't so bad, he told himself. Most of the time. He and the Joker would be friends. Secret friends. It wouldn't matter if he stuttered in front of the Joker or not. Only the two of them would know if he did. His new friend would see lips quivering, a tongue darting in and out, a face twisting in torment, but that would be okay.

Brian snuck his mother's playing cards out of the top drawer of her bedroom dresser. They smelled pretty, like her perfume. He sat on his parents' bedroom floor, spilled the cards onto the rug and searched for the Joker. He was thin with a pointed chin and sharp nose. He wore a floppy hat of many colors with a tassel at its end. Brian returned the rest of the cards under his mother's underwear in the dresser. Brian hid the Joker in his own dresser. He worried that its perfume scent might give it away when his mother put his clean clothes away in the top drawer.

*

"Brian, dear," his mother said to him one hot afternoon. "Your friend Mary is on the phone for you." He was closer to the phone but hadn't answered it because he never did. His mother was panting because she had rushed into the house from the clothesline. She kept the back door open a crack, even in winter, in case it rang.

"Hi, Mary," he said into the handset. She wondered if he'd like to go to the rodeo together.

"I think my *pah-pah*-parents will let me. *Huh-huh-huh*-how about yours?"

"Of course, that's why I'm calling. They want me to bring Jim along."

Brian minded the addition but didn't say so. He wasn't comfortable in the company of other stutterers. "*Shuh*-sure, anything's okay with … *muh*-me." He wanted to make Mary happy. He said he'd talk to his parents.

"Why, Brian!" remarked his mother, who had stood nearby during the conversation. "You got that out on the telephone with no problem!" She often pretended her son's stutter was getting better and not worse.

Brian turned to the Joker, who was sitting on the counter next to the phone. The Joker saw anger on his face even if his mother didn't. He hated being congratulated for not stuttering, especially when he had. Or being told someone else's stammer was "far worse." Compliments were a problem. Hear one, and he'd mangle the *thuh-thuh*-thank you. He knew everyone expected him to stutter. So why not.

He also hated, with a fury he could hardly contain, adults finishing his sentences for him when he stuttered halfway through. They always came up with the wrong thing, the wrong words.

"*Muh-muh*-mrs. Cosini," Brian once asked in school. "Can I *guh-guh-guh-guh* . . ."

"Go to the bathroom, dear? To the boys' room? All you have to do is ask!" she replied with a flutter in her fluent voice, handing him one of hall passes she kept in a pocket sewn on her dress.

All he had wanted was to get up from his chair and sharpen his pencil in the sharpener. Shamed as well as angry now, he took the pass and stormed out to the bathroom. He paced the tile floor back and forth. "They should shut up, those *sentence-completers*," the Joker whispered to him. Brian glanced in the long mirror above the sinks and didn't see the Joker's reflection because, of course, the Joker wasn't real. He nodded in agreement anyway. *There is no way to say anything correctly, even if you don't stammer, even if you mean what you're saying. Well-meaning people will always fill in the blanks for you. No word matches up with what it names.* Words were soft blurs of dishonesty obscuring sharp edges of truth. From now on, anyone who tried to rescue him from stuttering was going to a special hell where the devil would interrupt *them* in the middle of everything. "And those people who, when they hear you stumble over a word, walk away to spare their uncomfortable feelings?" the Joker added with a devilish grin of his own. "There's a special place for them, too, one twice as hot." Brian turned away from the mirror and this time saw the Joker standing in the middle of the restroom because, of course, there were times he was real. He left him there and shuffled back to class, wondering what new line his secret friend was now tempting him to cross.

CHAPTER FOUR

Christmas in 1956 promised to be great. Everyone was talking about the polio vaccine. Brian's mother whispered to him that his father had gotten a big raise at work, but to keep it their secret.

He had his heart set on an erector set. Brian liked to build things, as his father did at the plant. He also liked to take things apart just to put them together again. An erector set had lots of pieces of stamped sheet metal with holes in them for little nuts and bolts, clamps and hinges. Fancy ones came with electric motors. Too old to believe in Santa Claus, Brian made a list for his mother. It had two things on it: Erector set and electric train, neither of which he could pronounce without stuttering.

Christmas morning, his father, with a silly elf's hat on his head, brought a big wrapped box to Brian on the sofa. It looked light in his father's arms. He knew it wasn't an erector set or an electric train.

"Open it, dear!" his mother burst. "I can't wait to see

your face! Art, get the camera. Is the flashbulb in it?"

He opened the package with less speed than he might have, both to give his father time to ready the Brownie and to signal his disappointment. Wrapping paper removed, he tore the cardboard box open.

"A basketball! Brian, darling! Look, it's already inflated!" exclaimed his mother, ignorant of the fact they came inflated.

Brian did not play basketball. Brian was short for his age, a good four inches short of where he thought he should be. The Moriarty family had a hoop above the garage door. No one ever used it.

"There you go, tiger!" his father boomed behind the bright flash that temporarily blinded his son.

"You'll be tall like your old man," his father continued. "You'll be sinking baskets in no time. Like the Celtics! Like I did!"

His eyes refocused. His father was not tall.

"We'll go out later today and sink some baskets," his father added, oblivious to the rain outside. His mother stooped to pick up the wrapping paper and threw it into the fireplace.

Still, basketball, he discovered playing with his father, had its advantages. You didn't have to talk. His father barked out instructions. Not long into it they mastered gestures to signal each other. *No traveling.* He seldom looked into his father's eyes. Now he had to. *Basketball isn't about you; it's about the ball.* Body language counted, too. *Don't think, just play.*

His father dribbled the ball for a while. They moved around the driveway, tracing figure-eights. He waited for his father to pass it to him. He moved in once he realized he'd have to take it away. His father made a quarter turn to keep him at bay. He lunged at his father and touched the ball for an instant.

"Dad! Let me have it!" said Brian, not stuttering. His father dribbled the ball backwards toward the garage door, stopping underneath the never-used hoop. He moved slowly, inviting Brian to come take it away from him. He gave his son a belittling grin, as if he were his age and they were meeting as equals on the court. Brian, suspicious of the grin, didn't take the bait. He realized he'd have to make the attempt or lose something important today: The chance to challenge his father and win.

"Come at me, Son. Come get it," his father tempted in what was close to a whisper.

He headed straight for his father and not the ball. Were it an actual game, Brian would have fouled by touching him harder than he had to. It worked. His father relinquished control of the ball; he seemed to have decided his son should have it. He'd proven his son could not steal it from him playing by the rules.

"I *guh-guh*-got it, Dad!"

"Guess you did," his father said, standing erect and motionless. "Now let's go inside. You're wet." His father turned and walked to the front door. Brian stood alone on the driveway. His father hadn't even waited for him to sink a basket. This was the first reason why, that evening, he'd rethink the rules for the games he'd henceforth play in life.

*

The clang of pots and the clink of dishes followed the sound of water filling the sink. Brian, sulking on the living room sofa, recognized the noises his parents made when they did the dishes together after holiday dinners. He leaned toward the closed kitchen door to make out what they were saying. Bits and pieces of words came through. He tried to connect their consonants and vowels by adding more consonants and vowels in between, just as they did when he stuttered in front of them.

His father emerged from the kitchen and told Brian to come along on his daily walk around the neighborhood. It was midafternoon and still Christmas day. "Your mother says you and I don't spend enough time together. Let's go."

His father wore his old army jacket with the aviator sunglasses Brian thought made him look like a pilot. It was impossible to tell if his father was ever looking at him. Brian didn't mind. He thought his father looked neat, and he was proud of him. He struggled to keep up with his father's quicker stride.

Decaying leaves covered the sidewalk. They were wet and stuck together. Brian kicked them aside with exaggerated motions intended to signal to his father that he was still by his side. He didn't know the names of the bare trees that had dropped these leaves, but they stood at equal distances in front of everyone's home. The leaves stopped where the bare trees and the concrete ended, as well. They gave way to larger conifers which had no leaves to drop.

Without leaves to kick, he might have tried talking with his father. He didn't dare risk starting only to fail. Mangled syllables jammed in his throat and choked him with consonants as glued together as the wet leaves. Fortunately, they were no longer alone with each other when they came upon a cluster of men gathered in a circle in the middle of the road. He and his father approached. They saw the men were standing around a mottled green snake. It was longer than the garter snakes he sometimes found in his backyard and picked up to scare his brother. This one was as long as Brian was tall. The snake was slimier than the leaves on the sidewalk had been.

Brian and his father joined the circle. They watched the snake curl itself up into a tight mound nearly the size of a soccer ball. It made no sound, and neither did the adults. Everything was quiet until there was a plop on the asphalt when another man arrived with a bright yellow pail, the kind Brian used to wash the Moriarty station wagon, and dropped it onto the road next to the snake.

The man had a long wooden pole with a metal hook at the end. He prodded the snake into uncoiling. Once it had, he extended the rusty hook to lift the snake up by its middle and dropped it into the pail. The pail rocked back and forth. The snake was thrashing in its confinement and made dull thumping sounds. His father, eyes invisible behind his sunglasses, nodded to signal they'd be resuming their walk.

The man with the pole used it again to lift the snake out of the pail and spill it sloppily back onto the road. The snake writhed. His liberator stepped forward, raised one of his work boots, and brought it down hard on the snake's head. Brian heard a crunch. He didn't know snakes had skulls. A couple of the men giggled in low voices. His father tapped his shoulder and led him away from the men's circle to resume their walk.

"A whip snake," his father tossed off. "Harmless." Brian asked why they had killed it. He faced his son and said, "A snake is not part of their world." Brian observed but did not say to his father: Here is another lesson for me today and another reason to rethink the rules. If something is not part of your world, you are free to destroy it. Brian now had official permission.

*

In ninth grade, Brian began to play hooky. High school was different from junior high. As a freshman he was at the bottom of the totem pole again. If he was not going to do well in school, he decided, he wouldn't show up for it. The office would call his mother and report his absences. Several times, they had to go to school to meet with the assistant principal. The Joker made Brian laugh when he said the assistant principal looked like the Penguin, one of Batman's supervillains. They convened in the Penguin's airless office, drab except for a framed photo of an American flag and his bachelor's diploma from Washington State that hung on walls the color of pea soup. Each time Brian explained that he stuttered, and each time the Penguin replied it was no excuse. The admonishment was invariably, "Other students have problems, too, Brian, and they come to class." Brian sheepishly said he was sorry, and he was. He wanted to succeed in school. He wanted to go to college. He wanted a choice whether to get out of Tummus or not. He wanted the option to start from scratch.

Instead of skipping classes, Brian adapted by becoming adept at never having to speak. If he was called on to recite in class, which was rare, he mumbled something which may have corresponded with the assignment or not, and the teacher moved on to the next student. If a substitute teacher called on him, he'd say he'd forgotten his reading glasses, which always got snickers from his classmates because he didn't need any.

One day his homeroom teacher told him he would be excused from class once a week to spend time with a speech therapist in the nurse's office. *Great*, he thought, *therapist, another word I can't pronounce.* In the following week he went to the small, windowless room to see the therapist for the first time. The walls were the same pea color as the assistant principal's office. Nothing hung from them other than a good health chart featuring cartoonish drawings of a young boy and girl missing their genitals.

There were three other boys. Brian recognized them, but he did not know their names. One was older than him and had the start of a wispy beard on his chin. *Why didn't they send me to a therapist when I was younger?* he wondered. The thought made him realize he was hoping this might actually help him.

The boys sat there, saying nothing to each other. A woman walked in and set up a folding easel. On it she placed a chart with colored pie sections. She explained why it is important to eat a balanced diet. One of the pie sections was vegetables. It was green and bigger than the others. The older boy made a face the others could see, but the therapist couldn't. Brian thought: What were his parents going to make him eat more of now?

The therapist talked for just short of an hour. She didn't ask them to say a single word, other than their names. To his surprise, he answered "Brian" without stuttering. Maybe this meant he wouldn't be back next week. He enjoyed being out of class, and he liked the idea of not stuttering, but he concluded he wasn't going to like this lady doctor. He had a funny feeling that, despite her job, she didn't care for stutterers much or believe she could help them. She'd come into the room with an unenthusiastic look on her face to begin with.

She wrote something on her clipboard and asked each of the boys to say his name again. She said they could go back to class. All the kids in his classroom looked at Brian as if he had been in prison for the past hour serving a sentence. He sat down in his seat with a deliberate thump.

*

At home, his brother Bam was talking a lot for a boy in the

second grade. His parents were on the lookout for any sign of stuttering. Brian was on the lookout, as well. He wasn't sure what another stutterer in the family might mean for him. Brian would look at his brother's face for hints of future trouble. There was always that funny eye, the unanchored one that stared into space. Brian sensed something else was abnormal, but what or just how abnormal, he didn't know. Was Bam going to stutter as well? Brian took some perverse pleasure in knowing his little brother's fate was sealed, whether it would be with his affliction or another.

Bam did stutter, for a while. At age eight and for less than a year. Brian wondered if Bam was just imitating him for the sport of it. A lot of children outgrew their stammers, but the Joker told Brian his brother had just become bored with aping his *buh-buh-buh*s and *moh-moh-moh*s. Brian figured that whatever happened to him had not happened to Bam. Or Bam had done something to cure himself that his brother had not. He and Bam never talked to each other about stuttering. Stutterers are like that. The slow kids in special ed hung out with each other, but not the stutterers. Brian didn't quite trust Bam. There was too much at stake to start confessing to each other. Later, when they were teenagers, Bam would insist he had never stuttered. "I wanted," he would say to Brian, "to be perfect, and you knew it. So you convinced yourself I was going to be a stutterer like you. Wrong." Brian did not believe this. He knew his brother shared too much of the same blood with him to have ever imagined he could be perfect.

*

Bam's brief career as a stutterer had just ended when, one Saturday, their mother was running around the house in her frayed nightgown. She looked up at the clock over the kitchen sink, halfway through washing the breakfast dishes. Brian could hear her talking to herself.

"Brian? I have an errand for you."

He was sitting at the kitchen table. He looked up from his math homework and waited for his mother to continue.

"Would you go to the grocery store for me? We need some some things for dinner." She stood at the counter and wrote out a list after wiping her hands dry. She waved it along with a ten-dollar bill.

"And take your brother with you."

Brian stood up and stretched his arms. "He's not around."

"Yes, he is. Bam!" she said in a voice loud enough to reach her sons' bedroom. "Come here! I need you to go to the store with your brother."

Bam appeared as bothered as Brian did.

"Bam, you said you wanted something new in your sandwiches for school. Go with your brother now and pick out something you like. A quarter of a pound. Sliced thin. I'm going next door to Mrs. Borowski's after I change."

Brian shoved the list and the money into his front pocket. "Let's *geh-geh-geh*-go," he said to his brother.

The grocery store was a good ten blocks away. They said

nothing to each other on the way. The doors into the supermarket slid open automatically.

"You go to the deli. Get what you want." Brian looked at the list. "I need to go get eggs and . . . *fuh-fuh*-flour."

"There are lots of kinds of flour," Bam said. "Don't mess up." Brian raised an arm as if to strike his brother, but he made a face that said he was kidding, probably.

"I'll mess up if I want," Brian said, looking at the list again. They found each other a few minutes later and headed for the shortest checkout lane.

"What did you get?"

"Cheese."

"Not baloney? You're full of it," Brian snickered.

Bam fumbled with the wrapping around his deli package, no doubt to eat some. Brian stopped him with a hard slap on his hand.

The checkout lady smiled at them when their turn came. She had seen them with their mother for years.

Bam elbowed his brother from behind.

"I want some of those cigarettes behind her."

"No."

"I said yes. And you're old enough to ask for them."

"I'm not. And there's not enough money."

"Yes there is."

"We're not supposed to smoke."

"Not your business." The brothers locked eyes.

"Ma'am," Bam said to the lady. "My mother smokes, and she'd like us to get her cigarettes."

The checkout lady looked up from the register.

"Cigarettes? For your mother, boys? Well, I don't know. Is your mother here with you?"

"She sent us here, ma'am. She told us to get cigarettes."

"Is that so? Well, all right then. Now, what brand does she smoke?"

"I'm not *shuh*-sure," Brian replied. "My *bruh*-brother knows." He handed the woman the ten-dollar bill.

"She smokes Marlboros, doesn't she?"

"No, that's my dad," interjected Bam. "My mother smokes the kind that tastes like candy. That's what she says."

"Oh, you mean Kools! Is that what you want, dear? Well, you better get some if that's what your mother wants." She looked at the older of the brothers for confirmation. Bam had set a trap for him.

"Yes, ma'am. She smokes . . . *Kuh-kuh-kuh*-kools."

Bam erupted in laughter. The checkout lady looked confused.

"One pack of . . . what was it you said? *Kuh-kuh-kuh*-kools?" Bam laughed again.

The lady put the cigarettes and the groceries in a small brown paper bag. She handed Brian the change. He made a show of shoving it in his pocket with great force, hoping the woman and his brother got the message.

Outside in the parking lot, the boys faced off. Brian started it by lowering the bag onto the asphalt between two potholes filled with rainwater. He crossed his arms and waited.

"Gimme those cigarettes," demanded Bam in response to his brother's challenge. He extended his hand palm up.

"Fat chance, asshole," tossed back Brian, unfolding his arms.

"You can't give them to Mom. She didn't ask for them. Give 'em to me. They're mine. She won't miss the money."

Brian saw Bam's bad eye, not the usual good one, focused on him. He'd been pissed off at his brother for a long time and was angry at having been set up in the supermarket. *Now he's giving me the evil eye curse.* Later, Brian would reflect, Bam wasn't to blame for anything he actually did. It was the very fact of Bam. To stutter like Brian for a short while and then stop—it wasn't fair. His parents' relief at Bam's quick return to normalcy was nothing he shared in. He put his own shame front and center. Ruminating later, he realized that as two stutterers, one reformed and the other chronic, occasional violence between them was the best they could do to be literally in touch.

Their contest was brief. Brian had several inches and many pounds over Bam and easily knocked him to the ground, where he kicked him a few times with his foot. Bam tried to defend himself with his arms. He did not cry out. They knew better than to attract too much attention in the parking lot.

"Get up. Let's go." Brian extended a hand to help Bam off the ground, but the last thing Bam would have done was take it.

*

Bam brushed the dirt off his clothes before going through their home's front door. Brian put the bag and the change on the kitchen counter minus the Kools. Their mother was still at the next-door neighbor's. Brian went back to his math book. Neither he nor Bam said a word about the cigarettes or about Bam being beaten up to their parents that evening at dinner.

Back in their bedroom, he on one twin bed and his brother on the other, Brian thought about what it meant that his latest outburst of violence had found its target in the person most like him. Had throwing Bam to the ground been throwing himself?

*

Brian was sent to speech therapy every week until he graduated from Tummus High, Home of the Fighting Indians. At some point, a second therapist followed the first. He liked her even less. The new one, Miss Edwards, never told him he needed to follow a proper diet. But she made him do things she must have known he couldn't, such as repeat the phrase "Methodist Episcopal," or attempt tongue twisters like "I wish to wish the wish you wish to wish," or "she sells seashells down by the seashore." The worst for Brian was "tell the bewilderingly bad boy dinner was delicious" because of the *b*s. After a few exercises like this, he decided this therapist meant to torture him, and he crossed his arms often to signal that the days of his active cooperation with her were over.

Miss Edwards advised him to keep what she called a "stuttering diary." She wanted him to write down not just those things he had difficulty saying, but how he felt at those moments.

"Brian, I don't want you to be too concerned if I explain that you, like many young people, have an inner condition. Something troubling you deep inside. Your problems talking are your particular outward manifestation of that something. Writing will help the two of us identify it."

That day the pale green paint on the walls looked more olive than pea, and looking at it turned Brian's stomach sour.

"Miss Edwards, I just *stuh*-stutter." Brian was in the mood to dispute anything she said. "I don't feel anything wrong inside. The *puh*-problem is my *muh*-mouth."

The therapist smiled weakly and told him it would take time to understand things. "Here's a notebook for you, Brian," she added, pulling one out of her desk drawer. "Start today, would you?"

"I *kuh*-keep a list of *wuh*-words in my *muh*-mind that I can't say. I *kuh*-call them my unpronounceables. I *kah*-can write those down, if you *wuh*-want."

Miss Edwards' weak smile turned into a weak titter. "Why don't you concentrate on telling me your feelings, Brian?"

That night he told the Joker what she had said to him. His secret friend snickered.

"She's trying to get into your pants. She's hot for you." Brian blushed at the thought, but he did not dismiss it. He was well into finding girls interesting, and the Joker teased him about it. "The bitch wants to fix your inner condition all right." Brian wondered where these thoughts came from. "If she were any good, you'd be getting better, not worse."

At every session, Miss Edwards asked him how school was going. One week, he was irritated enough that he decided to tell the truth. He told her school was one long fight.

"Fight? Fight with whom?" She leaned forward over the desk close enough for Brian to smell her perfume.

"Everyone."

"No," corrected Miss Edwards. "It can't be everyone. Tell me who in particular." She glanced over her shoulder as if making sure no one else was in the room.

He pulled a name out of thin air. A name he could say without stuttering.

"Tom."

"Why Tom? Why do you fight with Tom?"

He was trapped. There was no Tom. Well, there was, but he didn't want to get the real Tom in trouble. There was no one in particular he fought with. He felt like fighting, more or less, with everyone.

"Did Tom bully you?" she asked.

Brian thought, yeah, the other kids he'd been in therapy with had been bullied a lot, and talking about it aggravated their stutters. That Black kid got picked on more than the rest of them. The new guy with the lisp didn't last long. Brian

51

thought back to Susan, and to his brother in the supermarket parking lot recently.

The Joker, sitting on Miss Edwards' shoulder with his legs crossed at the knee, spoke to him. "Tell her the truth."

He obeyed the Joker this time.

"It's just a fight. I . . . *duh-duh*-don't fit in."

"Tell her more," the Joker said.

"I don't want to go to school. Not anymore. *Ai-ai*-I've had enough."

Miss Edwards sat back in her chair. "Not anymore? Has something happened, Brian?"

He thought of making up a story. One to make her happy. Like he did when he told the priest fibs in confession. If you didn't have any real sins to tell the priest, you made some up. Brian had gotten good at inventing stories.

"Skip it. Let me go . . . *buh*-back to *kuh-kuh*-class." He could tell the Joker was not pleased with him. Brian would hear about it later.

Miss Edwards pursed her lips.

"Brian, I want to explain something to you." As if it was a diagnosis she'd been saving up for a special occasion or a secret pleasure she had long denied herself, she told him he suffered from spasmophemia, a word he neither understood nor could pronounce in a million years.

"Spaz what?" he chuckled. "Yeah, I'm a spaz all right."

Miss Edwards explained it was a condition like a disease. Not his fault. Something he could learn to control and live with. He had heard what was wrong with him called a "condition" his entire life.

"Same as stuttering?" he said.

She stared at him. "The scientific term. Doctors are researching it."

That night he tried to spell out spaz-whatever in his stuttering diary, but he couldn't remember all its syllables. He threw his pencil hard over Bam's head in the next bed and saw it fall when it hit the wall. Bam ignored him. He fell back against his pillow for a moment. He wrote in his stuttering diary:

Thursday. I didn't answer the phone when I came home from school today. I try never to answer the phone, but sometimes I'm alone in the house. Even then, I don't answer it much. I ignore the ringing. Sometimes it stops, only to start up again. It's some kind of emergency but I still won't answer it. Something's happened to my mother or my brother and they need to tell me. I ignore it mostly. I can't say hello.

He could feel the Joker breathing on the back of his neck as he scribbled.

When I don't answer the phone, it seems to ring forever. Even when it stops, I keep hearing it in my head. It's like the shrill sound of a dentist's drill. Promising pain. I hate the ringing phone, like I hate being sent to the store to ask for something I

know I can't pronounce, whatever it is. Hamburg.
Haddock. Hot dogs. Kools. Having to answer
the phone is hell. You have to pick it up and say
HELLO except that I don't. And unless you say it
fast, the other person hangs up. The person at the
other end freaks when she doesn't hear a voice.

He put his diary down and resumed lying flat on his bed. He stared at the ceiling. His mother knew he had a lot of problems. She often had advice for him. He wondered where she got it. Once she read aloud to him from the *Reader's Digest*, "'Think before you speak.' That's helpful advice, dear." But think was all Brian did.

*

He was an adult twelve now and, during the daytime, allowed to go anywhere he wanted. One Saturday, Brian found a book at the town library with the longest title he'd ever come across: *The Cause and Cure of Speech Disorders: A Text Book for Students and Teachers on Stuttering, Stammering and Voice Conditions.* The cover was worn at its edges. He looked at the inside back cover of the book and saw it had been checked out many times.

His morning chores done at home, he had walked to the library, an older brick building surrounded by a smooth green lawn clipped close. A black iron statue of some man holding a coal miner's pickaxe stood tall in the middle of it. The library's heavy glass and brass door pivoted on greased hinges when he tugged at its handle. The library had just opened, and he was the first person there, aside from two ladies behind the desk.

This was not his first trip to the library. He'd gone before, sometimes to look at the drawings of women's bodies in the anatomy textbooks, sometimes to see if there were new things about stuttering. He wouldn't ask either of the librarians for help in locating any books. Brian wandered around pretending to be interested in other things until he found them. The books filed under Speech Pathologies in the card catalog looked too technical for him. He stumbled upon things by browsing. He'd take a book or two off the shelf and scurry to the chairs in the back of the stacks. He'd thumb through them there. He was as nervous about the speech books as he was the anatomy ones.

One short book he had found on a trip to the library, *A Parents' Guide to Your Child's Stammer*, explained a lot. The language wasn't too hard. It described the different kinds of stuttering, and he found his right away. Repeated sound and syllable. The others were interjections, word repetition, phrase repetition, revisions, incomplete phrases, broken words, and prolonged sounds. He was relieved he didn't have them all.

He checked the card in the back of the book again. Someone must have just returned *The Cause and Cure of Speech Disorders*. He flipped through it and found that someone had underlined passages, sometimes in pencil, sometimes in pen.

Our experience indicates that stuttering children, to begin with, are the victims of sensitive, impressionable, high-strung, excitable, or emotional temperaments. I guess that means me, though no one ever said it like that. *Stuttering never had its right place in history, in practice, in science or thought, but was always considered rather a mannerism, like wearing one's hat at an angle.* I don't wear hats. *It was not considered in its true light as a prominent symptom of an emotionally unstable nervous individual, and prominent symptoms are not lightly brushed away.* Unstable? Maybe. *Why does the stutterer have such dreams of being a hero?* I never dream of being a hero, Brian thought. Sometimes I have a funny feeling one day I might be, though. One day I might save a million people. If I had a pencil or a pen on me, I'd underline that part again, under the thin blue line already left there by someone else.

The sooner the stutterer realizes that he is just a regular, common garden variety of neurotic, with a stuttering symptom, the sooner he will be in the right mood to begin working himself out of his undesirable state. I am just a regular kid; I know that. *Let the other man do and be what he chooses; but the stutterer must realize his limitations.* I know my limits: I don't do as well in school as everyone wants, and I'm bad with girls. *Remember that during the period of your sickness you have lost years out of your life, that although you may be an adult in age you are a child in experience, as far as speech is concerned, and that this has caused an underdevelopment in many other ways.*

Gripping the book, Brian's hands sweated. He skimmed it, skipping parts such as these. He closed the book when one of the librarians walked by him and reopened it when he was alone again.

The stutterer's handicap and circumscribed experience often lead him to harbor animosity toward others, because he feels deep down in his mind that he cannot meet them on equal terms in friendly competition. Is that why I get into fights? *But neither can he cope with them in active battle on equal terms, so the animosity is suppressed, the whole process frequently taking place in the subconscious mind, without the individual ever suspecting it.*

Brian felt a familiar anger rising up inside him. He flipped the pages faster. Before throwing the book onto the library floor and walking out, he read what, if true, had been unclear to him: *The stutterer's sacrifice is his salvation.* The experts had their idea of what sacrifice and salvation meant. It was all very clinical. Brian had his own take. He'd cross more lines in the future. He would do terrible things until the balance of the world, with him at its center, fit within his growing understanding of right versus wrong.

Chapter Five

Brian was going to catechism classes on Saturdays. There he learned about his upcoming sacrament, confirmation. It promised to be risky. His First Communion hadn't required him to talk. This time, a bishop would be there to ask questions. He couldn't sleep the night before the ceremony. His parish priest with the ruddy face and an Irish accent, Father Thomas, had chosen him to recite an opening prayer. And now, the Joker wasn't helping any. He was on Brian's bed, pantomiming what would happen the next day. He marched across the bed like a toy soldier, mimicking Brian walking into the church but exaggerating every move. He plopped down on the bed, imitating the fat bishop in his chair and blessing the non-existent congregants with a blasphemous sign of the cross delivered with a middle finger. The Joker jumped up and down on the mattress with his mouth gulping wide, his familiar way of mocking Brian's inability to say the simplest words. *Holy. Heaven. Hell.*

In the morning, his mother wouldn't let him eat

breakfast. She said the family had to fast. There would be lots of food at the party afterward. She relented and let him have a little of her coffee when he said he hadn't slept much. He put on the new suit his mother had bought for him. She made sure his bowtie was straight. He looked in the mirror and thought he looked grown-up. They would leave Bam with a neighbor. It was raining. Everyone in the car was quiet. He listened to the tires squish on the wet road. His father turned the radio on and listened to the game for a few seconds. News came on about the Berlin Wall going up. There was going to be an airlift and it would be risky for U.S. aircraft. Eve told Art to turn the radio off when he started mumbling angrily under his breath. After that, no one said a word.

His father caught his eyes looking at him in the rear-view mirror. "Excited, son?" he said. Brian squirmed in his seat. "You're going to get a great new name. A confirmation name. A new Christian name!"

His parents had decided his confirmation name would be Paul. They only asked him if he liked it after choosing it.

"Do I have to have that *nuh*-name?" he asked when they told him. His first thought was: *P*s are right up there with *b*s and *h*s.

"Paul? Why, it's a beautiful name!" his mother exclaimed, beaming. It was the same beaming face that told him Brian was a beautiful name, too.

"Did I have an uncle named Paul, Mom?" he next asked. If Brian was the name of an uncle who died in the war, Paul might be another dead one.

"An uncle? Named Paul? Why, why do you ask, darling? No." Paul was one of her favorite saints, she explained. "He converted to Christ on the road to Damascus," she said. "He cured the sick without touching them. He spread the word of Jesus everywhere."

That meant, Brian figured, Paul must not have stuttered. How could you convert people if you stuttered? Well, maybe *this* Paul would cure him, too. Maybe he wouldn't stutter after his confirmation this morning. Maybe that was all it would take.

They dropped Bam off at the sitter's and made it early to St. Joseph's. They parked in the nearby Dairy Queen lot. His mother led him by the hand across the street. The kids were assembling on the front lawn. Families were taking pictures. The boys wore suits and the girls dressed in white. He didn't say hello to any of them. His mother took him aside on the lawn and helped him with his robe. It was long for him and scraped against the ground. He got the red stole around his neck by himself. He got in line and made his impatience clear by fidgeting. "I *wah-wah*-want this to be over," he complained to the girl in front of him.

He grew more nervous when the ceremony was about to begin. Some families were moving inside the church. The Moriartys entered, too. Brian left his parents and went to his assigned seat. He was not far from the votive candles underneath a stained glass window of the Crucifixion. He turned around to see where his parents had chosen to sit.

They weren't in the front section but close behind it. His mother was holding an unlit candle in her hands; his father was wearing one of the same two suits he wore to work. The necktie looked new. Mom had a thin veil over her face. Brian felt hot in his robe and wished he could loosen his tie.

The altar had a white tapestry covering it. Big red letters read THE HOLY SPIRIT LET OUR FAITH SOAR. The Bishop and other clergy, including Father Thomas, paraded down the aisle while everyone stood and sang a hymn. They sat and the service commenced. Brian didn't repeat the liturgy. He was saving his voice in case he'd have to use it later.

The mass ended and the bishop moved to the big chair in front of the altar. It was what he imagined a bishop's throne would be. The bishop wore an immense hat, what Brian guessed was his crown. Father Thomas sat to the side with other priests in plain cassocks. He thought Father Thomas glanced at him now and again. Brian didn't want to embarrass Father by screwing up the prayer. His palms were sweating. He wished Mary were sitting next to him. She was several rows away. They had nodded to each other walking in. It was her confirmation, too, but the boys were separated from the girls. The Joker was sitting next to him, in the lap of some kid he didn't know. He knew Brian was going to be asked a question.

Father Thomas stood and welcomed the congregants in his Irish lilt. He gave a special greeting to the young people making their confirmation. "I have asked Brian, from my parish, to begin by reading the *Anima Christi.*"

Brian stood. He held the paper in front of him. It was so crinkled from folding it over and over it had become hard to read. He thought back to his audition for his school's Thanksgiving pageant.

"*Suh-suh*-soul of Christ, sancti-*fai-fai*-fy me." His face grew hotter. He paused, gritted his teeth and stared down at the paper. He avoided meeting anyone's eyes.

"Body of . . . *kuh-kuh*-Christ, *sah-sah-sah*-save me."

He kept going. Nothing was going to stop him.

"Blood of Christ, inebriate me." He didn't stutter on this sentence, even though he didn't know what *inebriate* meant. His mother had helped him practice at home.

"Water from the side of *kuh-kuh-kuh*-Christ, *wah-wah-wah*-wash me." The stutter was back. He felt his face grow incandescent.

"Passion of Christ, *strah-strah-strah*-strengthen me. O Good Jesus, *huh*-hear me."

Good, two lines out. Quick. Go faster now, he urged himself, the exact opposite advice he and other stutterers were always given.

"Within Thy . . . *wuh-wuh-wuh-wuh*-wounds hide me."

Brian wanted to hide. There was nowhere to go.

"Suffer me not to be separated from thee."

Halfway through now.

"From the *mah-mah-mah-mah*-malignant *en-en*-enemy . . ." Brian couldn't finish the line. He froze and stared down, not at the piece of paper but at the stone floor beneath his polished shoes. The church was silent. No one in the church could know how he felt. When other people stopped talking, it was because they had nothing else to say. Brian had plenty, his assigned prayer and a lot more. Stopping was different from not being able to start at all. This was worse. A halfway sentence was a sentence that came only partly into being and was left broken, severed, undone: The bloody stump of an amputated limb. He felt the boy next to him gently pry the paper out of his hands. Brian could hear the Joker sneering. He kept looking at the floor and didn't sit down. The church was still silent. At last, the unknown boy read the last line, and Brian sat. The ordeal wasn't over yet.

The priests took turns announcing their congregants to the bishop by his or her new confirmation name. Brian's turn came. Father Thomas said, "Bishop, may I present Paul."

"Paul, be blessed with the Holy Spirit."

"Amen," Brian rejoined.

"Peace be with you."

"And with your *spuh-spuh*-spirit."

That last stutter made Brian a target for special attention. Father Thomas and the bishop were studying him.

"Paul, when does the Holy Spirit first come to us?"

Paul. He should have been prepared for this. It was one of the sample questions in his catechism class. Brian's mind went blank. He could see the Joker smirking at him. *Paul.* Brian was inside his mother again, in the company of another fetus who would do his talking for him. The baby who slashed his face. The brother Brian left behind.

Defeated, he looked at the bishop in silence. If bishops had special powers, he didn't use them on him. The bishop's face drew itself up into the same sneer as the Joker's, more humiliating because everyone in the church could see it. Brian turned his head to find his parents. His father was staring into space. His mother, like the bishop and Father Thomas, was looking at him. Her face had a small smile on it. For a second, he was happy. Her lips moved, wanting to supply him with the answer to the bishop's question. *At baptism.*

"At *beh-beh-beh*-baptism."

The bishop nodded and motioned to the parish priests to continue. It was Brian's turn to study their faces. The bishop's expression was disapproving, but Father Thomas' face said something else, halfway between a job well done and you're not fooling anyone. As if to say, *I know that sin has made you a stutterer.*

Brian lined up to receive an unexpectedly sharp slap from the bishop to make him a full congregant of the Roman Catholic faith.

For a few months after his confirmation, Brian would put his weekly allowance money, fifty cents, in the collection basket every Sunday. He would punish himself for stuttering, and at the same time would want to show gratitude for the small part of Father Thomas' smile that was less contemptuous than the bishop's, and perhaps even kind.

*

His parents threw a party at their house after the ceremony. None of his friends were there. The party might have been in his honor, but no one paid Brian much attention. Some old people said hello. A few handed him envelopes with money. The envelopes that fit, he slid into the inside pocket of his suit jacket. Those that didn't, he sat on.

Bam circulated around the living and dining rooms. He got the attention Brian did not. He was ashamed these people had heard him stutter. They were punishing him by ignoring him. They thought he'd stutter again if they asked him questions. He saw some people give his mother or father the envelopes they should have been giving to him. In his stead, Bam charmed the old ladies, who told him he was so cute. Brian was fidgety. He wanted some of the party food his mother had laid out. But he didn't risk leaving his chair with the envelopes of money on it.

From the far corner, talking to a man in a suit like his own, his father was observing him. It was the look he got when he had done something wrong. His father's eyes bore into him. The man his father was talking with didn't notice Art's gaze was fixed elsewhere.

His father, after placing his hand on the other man's shoulder and whispering into his ear, set out across the room toward Brian in his chair. Several of the guests crossed his father's path. He moved them gingerly aside, never taking his eyes off Brian. His father halted just in front of him, forcing him to raise his head up to look. His father's five-o'clock shadow was thick. Brian could see into his nostrils.

"Let me tell you something, Son. I want you to remember it. I won't be saying it again."

"Yes, sir," Brian said, gulping.

"If you don't dwell on a problem, it goes away." With that, his father turned and walked back to his guests. Of all the lies Brian had been told as a child, as a stutterer, as a therapist's charge and as a Catholic, this one hurt the most because it was so patently untrue.

He nested atop the gift envelopes beneath him for the rest of the reception. Brian was not yet done with religion and its rituals. He would not be done with them for years, even after renouncing all faith after one coming afternoon in the church vestry. But from today on, Brian was done with his namesake Paul, any saint's miracle cures, and one of his fathers.

*

"Mom," Brian said when the timing was right. "Can I ask a question?" His mother put her needlework down.

There was a kid in a grade below him who was missing an arm. People would ask him what happened. There was a stump you could see whenever he wore a short-sleeved shirt. He had heard the guy was born that way. The boy never seemed bothered by it. When they took showers at the end of gym class, Brian discovered some boys, the armless kid included, had a flap of skin hanging off the end of their dicks.

He and his brother did not.

He was alone in the living room with his mother. She was sewing a button onto one of his father's dress shirts. He had his history textbook in front of him.

"Of course, dear," his mother replied with a little chuckle. "What is it?"

He wasn't sure he should continue, despite the permission. He had a theory he needed to pursue. Several things made him different from other boys, and he swore he'd discover which one of those differences had forced him—and, for a while, Bam—to stutter. As expected, he stammered badly in asking his mother a question about his penis.

She shifted in her chair and coughed slightly, a sign this was not the kind of question she was prepared for. "Oh, the doctor took that little thing away from you after you were born," she explained, surprised. "They do from almost all boys."

"Do what?"

His mother gulped. "Take it away."

"Is Dad missing that piece of his skin, too?" he asked. His mother blushed as she moved back into her earlier position. She looked down into her lap, wrapped thread around a spool and smoothed her dress. This would be another question, a humiliated Brian realized, no one would answer.

"Did it hurt when they took it away?" he asked, persisting.

"You cried, I think," his mother replied with her own embarrassment. "I think you cried. Babies cry all the time."

She paused. "Actually, I don't know, Brian. I suppose you cried."

"Is that *wuh*-when I started *stuh-stuh*-stuttering? Is that *wuh*-what . . . *muh*-made it *huh*-happen?"

"Oh, darling, you didn't know how to talk yet!" She placed a hand on her forehead and ran it back over the headband holding her hair in place.

I still don't know how to talk, he wanted to shout. Instead, in the bathroom, he examined his cock while rolling it in his hands, wondering if touching the faint scar would revive a memory. Something that made him a stutterer. Something that could have happened to anyone, except that anyone was him. There had to be some original event when he had lost control of his body, when someone or something had seized command. If not his circumcision, then the bite of a mad dog; or someone dropped him when he was a baby; or his mother had been frightened by a ghost while pregnant with him. They say left-handed people stutter. They say shell-shocked soldiers and homosexuals do, too. Drunks, drug addicts. He was none of those things. He had to retrieve from history just what it had been for him, or stay a victim of his disquiet forever.

Maybe nothing had caused him to stutter. Maybe he had *chosen* to. He couldn't imagine that being a good idea. It was possible. There was an odd power in simply deciding who you were going to be. An astronaut, a superhero, a fireman, a crook, a rodeo cowboy, a spy. Did it matter which? A first-grader throwing a tantrum in the hallway, a son who disappointed his father, a boy who pushed girls to the pavement, a schoolyard bully: A stammerer.

But then why was he so upset that his stutter was getting worse? His list of unpronounceables was getting longer. Other things were going wrong, too. Now, if especially nervous before talking in class, he'd break out in a fit of hiccups. He told his therapist he was getting more frustrated.

"I have some new things for us to try, Brian," Miss Edwards replied, as if she didn't want to hear any more. "Some games."

Over the next few weeks she had him do a number of exercises. He talked with a coin on his tongue. He crawled on all fours. One session, he was instructed to speak in a higher register, and the next told to speak in a lower one. His voice sounded different but not any better. These weren't games like sports, where someone gets to win. They weren't games with any rules.

One day, he asked Miss Edwards a question. "Do I stutter, or do I *stah*-stammer? Which is it? A *stuh*-*stuh*-stutter or a stammer?"

Miss Edwards pushed her chair back and sat upright. She did this when she had something to explain but wasn't sure Brian would comprehend it.

"Stuttering results from a nervous disorder," she began, counting out her words one by one, just as she told her stutterers to. "Stammering results from uncoordinated vocal items."

He wondered which of these he was. He wondered if

he was going to get sicker.

"Brian, you have both." She paused. "You have multiple problems. Don't fret over them."

Multiple problems. Brian had known that ever since she told him he had an inner condition. *Old news, lady.* No, he wouldn't fret. He'd work more on the rules for his own exercises. He had to retool to navigate a world he knew extended beyond Tummus; one that, he was old enough to know, wouldn't always stay a game.

*

He and his father stopped by the local bait shop one hot Saturday. The fishing was going to be good. The shop was only a wooden shack leaning against a stucco Chevron gas station. Sammamish Bait and Ice sold only those two things. It looked as if it might collapse under its own weight. He had seen it many times from the school bus but had never been inside. The smells were potent. It didn't smell like fish, more like dirt after rain. Like mushrooms in the woods. The air was cool, like mountains covered with old-growth forests.

They were getting bait for the perch and trout in Lake Sammamish. His father was borrowing a small skiff from a coworker who lived on the lake. It would just be the two of them. His father wore his aviator sunglasses.

"We could've dug up some earthworms at home," his father told him. "But these will be better." He took out his worn leather wallet, preparing to order from the teenager at the counter, a kid not much older than Brian. "What kind

70

should we get, Son, the nightcrawlers? Minnows? Honey worms?"

The pimply teenager stood with his mouth half open, saying nothing, waiting to hear Brian's decision.

"Salmon eggs are best for trout," the teenager offered. Brian's father waited for his son to agree.

"*Huh-huh-huh* . . . *huh-huh*. No, nightcrawlers. Can we have some . . ."

The teenager nodded. His father spoke and stopped the teenager from reaching into the mound of wriggling nightcrawlers.

"Honey worms. I think my son meant to say honey worms. Didn't you, Brian? You were partway through it."

Brian's mouth opened. His tongue moved. His face grimaced. His shoulders hunched. His arms fell limp. His eyes darted away from his fellow teenager's. His terror returned. His cheeks grew hot. His panic closed his throat. His shame became everything. His voice was nowhere to be found. He thought: My father has humiliated me in front of this kid my own age. Brian closed his eyes and was back in class, asked to read aloud; he was back in church, asked to recite a prayer; he was back at the supermarket, trying to buy his mother her *Kuh*-kools.

"We'll take some of them," his father ordered with finality, looking down at Brian with a slight grin.

He looked away. His father prepared to pay for the worms. He fixed his eyes on the wall behind the plastic bait bins. There was a large map of Alaska pinned to it with rusted

71

tacks. The edges of the map were yellow and curled. He didn't recall ever seeing a map of Alaska before. It looked big, with a long, skinny tail that led down to Washington state. Alaska, he thought. A word he could pronounce. *Ah-lass-kah.*

Brian couldn't remember much about the fishing that day, but his dream that night was vivid. The Joker led him by the hand to *Ah-lass-kah.* He could picture it clearly, having just seen a map in the bait shop. They kept going north, flying like a jet airplane but faster. The sky grew darker and the temperature colder. The moon rose low in the sky and cast little light. He and the Joker descended to a small town on the ocean. He had no idea where they were. It didn't worry him. Dusk silhouetted mountains.

There were no people on the streets. He saw a few houses, some storefronts, a gas station with a lean-to shack attached to it and a little park with damp, moss-covered wooden benches. He looked around for polar bears and eagles. What he saw were trees: Immense, dense, damp, with the strong scent of mushrooms in moist earth. Trees behind the buildings, trees alongside them, trees in front. Trees everywhere. Spruce, the Joker told him, and cedar. Hemlock. Then it was nighttime. Faint moonlight seeped between the trees, whose lower limbs had fallen off to expose straight trunks. Everything was dark green shading into black. On the forest floor large ferns sprouted up to form a canopy almost Brian's height above an unbroken carpet of thick, luminous moss. The earth was wearing the fur of a creature from another planet. If I walk into this forest, Brian thought, I would soon disappear in it. If I moved here, he thought, I wouldn't stutter. I wouldn't have to talk at all. It would be utopia.

*

A new teacher, Mr. Reynolds, picked Brian for an oral report in tenth-grade English. He had to talk about Nathaniel Hawthorne's *The Scarlet Letter*. He was given one week to prepare. Brian panicked. The timing was bad. He was busy studying the rules of the road for his driver's exam. He liked these rules. They were clear and rational. They were meant to keep both him and other drivers on the road safe.

Now he had to put that aside. For a while his anxiety hadn't been this bad. *Hah-hah-hah*-thorne. He told his mother about the assignment. She offered to help him. He said no. He was too old for help from his mother. He would deal with it, he decided, by writing out what he was going to say and practicing it until he could recite it smoothly.

On the day of his report, he resorted to an old trick. He stood at the front of the class and struck his left thigh repeatedly with a fist. Hitting himself like this helped, even if it earned him odd stares from teachers and his fellow students. Later, his gym teacher spotted a big bruise on his leg and asked about it. Brian pretended not to have noticed it. He had to hit himself hard for the trick to work. This time it didn't. He stuttered as badly as ever, beginning with *Heh-heh-heh*-hester. He had been assigned a novel about shame, and now here was shame. He wrote in his stuttering diary that evening:

Mary was there. She watched. I saw her move her lips silently, mouthing the words I was supposed to be saying and somehow I would. Well, it didn't work. It might have. Good try. I was glad she was there today. After class, we talked in the hallway. She told me I did good. I told her not to lie. You know what happened. I'm a stutterer, you used to be, your little brother is, my little brother used to be, and that's just the way it is. Mary smiled at me and gave me a kiss. On the lips! I kissed her back and got hard. I think she felt it through my pants when I leaned against her but she didn't move away. That was all. I backed off and left her alone. We were in the hallway. Why does she like me? What is there to like? I don't think anyone saw us. Maybe I'm wrong. I want to spend more time with her. I want to sit next to her in class, but I don't want to embarrass her and I don't want the other guys to razz me when they figure out I like her.

Brian read over what he had written. Maybe he really could be a writer someday. There wasn't a mangled word anywhere on the page. He put the pencil down on his notebook and turned his head. Bam was asleep in the next bed. He picked his pencil up again, but instead of writing more he drew a picture in his journal. He drew a picture of what a forest in Alaska might look like at night, a forest full of cedars, spruces and hemlocks. He drew a canopy of ferns and their spiderweb-like fronds, where, if he walked into them, he'd disappear forever. The Joker wasn't there, so he didn't draw him. Brian knew he was too old to have an invisible friend. There weren't any houses or storefronts or gas stations to draw, either. He used the side of his pencil's tip to shade in the spaces between the trees he'd drawn. Lastly, he made the ground's moss as dark as he could, until his pencil was no more than a dull wooden stub.

*

"Want to eat our sandwiches now?" Mary asked.

She and Brian were at the small lake just over the Tummus town line. They had ridden their bikes and left them at the head of the short trail. The sun was high. They found a small clearing in the shade on a hill overlooking the water. They sat near the foot of a cedar made fragrant by the warming sun. It hadn't rained in weeks. The undergrowth beneath the cedar's branches was dry and brittle.

"Sure, why not," he answered. He swatted a fly away.

She unwrapped two of the four tuna sandwiches she had brought in her knapsack. He took out the two cans of soda he'd carried in his. He walked down to the lake's edge and placed them in the water to cool. They would explode if he opened them now. He walked back up the slope. He saw Mary was shielding her eyes from the sun with one hand.

"Let's start on the sandwiches. There's mayonnaise in them."

He nodded thanks. He took a sandwich from her

hands. Sitting next to each other, shoulders brushing, they looked straight ahead over the surface of the lake. They were too awkward to look at each other when this close. Perhaps they were absorbed in separate thoughts. Brian stole a quick glance and was struck all over again by how pretty Mary was. Her cheekbones, her oval almond-shaped eyes, the eyebrows framing them like a painting; her lips, neither large nor small, made a mouth he was eager to kiss. They were seventeen now. In the movies, seventeen was nearly adult. Her face sat atop a long, alabaster neck and led to shoulders narrow enough for Brian's arm to wrap comfortably around. Were there any imperfections? Irish freckles here and there added charm, as did an aquiline nose that might have looked better on a boy than a girl. Pretty wasn't quite the right word to describe her, just the first word guys reached for. You'd never find her on the cover of a magazine. She was handsome, but a weak chin made her vulnerable. Brian liked that. Was there a word for it?

Mary broke the silence by talking to him about her own stutter. It had appeared a year after she started talking. Her parents, alarmed, took her to a doctor. "Like mine," Brian interrupted. Unlike him, she was told she would grow out of it. She was a girl. They were right, though her cure came slowly. It was as if some part of her were more male and less female, Mary said, and so her stutter lingered in her longer. She admitted that even now, if she tripped up, it made her feel tomboyish.

Mary had also told him that though she outgrew

her stutter, mostly, her brother Jim's worsened. Her family changed. Her mother grew closer to Jim and their father more distant. Brian said it was the same in his house. His own father barely spoke to him. Mary told Brian a story. Once, when they were living in Flint, Mary had taken her brother into the backyard shed and told him to lend her his red pocket knife. She opened his mouth to look inside. It was too dark to see anything. She stuck two fingers in his mouth and felt around, thinking she'd find what was wrong in there, something she could cut out. She was about to use the pocket knife when Jim gagged and ran indoors.

"Did you get into trouble?"

"No," Mary replied, "Jim didn't tell." She explained to Brian that talking is only important for people who interact with the outside world. She wondered if she would ever grow up to be one of those people. Her mother hadn't. She stayed home and cooked and cleaned all day. If her mother stuttered, what difference would it make? "Except on the phone," Brian interjected.

"I'm going to be different, Brian," Mary insisted. "I'm brave for a girl, maybe part boy after all. I know how to bully other kids back." She raised her hand in a fist and laughed.

People who didn't like her stutter could just mind their own business. "I told them so, and so should you." Brian thought: she could tell people to mind their business was proof her stutter was never going to last all that long.

"Well, you don't stutter anymore, so you can just put your fist down." This time, they both laughed.

Now, everything was so quiet Brian could hear the two of them chewing their sandwiches. He watched a bird, a blue heron, skim over the far end of the lake, scouting for a fish near the surface to capture with its beak.

"Brian?" Mary said without turning her head. "Let's make love."

He kept chewing. His heart thumped, then skipped a beat. He looked at the ground between his legs, too embarrassed to look her in the eye. Brian was excited and frightened at the same time. He prayed all the parts of his body would work but wasn't sure they would. He didn't hear her eating her sandwich anymore, just himself.

What followed, on an uneven bed of cedar needles mixed with bits of paper and plastic, trash tossed aside by other picnickers, proceeded largely clothed. The ground was rough. They were shy with each other. It was his first time and, he was sure, Mary's, too. Brian had wondered when this would happen. He had thought it through. He assumed it would unfold as he had rehearsed in his mind: Wordlessly. There would be sounds, but only sounds never rising to the level of language. He'd be spared his stammer.

But he was wrong. When they coupled, neither pantomimed. There was no stuttering. They spoke to each other in complete sentences. "Is this okay?" He was this comfortable with her. "Hold me tighter, Brian." Phrases came to him from out of nowhere and helped. "Is this good?" In the years ahead, he would stutter in front of Mary many times, but not now. "Am I hurting you?" Words came to him, though not the ones he had set aside for this day. "I love you." Unexpected syllables traveled the length of his throat and escaped from his mouth. They fused into words possessing a life of their own, aloud, and echoed in the compressed space between them. They wrestled under the cedar's canopy. "Don't stop." In his recurring daydream of making love to her, he hadn't said anything. Here by the lake, as close to dreaming as he would ever be in his waking life, the things he heard himself say returned him to his mother's womb. "Kiss me." She didn't cry. He didn't stammer. "I like you, too."

Here on the mountainside with Mary, he enjoyed a respite from everything: From the dream of a harrowing birth, from the rise and fall of the first Moriarty son who gurgled happily in infancy only later to maul every other word; from learning that shoving girls could be just retribution according to his rulebook; from the tyranny of first consonants that hovered over him like winged predators eager to devour what little self-regard he had; from the doubts that he was ever meant to be complete. This was a high higher than any other, a personal best. Brian knew to savor it. He was no longer a virgin. He'd crossed a more important line—an initiation into what his life could be, if it were with Mary, once a stutterer no different than he.

They finished and struggled to sit up. Brian giggled as he peeled a square of plastic wrap stuck to the back of Mary's shirt. He showed it to her, and she giggled, too, but only after turning her head to check no one had seen them. He let his gaze follow hers. Out of the corner of his eye he saw his blue heron again, now with a struggling fish in its beak, a fish too large for it to swallow whole. The bird was making a slow circle in the sky when it dropped its writhing prey onto boulders at the far end of the lake, to kill it. Brian stood up and walked down the hill to get their two cans of soda out of the water.

Chapter Six

The Sunday before Bam's confirmation, the Moriartys invited Father Thomas to dinner. The adults had sherry in the living room. Brian and his brother were summoned to the dining room once his mother had set a big pot of Irish stew down on the table.

Art turned to his oldest son Brian and asked him to say grace. Brian was taken by surprise. Why not Father Thomas? Why not the priest? Isn't that his job? They never said grace except at Thanksgiving, Christmas and Easter. Today was none of those. He panicked. He didn't remember the words to grace. Something about being grateful. He was feeling anything but gratitude. Brian had been ambushed. His father had put him on the spot. He was guaranteed to stammer. This was a setup.

He opened his mouth wide. Bam opened his own in mocking imitation of his older brother. Nothing came out. His mother reached across the table to slip him a piece of paper, letting everyone see her do it. The adults planned this, he realized.

"Bless us, O Lord, and these ... Thy *gih-gih-gih*-gifts .. . which we are about to receive from Thy *buh-buh-buh*-bounty, through Christ our Lord. *Ah-ah*-amen."

He closed his mouth. So did his brother. There was silence at the table until Bam broke it with a whine that he wanted to eat. Everyone relaxed. His mother dished out the stew. No one thanked Brian. The conversation among the adults turned to other things.

Near the end of the meal, the priest spoke to him. "How is school going, Brian?" Father Thomas asked, picking at his dessert.

Holding a fork loaded with cherry pie halfway to his mouth, Brian answered with his first words since grace. "*Guh-guh*-good, *Fah*-father Thomas."

The priest sat back in his chair, placed his crumpled napkin on the table, and began the sermon his parents had invited him to deliver. Brian was about to be given guidance. He was used to advice. The world was full of advice. Swallow hard before you talk. Breathe deep before starting. He had heard it all before. But he hadn't. This was going to be new guidance.

"Brian, you were a good student in catechism classes. Remember? Aren't I right?"

Brian stayed silent. His mother leaned forward in her chair.

"In Exodus, it says Moses spoke to God, 'Behold, the people of Israel have not listened to me. How then shall

82

Pharaoh listen to me, for I am of uncircumcised lips?'"

"We didn't read the Bible in *kah-kah*-catechism class, *Fah-fah-fah*-father." The word *uncircumcised* made him uncomfortable in front of his mother. So this is why they made me say grace, Brian realized. To show the priest my symptoms at their worst.

Father Thomas chuckled. He sat back in his chair again. His mother moved her narrow shoulders further forward.

"But Moses spoke to the pharaoh. And the pharaoh listened, as everyone will to you. You are blessed, Brian."

His mother smiled. Brian did not. Bam became the table's center of attention for a while. Brian took care not to talk again, lest he stutter and have to hear Father Thomas quote the Bible again. He understood that by talking in front of his family and their priest, he was acknowledging their power over him. One realization followed another: Were he to join in the dining room conversation, his stutter would confirm their faith in a God whose existence was still on trial in Brian's mind.

*

The next day Brian's parents told him they were sending him to Father Thomas once a week for spiritual counseling. What they meant was for help with his stutter.

He met Father Thomas in the vestry. The small room was crowded with the priests' vestments hanging on a long clothes rack and from hooks on the walls. There were long windows lining the top of the room where they met the ceiling, designed to keep direct sunlight off the robes. He noticed a fat moth banging repeatedly against one of the glass windows, desperate for escape.

Father Thomas was wearing the dark uniform all the priests did. His collar had that bit of white on it. Brian hadn't looked closely at him before. Now he did. There was a sickly-sweet smell about him that said he had just shaved, a smell like his father's early in the morning but stronger. The priest's thinning hair was combed back with a shiny pomade, revealing a receding hairline. His temples were turning gray. Creases circled his eyes. His cheeks had faint brown spots on them. The skin around his neck looked loose. His teeth were small and stained. There was the hint of a small scar on his weak chin. Father Thomas was not wearing the frameless eyeglasses he usually did. Brian could see his eyes. The pupils were small and bright, as if lit from within. Bushy eyebrows topped them, and above that were deep lines in his forehead.

The priest's hands were plump, pinkish and lined at the knuckles. There was a gold ring on one finger. He knew priests couldn't marry, so he wondered what it meant. Priests always had rings. He recalled the sharp sting of the bishop's ring against his cheek when he was confirmed. He remembered being asked a question he couldn't answer: At baptism.

"Brian," started Father Thomas in a low, measured voice. "I want you to understand me when I say God loves you very much."

Brian fidgeted in his hard wooden chair. He shoved his hands deep in his pockets to keep them still. Once they could go no further, he clenched them into fists.

"But God has also withdrawn His love from you. That is why, like Moses, you have trouble talking."

"You mean my stutter, *Fah*-father," he corrected. "My trouble is *stuh-stuh*-stuttering."

"Yes, stuttering, Brian. Your stutter." They sat motionless for a while.

"Brian, do you have something you want to tell me? Your sin must be deep for God to have done this to you."

He tightened the fists in his pockets some more. Father Thomas paused before continuing.

"Brian, would you like to join me in confession? Let's get down on our knees and pray for forgiveness. Jesus encountered many sick and crippled people, and he cured many. Even the sinners among them."

Brian considered reminding the priest what they'd learned in catechism classes: We are all sinners. But that would be talking back. Instead, he took his relaxed hands out of his pockets and joined the priest already on his knees between their two chairs. Facing the dark plastic crucifix on the wall, they brushed shoulders. In front of them, and below the cross, hung the altar boys' garments.

He waited for Father Thomas to start the prayer. He did not. Instead, he continued to talk to him in the same slow voice.

"What is your sin, Brian? What are your sins? Tell me, and tell God."

He hesitated to say anything. He wasn't sure what the

priest wanted him to say. He had been raised to please priests.

"I tell them in *kuh-kuh*-confession, Father. My mother takes me every *muh*-month. Sometimes *muh*-more."

"We are in confession now, my son."

He knew it was Father Thomas who sat on the other side of the screen in the confessional booth. He had always heard his sins.

The priest raised his clasped hands from his chest to the edge of his weak chin. "Brian, tell me. God wants you to tell me everything."

"I *stuh-stuh-stuh*-stutter, Father."

"Then stutter, Brian. But tell me your sins. Your stutter is not a sin. It is God's punishment for your sins." The priest's shoulder rubbed against his. "Confess your sins, or Jesus cannot save you."

So Brian confessed. He invented sin after sin in his head and sputtered them out, just as he did in the confessional booth. "I drank alcohol." *I want to drink alcohol sometimes. I think it will make my stutter go away.* "I lied to my parents." *I told them I was studying with Mary. We weren't.* "I took the Lord's name in vain." *The Joker makes me do it.* "I missed Sunday mass last month." *I didn't feel well. I stayed home that morning.* "I bullied a kid in school." *He deserved it.* "I beat up my brother because I felt like it." *He deserved it, too.* "I had dirty thoughts about Mary." *She has them about me. Doesn't that cancel out the sin for the both of us?* "I stole a candy bar." *I didn't have any money on me.* "I cheated on my homework." *It's so easy to do.* "I played with my dick when I was in the bathtub." *The door was locked.* "I kicked a dog in the street." *It didn't get out of my way.* "I didn't give Jerry back the lunch money I borrowed." *It wasn't much, and he's always got money.*

"I can't remember any more sins, Father." He thought: This priest has heard my lies before.

Father Thomas was silent. Brian saw he had closed his eyes. Was he thinking Brian had just committed a sin when he said he had nothing more to confess?

The priest lowered his folded hands from his chin and let his arms fall by his sides. He rose to his feet but did not motion to Brian to do the same. Brian looked up at the older man standing over him, and the older man motioned they should take their seats again.

"Next week we'll pray again, Brian. And you will confess the new sins you'll commit in the coming week and those you refused, today, to admit to God, to your Savior, and to me."

He leaned toward Brian, who sat motionless in the chair across from him. The priest extended his right hand and placed it lightly on the young man's crotch.

"He has withdrawn His grace from you, Brian. Because you have sinned."

His mind raced. Yes, he had sinned. He had sins upon sins, sins he had never confessed. He had sins even the Joker didn't know about. But he had never touched another male's crotch.

"Let God admit you to His circle again, Brian."

The priest deftly opened Brian's fly. His hand pulled his

penis out. He felt he was floating in the air above what was happening. It was like floating over the stage when he auditioned for the Thanksgiving pageant. But this time, there was disgust. He was observing two strangers doing something too private to watch without the revulsion that accompanied the shame. He did not recognize either of the strangers. The older man lowered his mouth onto the younger man.

There was no more talking once Father Thomas began slurping. Brian gazed up at the vestry ceiling, thinking he might see himself suspended there. He started to get hard. He tried to recite his Latin prayers in his head, thinking it would deflate his erection. *Pater noster . . . qui es in caelis.* Things you memorize early in life, you never forget. *Fiat voluntas tua.* The priest made ugly sucking sounds with his unpleasantly moist mouth. Brian got harder and stayed that way. He was not aroused; he was repulsed. What was the priest doing? He couldn't be enjoying this. *Maybe this is a cure for my stuttering? Some old church ritual.* Maybe Father Thomas was trying to extract the evil out of him. Is that why his cock was cooperating? Is that why his cock was filling the old man's mouth?

He stayed still in his chair while the kneeling priest panted like an exhausted animal. Father Thomas appeared to him as a hateful *thing*, something that with one forceful kick he could leave sprawling on the vestry's tiled floor. Was this old man *swallowing* his sperm? The cough was proof he had. Now who was more abject? Brian wondered, and the answer came to him. The earlier shame and disgust were displaced by a fresh pair of feelings: Scorn and anger. He felt both for the groveling priest. The combination, for the first time in his career as a stutterer but not the last, gave Brian new scales of justice to weigh his sins: The righteousness of deserved contempt for other people.

*

While everyone else in the house was at Bam's confirmation ceremony, Brian watched *The War of the Worlds* on television. He had lied to his parents and told them Father Thomas said his guidance sessions were over. He'd gotten some useful advice. Yes, it was helping. No, no special prayers to say. His parents seemed mildly surprised.

He'd seen this movie before. Bam liked it, too. They knew how it ended. The Martians would die and the world would be spared. *By the littlest things.* This time he watched it with a new interest, even the commercials for cars, detergent and cigarettes. The people in the ads were so fluent. They spoke about this new brand or taste delight with such fluency. The people in the movie talked easily, too. "It's a *bah*-bomb." The only stutter in the film, when the death machine emerged from the first alien pod. When one of the three men guarding it stammered out his guess what it was. "We'll talk to them in sign language." Brian thought, damn, I'd stutter, too. "All radio is dead." They aren't stutterers in real life, he reminded himself. They were actors paid *not* to stutter unless the script said to. The movie was about people being struck dumb for a moment—outside the alien pods, in front of ray guns shooting flames, in a bunker where they learned even an atomic bomb could not stop the Martians. "It's the latest thing in nuclear fission." Birds and animals fled "fields and forests" ahead of the machines. "If you have no goggles, turn away."

You never hear the aliens talk in this movie, Brian noticed. They can't speak. They have evolved beyond speech. They probably communicate via telepathy without words. They don't have mouths. They were powered by nuclear energy and didn't need mouths to eat, either. "We'll get out of here safely." Brian was back in his mother's womb, when he didn't have a mouth, either. He raised his hands and counted his fingers. Five on each. Not three. "It's dead." The cities stopped burning. Mankind was saved. Bam and his parents came home late that evening, because Father Thomas had invited them to stay for supper at the rectory.

CHAPTER SEVEN

Eating a grilled cheese sandwich in the student union cafeteria, Brian got some unsolicited advice from a guy in his dif-
ferential calculus class. You should box, he was told. You've got
the build for it. At the time, he didn't stop eating to respond,
but not long after he joined the University of Washington's
junior varsity boxing squad. He was thinking of majoring in
Russian and French. They weren't hard. He figured he had
some time to devote to a sport. Mary had chosen Spanish
to be near him in the same foreign language department, so
he was already seeing plenty of her. In high school, he had
been too intimidated to try out for a team. None of them
spared him from speaking. He felt differently about boxing,
a college sport they hadn't had at Tummus High. And being
a little short was finally an advantage.

Brian earned a spot on the squad more for his spirit
than for any skills he had, which were zero. He had to learn
to box from scratch. Where to position his feet to stay stable.
Left under the cheek, right under the chin. Cross punches to

defend from jabs. How to throw a hook. How to be *present* in the ring, if not the world, he thought. Boxing was instructive and useful.

Was that the appeal of boxing to him? Or was it the rubber mouth guards making his squad mates' speech as garbled as his own? Perhaps it was the flirtation with injury, even death. Maybe the allure lay in the spectacle. He'd graduated from kicking boots as a first grader to landing punches as a college freshman. Like being on a Thanksgiving pageant stage without having to talk. It was a zero-sum game. Boxing required violence to generate drama. Boxing made him feel strong.

The coach, Mr. Jones, stuttered himself. When he did, he'd grab anything close at hand, a pencil or a small barbell, and squeeze it so tightly Brian could see his knuckles turn white. Once he saw that Brian stuttered as well, the two bonded. Mr. Jones' father, he learned, worked as a barber but went to prison when Coach was a boy, taking the rap for a guy higher up in the mob. Something about loans. Mr. Jones' name wasn't always Jones. It was something Italian before his mother changed it out of shame over what her husband had done. Mr. Jones told most of his team he had boxed as a teenager hoping to go professional. The real reason, he let Brian know, was that at a young age he had bought a book, *How To Stop Stuttering*, and it mentioned boxing as a remedy. He was good at it. He boxed in the army. After a few years at a teachers college on the G.I. Bill, Mr. Jones ended up the Huskies' boxing coach.

He noticed one of Mr. Jones' eyes was glass. Brian liked that. It was cool, unlike his younger brother's queer eye. Coach wore his scars for all to see, like Brian's scalp gash. His parents, Art and Eve, met Coach after one match. His mother said he reminded her of Spencer Tracy. The next time he visited the school library, he looked up who that was: *American actor . . . Played an Irish priest who sparred in the ring with Clark Gable in San Francisco (1936)*. Even cooler.

Brian was at home in the ring. Inside the ropes he could fight and not get into trouble for it. Unless he broke the rules, of course, and then his punishment was only a penalty, at most a forfeit or a reprimand from Coach Jones, who often delivered it with a wink. He learned a reputation for breaking rules was not necessarily a bad thing to have. Despite the bravura, he became an amateur boxer for the same reason Mr. Jones had: A stutter that had him thinking he was weak. He hoped boxing would help. But Mr. Jones had been boxing his whole life, and he still stammered.

He was popular on the squad, though he often lost his matches. He made mistakes. Once, up against a guy from Washington State, he got knocked out. His teammates told him he was felled like a tree in the forest. The knockout added to his reputation. Some of the other boxers imitated his swagger in the ring. Some of the girls who came to matches doted on him for a few weeks. He was glad Mary didn't come. He wasn't always proud of the way he boxed in the ring. Sometimes, in a bar with the other boxers, he'd think of starting a fight because he thought he could win.

The thought of a boxer on another campus training to break his jaw excited Brian. He was keen to disappoint his challengers. But his career as a boxer would end his junior year, just when he'd made it to varsity. One day Mr. Jones didn't show up for practice, and that was that. The university had trouble finding a replacement. Brian gave up waiting. He heard a rumor that Mr. Jones had gone to prison. Something about loans. Something about breaking someone's face. He wished for a moment he'd learned to box before encountering Father Thomas in the vestry. Brian was older now, and his list of dos and don'ts had evolved to become principles of the just and the unjust. Violence, if played by the rules Coach had taught him, was a way to enforce the difference between the two. He was now allowed to break up faces, too.

*

"I'm going to major in foreign languages," he told his parents one weekend. It was a cool, crisp November day in his sophomore year. He interrupted his parents after watching the Huskies beat the Oregon Ducks in the campus stadium. He walked in the back door and hadn't even sat down in his chair at the kitchen table before making his declaration. His mother stopped pasting her S&H green stamps. His father, paying bills, looked up from his checkbook.

"Which one, darling?" his mother began.

His father stared at him, the corners of his mouth downturned. The unspoken subtext around the table was that Brian was a stutterer, and if speaking in English was often beyond him, what was he doing learning *other* languages? Brian gazed out the kitchen window.

"Weren't you interested in engineering, dear? All those math classes," continued his mother, now with an element of optimism in her voice betrayed by hands fretting with a damp sponge. Brian was reminded of how she fidgeted with rosary beads in church.

"Wasn't Spanish tough for you in high school?" his father finally contributed. "That's the way I remember it."

"*Duh-duh*-dad," he stammered, proving his father's point even though he was about to say he'd done well in Spanish class.

His grades in college were good, too. He did stutter in his French and Russian classes, for which his parents continued to pay tuition without enthusiasm but also without objection. Unlike in high school, his college teachers and classmates were circumspect about his problem. Still, there were reactions. One time he was stuck halfway through reciting a Russian poem. He glanced up from the page for a split second and saw eyes downcast all around him; a class embarrassed at the trouble he was having but aware they couldn't help without making him feel worse. Another time, his French teacher hesitated in deciding who would get saddled with him as a practice partner.

Languages were fine. It was speech getting in Brian's way. His teachers had the conviction that language, foreign ones, too, were mediums for communication. Brian did not. Words were a recording of his humiliation, a confirmation of his ineptitude, an indicator of his abnormality, a violation of what everyone else considered minimally human. He was not studying French and Russian because he "loved" them, as some of his classmates liked to say. They were the enemy. They were boxers from other universities. When he said his ambition was to "master" them, it meant something different from when his professors used the word. For Brian, it meant acting on his contempt for speech.

He was best at composition and translation, so good that teachers often called on him to read out loud in class. *Bégayer*. Brian stuttered less when reciting homework, and the teachers knew it. *Zaikat'sya*. He knew it wasn't on account of having practiced the night before. It was because these words did not come out of his own head. They came from those of others. In his literature classes he read French poets and Russian novelists who owned the words. They were lending them to him. *Balbutier*. He understood he was a kind of machine, one that reprocessed things other people had assembled. His English versions were not as eloquent as the originals, but who cared. All he had to be was accurate. *Zaikaniye*.

By the time he graduated, his French and Russian vocabularies were large. He was proud. He was pleased because, unlike his classmates, he hadn't spent a year or even a summer in Paris or Leningrad. The cost was one reason, but the bigger one was he lacked the ambition to speak a foreign language. Reading and translating were silent tasks. They appealed to him. Stutterers stutter less in foreign languages;

he should have lived with a family in Provence or Moscow. Learned to make small talk around the dinner table. Had a French or Russian brother to teach him the dirty words that weren't in any textbook. He did not.

He had one ambition, though. One day, he learned many famous authors were stutterers. He toyed with the idea of becoming one. He had no idea what he might write about. But the words would be his and no one else's. There was a problem, though. He'd had no adventures in his life and no prospects of any. And, he concluded, writers had to give readings, stand before classes or bookstore audiences, mesmerize the public with their voices. Translators, he figured, never had to speak. They worked alone, in offices behind the scenes. He didn't want a job in a big company. He'd never make it anywhere near the top because he was a stutterer. So here he was, armed with a pencil, bent over printed pages lined with words next to blank paper, waiting for the inspiration—or was it simply the discipline?—to substitute his words for theirs.

*

"Translate?" Mary exclaimed when Brian told her, too, of his decision. "I get good grades in it," he offered, which was no explanation. Maybe she'd been hoping for a lawyer or doctor. But she had to have known he'd never go into anything where oral communication mattered.

The two of them had never talked about their majors. They had just fallen into them. His options as a stutterer, and maybe those of a former stutterer such as Mary, were limited. All Brian needed to translate words were his eyes, his hand, and a pen and paper in front of him. In translating he experienced a release, a catharsis, a revelation, a flight, an escape. This was both his freedom and his necessity. He had to specialize, as all handicapped people do. They need their own tools to make themselves indispensable in a world pleased to discard them.

Indispensability takes a toll, Brian came to realize. Graduation was around the corner, and his projected career was using one language, English, to replace two others, French and Russian. Technical documents were dull but straightforward. They were regular, unambiguous. Perfect for him. One day, he knew, machines would do this. For the time being, he'd dedicate himself to doing a good job. Good would be good enough. He knew he was mediocre. The world was satisfied with mediocrity, including in his translations. He had dreams of translating one day a French or Russian masterpiece, of being in the audience when its author won the Nobel Prize. That was not the translating he would do for now, however. There was a demand for technical translators out there, even for a green freelancer. He would translate bills of lading, ingredient labels for imported jars of caviar, court documents, licensing agreements, wills and last testaments, citations, birth certificates, and death certificates. He fancied himself a god at times. A small one.

In his worst moments of tedium, Little God Brian would daydream, toy with the idea of deliberately mistranslating something, something that, due to his willful sabotage, might result in tragedy. The pilot's manual for a new passenger aircraft. Or the instructions for a new piece of heavy machinery. People could die if his translations were less than perfect. He fantasized about such things. But his disdain for the world did not yet extend that far; not to the anonymous others who'd never laughed at him or who enjoyed their fluency of speech without reflecting what its absence might entail. The small god in him was a benevolent one, or so he liked to think.

Ducks was his private, dismissive word for the non-stutterers of the world. Quack, quack: No duck ever had trouble making honking sounds. Brian awarded fowl the humanity he did not possess: *Quack*, a word as devoid of meaning as any animal cry. He concluded he could not comprehend what being a normal person was like. Lack of imagination was the reason he could never be a writer. Translating was the best he could hope for. Translating was akin to stuttering. A stutterer knows words as obstacles to be dealt with one by one. Like a translator, the stutterer limps from one word to the next. Speaking with a stutter and translating a foreign language required equal degrees of concentration. Brian had to get each word right as best he could. What he translated didn't require art. It required fidelity and precision. These things were in his grasp.

*

Less than a month after his graduation, a letter from the

government showed up in Brian's mail. He had to report the following Thursday for his draft physical. He wasn't surprised.

Mary had just found work at a Spanish-immersion daycare, but she took time off to drive him to the induction center. Flowers were blooming. They were headed to Seattle's Interbay neighborhood, where neither of them had been before. They became lost in Magnolia, and he panicked. He had no idea what they did to you if you were late.

"You won't be drafted," she said, turning left onto 15th Avenue West.

"Oh, yeah," he said, in a tone of voice halfway between telling a joke and revealing his nervousness. "How do you know that?"

"I did research. Thinking about my brother and the army. Stutterers can get out."

It hurt to be lumped in with other stutterers, most of all one as bad as Jim. Brian wasn't sure he wanted to, as she put it, "get out." He didn't relish the idea of going to Vietnam, but neither did he look forward to being less a part of life, once again, just on account of something he couldn't do.

Mary pulled into a large parking lot next to two school buses lined up outside a concrete and sheet metal building the size of an aircraft hangar. There was no shade to park under.

"I'll wait here for you."

"May be a while."

He walked in behind the young men who had gotten off the school buses.

"Seattle?" one said to him over his shoulder.

He nodded, though he wasn't from Seattle. He didn't want to risk stammering.

"We're from Renton."

Inside, some fifty young men sat on bleachers. Everyone was talking in low voices to whoever was next to them if they were fearful or in elevated voices if excited. He felt shyness oozing out of his pores.

An older man in an army uniform appeared. He stood in front of the bleachers wearing sunglasses. Pointless in a dimly lit building. He started calling the roll.

"*Huh*-here!" Brian said when he heard "Moriarty, B."

"Are you getting drafted?" asked one of the Renton guys sitting above him on the bleachers. Dumb question, Brian thought. He's one of the nervous ones. Real nervous to have asked me that. Before he could answer, the officer finished with the roll and barked instructions. Several other soldiers appeared and distributed booklets and short pencils.

"You'll take this written test. You college Joes who think you can fail this test and get out of the service, forget it. We're going to keep you here until you pass."

Two young men in the bleachers guffawed and then looked embarrassed they had.

The questions were multiple choice on the level of *What color is a blue sky?* Despite the simplicity of the questions, some men near him had trouble. They whispered among themselves. Brian finished quickly. The rest of the bleachers were still scribbling when the soldiers came by to collect the booklets and pencils.

"I hope they make me a medic," said the fellow who had asked him if he was here to be drafted. Medics get creamed in Vietnam, too, Brian thought, but did not say.

They were told to go into a locker room and take paper bags from the pile by the door. They were instructed to strip to their underwear, put their shoes and socks back on, and leave their shirts and pants in the bag. Any "supporting materials" were to be carried by hand. He had no such materials. Many of the guys had manila folders or even briefcases: Dozens of guys in their underwear, all carrying paper bags, and a lot of them with "supporting materials."

Back in the big room, they were herded into four lines leading into several white tents erected at the far end of the hangar. Two men at a time entered a partially curtained-off room. He heard someone say that's where they'd get their physical examinations. Brian, last in one of the four lines, would be there a long time. Some of the guys were shivering without their clothes on, but his thoughts were about Mary getting overheated in the shadeless car parked outside.

Eventually he and one other were summoned into the smaller, curtained room. They were the last of the day. A doctor with a stethoscope lazily draped around his neck sat behind a folding table. He told the other guy to step up and gestured to Brian to stay back behind the line marked with black electrical tape.

The fellow ahead of him handed the doctor a set of papers. The doctor thumbed through them. "What's your problem?" he asked curtly.

"Car accident," he responded. He gave the doctor more papers. "Damaged vertebrae."

"Anything else?"

"Psychological trauma." No chance that guy stutters, Brian chortled. He passed the doctor more papers. The doctor leafed through them slowly this time, irritation showing on his face at being fed the papers in stages.

"Okay, you're out," the doctor said, giving him a slip of paper. "Go back to the main desk with this."

Brian's turn came. The doctor began the exam asking none of the preliminary questions he had the fellow in front of him. Brian guessed the day was getting long.

"Rheumatic fever?" the doctor asked. He palmed Brian's balls and told him to cough. He didn't hear the word clearly only because he was already coughing.

"*Ruh-ruh-ruh* . . . ?" he stuttered.

The doctor sat up straight in his chair.

"Rheumatic," he repeated. "You stammer, son?" He thought of lying, that he was stuttering because he was nervous. But he did not.

"Anything from a doctor?" he asked. Brian shrugged.

"Recite the Pledge of Allegiance."

Brian was three words into it when the doctor waved a hand. He was glad he was the last guy in the line and that no one had to overhear what was coming.

"Give this to the front desk," the doctor sighed. "You're

out, too. The army's not having a very good day today."

Back in the car, he asked Mary why a stutter got you out of the draft.

"Because you might have to say something important in battle, like an order or a warning, and it won't come out."

"*Puh*-privates don't . . . *guh*-give orders," he lectured.

"Warnings, then."

She handed him a sheet of paper, larger than the one the doctor had given him a few minutes earlier. It was in her handwriting. She started up the engine.

Stammering, if excessive and confirmed; to be established by satisfactory evidence under oath.

"I did research," she said.

"Yeah, you told me. Well, it wasn't an oath, it was a pledge."

He stayed quiet on the drive back to Tummus, feeling diminished. A part of him wanted the chance to kill a man and get away with it. The directives and prohibitions in his system of justice had advanced to permit that now. He fantasized about going back in time and murdering those who had abased or abused him. Those were now capital offenses in his book. The incipient lethal violence in him had more innocent origins in his early failures to let the world know how he felt about the simplest things: That he was *thuh-thuh*-thirsty after playing outdoors; that he wanted to stay up past his bedtime to see how the *buh-buh*-ballgame ended; that he wanted an *er-er*-erector set for Christmas; even that he wanted Father Thomas punished for what he did. Looming now within him was the pugnaciousness of the heretofore sequestered brute Brian had cultivated since childhood. The army could have used him. And he could have used the army. That was another thing to be denied him. Brian would have to look for other opportunities.

CHAPTER EIGHT

Brian proposed to Mary just before his twenty-third birthday and just after hers. Their friends wondered what had taken him so long. For kids who had gone to Tummus High School in the sixties, this was a late marriage. Their families had let on they were worried. In fact, Brian had not proposed to Mary. She proposed to him.

"We're getting married in the Catholic church," she had informed him. "My mother reserved it already."

"Which one?" he asked, not because there were now two in town, but because he was signaling to Mary that he didn't look forward to going to either.

"Why, the old one, of course." Mary's "why" and "of course" were there to remind him where their families' ceremonies were always held, St. Joseph's, where he had his confirmation, where he had stuttered in front of everyone and was treated to the cold, hard ring that smarted when a bishop's liver-spotted hand slapped him; the same church where the parish priest had pulled his soft penis out and sucked it until it was as hard as the bishop's metal jewelry.

A bridegroom does not say more than two words. One of those two words terrified him: *Do*. The Saturday morning of his wedding, he stood with his brother, father and uncles outside the church. The women were elsewhere. He had decided to go to war with *do*. It would not intimidate him. It would not defeat him. He would fight it and win. Brian would not embarrass himself or Mary. He would triumph. He isolated the *d* of *do* in his mind and plotted strategies against the menacing first consonant.

That morning one of his uncles led Brian out of his father's sight and took a shiny silver flask out of an inside pocket.

"Brian, boy, come on, take a swig. Take two. It's your wedding day."

An hour later, whether it was the whiskey, or his determination to vanquish all enemies that day, Brian performed his part flawlessly.

"I do."

The rest of his wedding day passed without incident as well. He behaved well at the brief reception. For their honeymoon they checked into the Indian casino resort in Marysville, where playing the slots required no talking. Later, though, he and Mary spoke for a long time in bed: How the day had gone, how happy they were, how there would be no insurmountable hurdles ahead. He stuttered a bit, but so did she. He took that as evidence she loved him.

*

A few months into their new life together, in the two-bed-room ranch they rented halfway between both sets of parents, Mr. and Mrs. Brian Moriarty talked about getting a dog. "There are two pounds we can go to," Mary suggested.

"Pounds? *Shuh-shuh*-shelters? Yeah, *shuh*-sure," he replied, showing his apprehension at the prospect of discussing something important with strangers. And at having a second living thing in the house he might have to talk to.

"Why don't you go, and I'll take a look if you find one you like." There was no doubt in Brian's mind what she was up to.

"Tomorrow?"

He nodded and swiveled in his chair to resume the work in front of him, a Russian space agency report he was translating for Boeing. He was distracted by the suspicion his new wife wanted a pet as a trial run for being parents. For a moment, he imagined his role in life from here on out to be instrumental, his sole obligation, besides being the bread-winner, was to fertilize an egg. He spent the rest of the day in the garage toying pointlessly with the lawnmower motor.

*

Dogs started barking as soon as one spotted them. They had driven to the local shelter at the end of a road with nothing but industrial warehouses and rusting silos on either side. Theirs was the sole car in the parking lot. The Joker, in a rare appearance, had been sitting between them since they had gotten into the car. Brian used his thoughts to tell the Joker to stay behind. He and Mary went inside.

An employee, a short, stocky woman with several large key chains attached to her wide leather belt, led them down an aisle lined with cages of various sizes. Each housed one dog or, if puppies, several. Their arrival was the big event of the day. As the animals barked louder, Brian laughed to himself that at least they didn't stutter. Well, maybe they did. *Woof* might be the start of some dog word they couldn't finish.

The smaller dogs attracted Mary, no doubt because they were cute. She lingered in front of a little white one with floppy, black ears.

"We're not *luh-luh*-looking for a cat, Mary."

"A what?"

"A cat. No cat, Mary. A dog. *Fuh-fuh*-focus on dog. Something *buh*-bigger."

"They're all dogs, Brian!"

"That they are," chimed in the Key Woman. Brian figured she must have those keys to warn the animals with their jingle that she was approaching.

They turned up the second aisle.

"We need a big dog, Mary," he said, unwilling to let his needling about a cat pass. After a pause, she asked why.

"Protection. We need a *duh-duh*-dog to frighten off . . . *buh-buh*-burglars."

"There aren't any burglars where we live, Brian." Key Woman turned her head to look at them, as if expecting an argument about crime in Tummus. "And if there are, you'll be there to defend me!" she said, throwing Key Woman a can-you-believe-men look. Mary was only teasing him, but Brian couldn't help feeling for the first time that his wife was capable of ridiculing him.

They reached the end of the second aisle. Mary hadn't stopped in front of any more of the cute ones. Key Woman turned to take them down the third aisle.

"They have their papers, of course."

"Papers?" he echoed, surprised he did not stutter over the word. "Even the strays?"

"Well, not all of them. But they've had their shots. Everyone up to date. Nothing to worry about there."

Near the end of the fourth and last aisle, one dog near the end caught his eye. It was medium size, certainly no cat.

Key Woman looked at him looking. A second later, Mary turned to see what had attracted her husband's attention. "That's a terrier," the woman informed them. It had a mixed brown and black coat of longish fur. Its ears stood straight up, and its eyes were large pools of dark water.

He bent over to study it close-up. Unlike the other dogs, this one wasn't yelping. Was it a mute? A stutterer? He stood to wrap his arms around Mary's waist and rest his chin on her shoulder. The dog looked like it had a gash on the side of his head like his. Then Brian saw it was only a patch of lighter fur.

"Does he—he's a he, right?—have a name?"

"We don't know. The name, that is. He was a rescue, not

dropped off."

"How old do you figure he is?"

"Hmm. We figure he's less than two."

"Too old to train?" he asked. Like the dog, Key Woman said nothing. He let Mary take care of the paperwork. There was no need to visit the second pound.

On the way home, they bickered over who should name him.

"You come up with a name," Mary commanded. "You picked him out." Her tone suggested he picked the wrong dog. Not darling enough.

"I thought you'd like him. He wasn't the biggest one. I would have picked a collie or a shepherd." In fact, he chose this one because he'd felt a private bond with him. He hadn't barked or whimpered in his cage. Brian felt ashamed of his little fib, but he needed to win at something. The Joker poked him in the side to let him know he wasn't getting away with anything.

They drove by St. Joseph's, the church where they married. An empty car decorated with pink crepe paper was parked in front. A group of men in ill-fitting tuxes with no women beside them stood in loose formation outside the entrance.

"Who's getting married?" Mary wondered out loud.

"*Truh-truh-truh*-tripitaka."

"What?"

"*Truh-truh*-tripitaka. Not who's getting . . . *mah-mah*-married. The dog's name."

111

"*Truh* what?" she said, repeating his stuttering first consonant, something she had never done before.

"*Truh.* A *t. Fuh-fuh*-followed by an *r.* An *i. Pih-tah-kah.*"

He made a sharp right turn past the church, as if remembering only at the last second where they lived. He knew she had no idea what he was talking about. Tripitaka was a word he had come across in a French article about religion in Cambodia. He wasn't sure if it was an English word or not. All he knew was that it was hard to say.

The Buick pulled into the driveway. Tripitaka jumped about in the back seat as the car rolled to a full stop. Brian let him out. The dog began running tight circles in the front yard. Mary went into the house by herself with the dog's papers and complimentary leash. Brian stayed outside to watch his new dog race.

The Joker strolled up to him now that they were alone.

"I think I know why you named the bitch Tripitaka," he taunted.

"He's not a bitch. He's a he."

"Okay then, some bitch with a ding-dong you named Tripitaka. There's an *a* at the end of it. You can really pick them. Anyway."

"Anyway what?"

"Anyway you wanted to give that dog a name you know you'll never be able to pronounce without stuttering. Not in a million years."

Brian nodded. The Joker had a point. Brian did want his dog's name to be a challenge, though not an impossible one. He practiced the syllables under his breath.

*

He was reading the Sunday paper around the kitchen table when Mary said her first words to him since they'd gotten up that morning. The headlines were still about four students shot by the National Guard in Ohio.

"Brian, our house is too small."

To have a dog? Brian thought. Despite her objections, Tripitaka slept at the foot of their bed from the start. Brian would let him out of the house without a leash. Mary objected to that, too, but not too strenuously. She had a favor to ask, and today was apparently going to be the day. They'd been in their rental all of six months. And her favor had nothing to do with the dog.

The following Saturday afternoon was their first tour of houses for sale. Brian worked at home, but nonetheless usually treated weekends as days off. Mary made him wear a tie, in case they found an open house to go into. It took him a while to find one in the closet. They left Tripitaka at home, despite his protests, and restricted themselves this first time out to familiar streets nearby. They weren't looking for anything different, just a home slightly bigger than what they already had. Brian paid close attention to the street signs, which he studied with a particular question in mind: *Can I say this?* He had been embarrassed too many times telling people his current address. No more *Hah-hah*-hollis Circle for him. No street beginning with an *h*. No street with a consonant apt to wage war on him.

"I don't like any of these houses," he told Mary after failing to repeat *Heh-heh*-heather Lane in his mind. "Too small," he said. "Or too large." The fact was, he didn't care much. Some things were important to him. Those things didn't include what men typically wanted—a two-car garage, a big salary, a beautiful wife and children. He'd be happy with not much more of a home than what he'd grown up in, enough money to feed and clothe his family, and a wife to help him skate through life with a minimum of hassle and humiliation.

"I didn't like any of them, either," agreed Mary. "Let's take the next left."

Third Street. The captain of his high school football team had lived on it. Gary. Good-looking. He was in the Navy now, Mary had mentioned to him.

"*Thuh*-third Street. Okay!" He stuttered it once, not twice or three times. He might be able to live with that.

A month later, they closed on a four-bedroom, one-bathroom ranch on Dogwood Drive, despite the trouble he always had with *d*s. They'd be easier than *h*s. He might have picked out the dog, but Mary chose the house. He just needed one bedroom as an office, one in which he could build shelves to line with the books, for the French and Russian novels he'd always wanted to read in the original. In time, one or more of their parents would no doubt be coming to live with them. Mary's parents helped with the down payment. Brian was ashamed, but he went along with it, saying nothing.

It had a big yard, around which he built a fence with surplus lumber he got from one of his building-trades uncles. He had let Tripitaka roam free at the old house, but now they were nearer the freeway.

Their old furniture fit nicely in the new house. Their parents lent them some of their own. Mary wanted bookshelves in the kitchen for her cookbooks. After nagging him for a couple of months, he chose one Sunday morning while Mary was out to go to the lumberyard and buy what he needed. When he got home, Mary's brother Jim was standing in front of the garage door. He wondered where Jim's car was until he remembered Jim didn't drive. Jim was the only adult he knew who didn't drive. Something about epilepsy, Mary had explained once. He must have walked the entire way. To Brian it seemed vaguely un-American and made a fellow stutterer even more helpless. Jim's father, an insurance agent, employed him. Meeting with clients was out of the question. He gave his son nothing more than busy work to do at the office. He couldn't handle even that. Sometimes he nearly writhed on the floor just to get out the first word of what he wanted to say. The O'Grady family had changed as Jim's affliction worsened. His mother grew closer to him, if not his affliction, and his father more distant once resigned to it. Brian told Mary it was the same with the Moriartys. What wasn't the same was that while Brian jostled with his brother, Mary had become Jim's guardian angel, his protector, his substitute talker, whenever they were together.

Jim had a hangdog look about him today. It was not unusual. He told his brother-in-law he had stopped by after mass at St. Joseph's. That explained the white shirt and dress shoes. Brian thought he could see the start of a faint mustache on his upper lip. It wasn't clear he was going to pull it off. He wiped his hands on his pant legs before shaking Jim's. They were a little formal with each other, despite being related. They were stutterers. They were alone with each other, but that didn't mean either would mention their shared debility.

"Hey, Jim, how are you *duh*-doing?"

Jim grinned. He gestured to show he'd be happy to help with the work. Brian let him do the easy things, since he was dressed up and, Brian guessed, not terribly handy. Jim passed tools to Brian when asked, like a nurse would hand scalpels to a surgeon.

The shelves went up faster with his help. Mary, back from her parents, beamed when she saw the progress in the kitchen. She looked fresh, as if she had just showered. When she turned, Brian saw the back of her neck was shiny with a fragrant lotion.

"Still gotta prime and paint them," Brian remarked, eager for any compliments. Mary nodded. She maneuvered around the men to put away the groceries she'd picked up on her way home.

"Why don't you stay for supper, Jim?" Mary offered. She knew he spent his weekends alone.

Brian and Jim drank cans of Rainier in the living room while Mary cooked hot dogs and beans. There'd be a freezer cake for dessert, she told them. She set up TV tables in the living room so the men could watch the Mariners on their small television.

Mary cleared the dishes away and began to wash them. Brian took advantage of her absence to speak with his brother-in-law. "Mary's *preh–preh*-pregnant, Jim. Well, she thinks she's *preh*-pregnant." Brian had known this was imminent ever since they started looking for a bigger house to buy. Mary couldn't have had another reason. What bothered him was that they never had a real talk about starting a family. Mary assumed it was the natural thing to do. No need to discuss it. Brian had worries he would have liked the chance to confess, since Mary seemed oblivious to them.

Jim played with his empty beer can. He moved his lips into a circle, the common prelude to a stutter. "*Buh–buh*-boy or a *geh–geh*-girl?"

Brian chuckled, not at Jim's stutter but at the question.

"Damn, Jim, no *wuh*-way to know that. We're not even sure she's . . . *preh*-pregnant. Much less whether it will be a *buh*-boy or a girl. Hey, who knows. Maybe *buh–buh*-both. *Tuh–tuh*-twins."

Brian dreaded the idea of twins. The new house was bigger, but not that big. Money was touch and go for them. He knew what was behind his brother-in-law's question. There was no need to elaborate. Most men want a son first, but for stutterers such as Brian and Jim, there was more to it. Both boys and girls could stutter, Mary was proof of that. Most girls who stammer outgrow it. But stuttering was in

Mary's genes, as it was in the two men seated across from each other. Brian and Jim were thinking the same thing. They could not say it out loud in earshot of Mary. They were hoping it would be a girl.

Mary rejoined them in the living room.

"Are *yu*-you . . . *preh-preh-preh*-pregnant, Sis?" Jim asked, gripping his seat cushion tight the way stutterers do when it is vital they get something out.

Mary laughed, flipped her hair, and turned her head to flash Brian a wide smile. "Well, someone's been talking!" He thought, yes, someone has been talking, and I hope it stays that way.

*

Brian was working hard on a new translation assignment. A client sent a series of French government reports on the state of the world's forests after a century of widespread timber clear-cutting and burning. He had a firm deadline.

One report mentioned an old logging town in Alaska, once a source for white pine but now passed over in favor of tree farms in Georgia. It had the name Utopia. He remembered his dream of a place in Alaska that seemed perfect at the time. He hauled out the big *Atlas of the United States of America*. There it was: A dot south of Juneau, north of Ketchikan.

He wrote to the chamber of commerce to request what information they could mail him. Utopia was too small to have a chamber of commerce. His request was forwarded to the Mayor's Office, which sent him what pamphlets they had. In the University of Washington library, he checked the card catalog for ALASKA; UTOPIA. He started a scrapbook entitled *My Utopia*. There wasn't much to paste into it. He used his imagination to picture what he wanted it to be, pristine and peaceful. He substituted photos of other places in Alaska, even of the Arctic, though Utopia was a thousand miles south. At the same time he had fantasies of it being destroyed by earthquakes, tidal waves, things more terrible—polar bear invasions, massive glaciers advancing from the east, a forest fire. Still, Brian knew he would go there one day. Before any of those things happened.

*

Brian's father died of a sudden heart attack on September 4, 1971, the same day an Alaska Airlines plane crashed. The Boeing jet had been approaching the Juneau airport with over a hundred people aboard. Bad ticker for Art, bad weather for the flying public. Brian was struck twice that day by what surprises can lie in wait.

Art was on one of the Boeing assembly shop floors at the time. He screamed out once in pain and collapsed. Brian wasn't in the hospital with his father at the end. His mother was. She said he died with a hint of a grin on his face. Brian doubted it. His father was not the grinning type even when enjoying himself. But why not go along and pretend his father had a good death; better than how a hundred-plus screaming airline passengers had scattered into bits. When

Brian traveled to Alaska, he'd take the ferry.

Brian felt somewhat sorry for his father. He wasn't that old yet. The cold concrete of a factory floor was not where anyone would choose to die. He and his father had never been close. Brian had been circumspect his whole life around him and his Irish temper. Art had lived just long enough to start weakening and growing forgetful. While it was an unwelcome preview into his own old age, Brian had to admit he enjoyed seeing the old man's strength wane.

Driving on his way to the funeral with Mary next to him and Eve in the back, he recalled the day he and Bam raked the leaves on their front lawn. They had nearly finished burning them when their father came home early from work. He parked the car behind the house and came over to his sons without stopping in the house first.

"Did your mother tell you? I've been laid off."

Still in his cheap suit and narrow tie, their father said he'd deal with the rest of the leaves. He turned on the garden hose to douse the fire's embers. Brian and his brother stayed to watch blackish water flow along the street, past their neighbors, until it petered out in the next block.

"We'll sweep this up later, boys. When we're sure the fire is out. After dinner maybe. Go tell your mother I'm home." But before they could leave, he leaned over them to say in a low, conspiratorial voice: "Worst day of my life. Me and all the other poor sons of bitches at Boeing." Brian remembered feeling pleased, even happy that his father was upset. Brian didn't worry about how the Moriartys were going to eat and pay their bills. He thought instead: Someone called my father into an office today and told him, in a few words, to clear out.

This began Art Moriarty's precipitous decline as the head of the family. Boeing called him back to the plant six months later, but by then his shoulders were permanently stooped like a man who knew he could be easily discarded. Brian took perverse pleasure in that. He knew all about Oedipal complexes, but this wasn't one of them. He was not so much his father's rival son as he was a reminder of how unexpectedly failures just happen.

His father's heart attack saved the surviving Moriarty family the expense of a long, lingering illness. You were supposed to grow up to be like your father, Brian mused to himself at the funeral. He never stopped stuttering long enough to be anything like him, and in hindsight he was glad. He had disappointed his father repeatedly. His father had disappointed him, too. He'd never worked hard to understand him. Or do all sons think that? He might have asked Bam what he thought, but there was no Bam at the funeral to ask.

The mourners, led by Brian, his mother and Mary, moved to the cemetery across town to watch the casket descend into the ground. Brian had another realization there. He and his father had never tied the score. His father was always his father. Brian couldn't help wanting his approval. What had Brian done wrong? Aside from his stammer, he never figured it out. Maybe his father got him as a consolation prize for another son who would have done better. Brian

121

thought of his old dream, the fraternal fetus left behind. Was his father any prouder of Bam? Unlikely. Bam had all his older brother's faults, plus he was lousy at sports and a lazy student to boot. Brian never saw the two of them together. He hadn't even taken Bam fishing, best Brian could recall. Bam barely made it out of Tummus High, had no interest in college, and would never make it as a singer like he wanted. No word of a wife or children, wherever he was these days. Their parents, Brian decided as he watched the casket disappear from view, should have had daughters and not sons. There would have been less stuttering, and by now more grandchildren.

Arthur Fitzgerald Moriarty's grave marker recorded he was a World War II veteran and the years he was born and died. Brian threw a handful of dirt into the hole in the ground. He was grateful for one thing, though. No Father Thomas here today, just the one father whom Brian came to say goodbye to.

On the drive back from the cemetery, he let Mary and Eve talk while he did some quick math. He calculated his share of the Moriarty sons' small inheritance after their mother was taken care of. He'd put Bam's into saving bonds, should he ever resurface to claim them. With his share, he'd start a special bank account to visit Utopia one day. This was the first thing he would ever keep secret from Mary. Aside, of course, from the details of his visit to the church's vestry for spiritual counseling years ago. The same church was named after the patron saint of fathers. Where, mindful of his stutter and other things, Brian had declined today to stand at the pulpit and eulogize his own father.

Chapter Nine

Blue things materialized in the house one day. Mary was writing thank-you notes at the kitchen table to friends who had come to her baby shower the evening before. They'd given her presents. Blue booties. A blue rattle. A blue bonnet and a blue knit cap. A little blue bunny rabbit toy. A blue hoodie. A blue scrapbook entitled *Our First Baby*.

Brian interrupted Mary's chore to ask her the question that had been bothering him since walking into the kitchen that morning.

"Did the doctor *sey-sey*-say something to you?"

She rapped the tip of her pen against the tabletop. "Oh, no. I just have a feeling. I told the girls I thought it's going to be a boy. I guess they took me at my word. I mean, look at all this. Not one pink thing! And they asked me about names. I said we hadn't decided. Hadn't even talked about it! But honey, if I'm right, it's going to be easier to pick a name, won't it? We won't have to worry about any girls' names. There are so many more of them. And fathers want their sons to be just like them. Brian Junior!"

Brian Senior stood and stared. Mary went back to her scribbling. He was seeing the female in front of him for the first time. Had he done anything to make her happy, other than to impregnate her? He wasn't happy, either. Not that it was Mary's fault. His happiness wasn't all that mattered. He was a family man now, and he barely supported his wife. He knew that. They lived from commission to commission. Nor had he given her a litter of babies. Her high school class-mates, the Catholic ones at least, had broods. Not Mary.

He squinted to look more closely. He did not know this person in front of him. Someone who until now may have pretended to be Mary. Now she revealed her true self. Whatever she was, Mary didn't look like his mother had when she was pregnant with Bam. His mother was beautiful back then. Pregnant women were supposed to be beautiful. This thing in front of him didn't look beautiful. It was hatching something, some egg having nothing to do with him. Where had this baby come from? What had this thing in front of him done? Who were the women who'd brought these blue things into his house? He didn't know any of these people. He wondered, who tricked me into becoming a father?

He coughed to make her look up. "Mary, I'm headed to New York soon. In a few days. It's work." He tried hard to make it look as if he regretted going. In fact, he had decided to go just that second, acting on a whim while standing in someone else's house full of blue things.

"New York! Oh, I wish I could go! How long?"

"A couple of days. I'll bring you something back." Mary asked no further questions and resumed writing.

*

Brian had never been to New York, or anywhere on the East Coast. At the last moment he accepted an invitation to attend a conference on new challenges in translating scientific Russian. The government was paying all the expenses. Once, he'd attended a similar workshop in Chicago. He went and came back without leaving the conference hotel once. New York was different. It was America's biggest city, and he wanted to see it. It was a city of many languages, spoken by immigrants from everywhere. Real Frenchmen and real Russians.

He hailed a taxi at Kennedy and handed the driver his hotel's address on a piece of paper. Brian had prepared for this. He didn't want to stutter. He wanted to be appreciated by his colleagues. He needed some recognition, just a little bit. Sure, he made a living as a translator, but what was in it for him except a paycheck? He seldom remembered for long anything he had translated. The French, the Russian, they melded into one long promiscuous stream of words, words he repackaged to sell. He might recall more, were he allowed to improve what he was working on, insert himself into what he was laboring over, be an actor on stage rather than seated amid the audience. Plenty of what he did, he did poorly; deep down, he knew that. Technical translations had to be done fast, not endlessly tinkered with. If he translated fiction,

126

he could edit what the authors had done. He still harbored the ambition of being a writer one day.

He checked into the conference hotel around his usual dinner time but it was already ten o'clock in New York. He was free to go anywhere still open. He walked down 42nd Street toward Times Square. There, he figured out how the subways worked and found himself in Chinatown. He thought the restaurants there would be cheap and open late. All this he accomplished without talking to anyone but the check-in clerk.

The restaurant he chose gaudily advertised itself with a neon sign: GOLDEN PAVILI N, the *o* burnt out. Brian raised a finger to make sure the Chinese woman at the register understood. "Just one." She led him to the smallest table in the center of the restaurant.

Another older Chinese lady in a red dress with black embroidery approached his seat. She was as unsmiling as the first woman when she handed him a large, laminated menu. Her gold plastic name tag read RUBY. His table was under a fancy red and gold decoration, like the ones in Seattle's Chinese restaurants, but, he decided, more authentic because this was New York.

He looked around the room. The restaurant was bright with fluorescent lights and sparsely occupied. Most of the other customers were white people such as himself, except for one large Asian family noisily celebrating something. He studied the menu as if he'd have to translate it. Ruby, chatting in Chinese with another employee, glanced his way to see if he was ready to order. He waved the menu in the air to signal her. She strolled over to his table, nodded, and waited for him to say something.

There were a million things to choose from. The print was small and streaks of grease on the menu made some words hard to read. He had no idea what most of the items were. There were no pictures on the menus like Chinese restaurants back home. He pointed at a few things tentatively, his gesture for help. He was by himself. I can take what's left over back in a doggy bag, he decided. I'm in New York and I want to try everything. Tomorrow night I'll go to a real Italian restaurant and do the same.

Ruby stopped looking at the finger hovering over the menu and turned her head to the next table. Six men in suits and ties had just sat down. They looked ready to order. One of them shouted for drinks. "Six beers. Heineken." Brian looked at the steel pot of tea Ruby set before him. He didn't like tea.

He stared at the menu some more. Mapo Dofu. *No. It starts with an* M. *Ditto Moo Goo Gai Pan, whatever that was.* Kung Pao Chicken. A *k. He might get it out.* Wonton Soup. *Definitely risky.* Yangzhou Fried Rice. *A possibility, but what is a* zh? Broccoli Beef. *Two* bs *in a row? Forget it. Beef Lo Mein would be less of a challenge. No to Buddha Delight. Potstickers? Too close to a* b. Barbecued Spare Ribs. *Why do so many things in Chinese restaurants start with* b? Egg Foo Young. Bingo, that's one he might manage. Piece of cake to pronounce, so to speak, with the advantage of knowing what it was. Cake. *Do they have desserts in New York Chinese restaurants?* It wasn't just his stuttering scaring him. He didn't want to look like a rube ordering the wrong things, whatever wrong might be.

He made up his mind, intimidated by Ruby leaning over him. "Sweet and *Sah-sah*-sour soup. *Puh-puh*-pork Stir-Fry with . . . *veh-veh-veh*-vegetables. Egg *Fuh*-foo Young."

"Rice?"

"No rice. *Thuh*-thank you."

The diners at the next table got their beers. Loosening their ties, they spoke louder and louder in accents Brian guessed were South African.

"That bloody stutter just now. Did you hear it? I mean, the fellow is an adult."

"My *broer* grew out of his. This *bakkies* must not try very hard. Americans. No different from the *Engels*."

Brian's cheeks flashed hot. He knew at once the Afrikaner with the brother had been a stutterer himself, just adept now at hiding it. He was talking deliberately loud enough that Brian would hear him. One stutterer finds another. There are telltale clues. Brian knew the tricks of The Clan of the Tangled Tongue. They were an international fraternity.

Ruby arrived with a tureen of soup too big for one person. After she ladled some into his tiny, porcelain bowl, he flashed her a smile that was not returned.

Broer-stutterer was not the only closeted one at the South African table. There was another, Brian ferreted, once he perked up his ears to listen in. He identified him through his word substitution, the changes in tone, the shifts in register, the measured beat between sentences. Brian hated these tricksters, the "reformed" ex-stutterers. He learned long ago there is a hierarchy of stutterers world over. Brian was nearer the bottom of the pyramid than the top. He would have liked to go over to the South fucking African table and have *words* with them. If he did, he might stutter and prove what they'd said about him. Brian had a choice. Sit alone at his table and be humiliated, or go over to theirs and be humiliated.

Why should he care? Let the whole restaurant know he was a stutterer. He clenched his right fist while his left gripped hard the plastic spoon he'd been given for the soup. In his younger days, he would have beaten these jerks up. They were half a dozen big men, but he still might have. He would have waited for their party to finish eating, pay their bill and leave. He'd have followed them until they were in the shadows and then jumped all six.

A pile of some multi-colored, stir-fried stuff appeared before him. He didn't recognize it as anything he had ordered. The spoon and the uneaten soup were whisked away.

He knew how the real world worked. Police would come and investigate the unprovoked attack. While he sat handcuffed in the back of a police cruiser, the Chinese waitress, suddenly able to speak perfect English, would identify him as the diner at the table nearest the victims. It would be better, he thought, staring at his food, to follow the dudes out and call them the bastards they were, but bastard was a *b*-word. He couldn't risk giving his prey another chance to snicker. He'd have to use his fists.

The Egg Foo Young arrived. Why, in his mid-twenties, did he still get so worked up? He knew every second pissed off was another second of his life thrown away, that knowing isn't always knowing. Other things gnawed at him, too. His so-called career had stalled at being a competent translator but nothing more. Perfect sentences never made it onto the page. It was like being on one side of a thick glass wall and watching the world pass by.

Interpreters could be famous, even glamorous, Brian thought. They're on stage at the Oscars when French directors win. Translators never are. Translators never have to look their best. They can be overweight. They can skip shaving if they work at home. Some days, if Mary didn't have errands for him, he never got out of his pajamas. There were many such days.

Translators, he thought while looking at his plate and not eating, are like stutterers. He had the impression interpreters got along fine with each other. He knew for sure translators did not. Interpreters form relay teams, they relieve each other. Who ever heard of translators working together? Put a bunch of us in a room and we'll kill each other.

Ruby was studying him warily out of the corner of her eye. A minute later, she brought him two fortune cookies wrapped in cellophane on a little white plastic dish. He hadn't touched his food. He wasn't hungry. Brian opened one of them and read the fortune: *YOU WILL COME HERE AGAIN*. He got Ruby's hint that it was time to go. It was late, even for Chinatown.

He motioned with a flap of his hand for the bill. Ruby nodded. She kept him waiting while she wrote out the bill for the South Africans, who delayed her by arguing about who was going to pick up the check. The six men rose from their seats. Brian threw down too much cash for what he had ordered. He didn't mean to leave a big tip, he was just in a hurry. He followed the South Africans outside, keeping his distance. They turned onto Mott Street and teetered this way and that on the sidewalk, brushing past Asian pedestrians and pushing the smaller ones aside. It had rained while Brian was in the restaurant. Everything was wet and shiny with reflected neon lights. None of the South Africans hailed a cab. Brian figured they were headed on foot to find another place to drink. New York had to be as unfamiliar to them as it was to him, but another bar couldn't be hard to find. He had to do what he wanted to do before they found one.

They turned down a side street. It was lit, but there were no other people on the block. Brian considered his options. There were six of them, but they were drunk. They weren't looking around. Their voices were loud, but Brian was glad his shoes made no sound on the sidewalk.

One of the South Africans stopped to cup his hands to light a cigarette. His friends kept walking. A stray separated from the pack. Perfect. Brian grabbed him by the back of his collar. The man was caught so unawares he didn't resist or cry out. Brian had him down on the sidewalk. The man raised his arms to fend off the coming blows. Brian looked up for a second and didn't see his victim's compatriots on the street anymore. They must have turned a corner and not noticed their colleague was no longer trailing them.

Brian kicked one of the man's raised arms. The South African lowered it. The round curve of his middle-aged beer belly, wrapped in a tight white dress shirt, was his next target. He glanced to the side and noticed a dead bird in the gutter. Brian's shoe transferred his body's weight to a fat South African stomach. The man puked all colors of Chinese food. The vomit-covered his face. He gagged on it. That was where Brian's dress shoe traveled next, and where it stayed until blood flowed from the man's nose and mouth. He could smell regurgitated beer.

Brian kicked a store's sandwich board sign out of his way as he retraced his steps. On the same subway line he'd taken downtown, he scraped his foot on the train's dirty floor to wipe off the man's vomit. An older Black woman across from him had a look of disapproval.

In the hotel lobby he spotted some of the other translators in town for the workshop. They were having drinks in the cocktail lounge. If there were a club for translators, he'd be the last to join it. But he nudged them to make room around their low table.

"Hey, Brian, come join us. Guys, move over. You all know Brian, right? He was in Chicago with us. Seattle, right?"

"Near Seattle," Brian corrected. He was on West Coast time, and it was too soon to call it a night, even after his downtown adventure. He was in New York and determined to get something out of his trip. Brian flagged down the waiter. "Rye with *wah-wah*-water."

Three drinks later, he wasn't stuttering anymore. He wasn't much of a drinker. He thought to himself: Is it this easy? Not that liquor cured stuttering. It was that alcohol, for a while, had the power to suspend his terror of stuttering. This had happened to him before. At his wedding reception he had gotten drunk and didn't stammer. Drinking shrank the boundaries of his world and let that happen. Mary took his keys from him when they left the party, embarrassing him in front of everyone. She drove the two of them to the Marysville casino.

"Gentlemen, that's enough for me," he announced. "What do I owe?" He wasn't stuttering, but he'd begun to slur his speech.

Back in his room, Brian realized he did not know if his victim had been the one to mock his stutter or not. Unable to sleep, he speculated whether a drink along with his Chinese food would have made him oblivious to the South Africans talking about him. If it did, maybe he wouldn't have mugged a possibly blameless man.

*

"Tied one on last night, *beh-beh*-babe," he stuttered on a phone call home during the next day's lunch break. "Drinking . . . *kah*-coffee now, heh heh."

"Well, be good tonight," Mary replied. "I want you back here in one piece. There's news I need to tell you. Big news, Brian. I'm not sure how you'll take it."

He did not take the bait. They'd been married long enough that Brian didn't jump at everything his wife said to him. She hadn't said good news or bad. Just "big." There was no mention of the baby. He was distracted thinking about how his meetings in the morning could have gone better. The workshop on new electronic vocabulary in Russian had nothing new to say, and his own contribution to the one on aviation terminology was stammered out in fits and starts. His stutter was back with full vengeance. Under the table he shared with his fellow translators, he beat his thigh with a clenched fist.

That next day, his last full one in New York, he skipped all the workshops. He said no thanks when housekeeping knocked on his door. No one seemed to miss him. He ordered room service twice, stuttering on the phone each time. It was raining outside. He wouldn't have gone out anyway. Brian forced himself to work at the small desk next to the bed. He'd brought an internal Airbus report to translate. Toulouse headquarters, something marked TOP SECRET, a French phrase as well English. Who knew how Boeing had gotten its hands on it? They paid Brian not to be curious.

He looked at it on the desk. Fewer than twenty pages and mostly diagrams and charts: He should have been able to finish it in one day. But he couldn't concentrate. The constant sirens racing along 42nd Street sidetracked him. Then it was early evening and he hadn't even brushed his teeth or shaved yet. He got up to piss and saw his round belly in the bathroom mirror. He lifted his shirt and rubbed it with his hand. If he were a woman, he could pass as pregnant. Back at his desk, he opened the French dictionary he traveled with to a random page and found a careless typographical error. *Ceint*, not *sain*. Brian couldn't trust the written word any more than he did the spoken.

His irritation at this trivial discovery provoked the ire smoldering in him over the past two days. Something was going to trigger him, and now it had. The Chinese restaurant with the missing *o* on its neon sign. His stuttering. The South African. His stuttering. Mary's "big news." His stuttering. The wasted day in his hotel room. His stuttering. The whole wasted trip to New York. The *baby*. He dared himself to make a few deliberate errors in his translation of Boeing's filched document. Technical ones. Metal stress tolerances. Temperature ranges. Wing strut fittings. He challenged anyone to uncover his mischief. He would enjoy this. Let Boeing fuck up. Let their planes fall from the sky. Let people pay if he put up with their bullshit. He hoped they would. But his guidelines for right and wrong still didn't countenance that. He might mug a blameless man in New York, but bring down a whole planeload of equally innocent passengers? He fancied he could do it and even rehearsed the necessary steps in his mind, but it was like playing a game for the sheer, horrible hell of it.

Later that night, not a word of his assignment translated, much less mistranslated, he packed his clothes and the untrustworthy dictionary. At JFK he paid a hefty penalty fee to take the red-eye back to Seattle. The 727 winged its way smooth as silk across America. Brian dozed off thinking about what new line he might have crossed in New York and what reorganization of the moral universe he'd need for the sort of man he was turning into.

*

Brian walked into the kitchen and dropped his suitcase onto the floor. He instantly realized he hadn't brought Mary back a souvenir. His regret didn't last long.

Mary didn't look up from her notepaper. Days later, and she was still writing goddamn thank-you notes. A scribbling pen was the only sound. What could have kept this woman at this mindless chore for so long? Was she writing to everyone in the phone book? Had she taken advantage of his absence to do other things? Brian saw baby shower gifts still scattered about the house, and his foul mood turned fouler.

Tripitaka sprawled on the floor not far from them. The dog's usual heavy breathing had gone quiet. The sole thing competing with the ballpoint's scratching noises were voices quarreling in his head. One was the Joker's, and it was the loudest and most insistent. Brian did as he was commanded and stepped closer to the table.

The next moment Mary was on the floor, her chair knocked over. Her hands shielded her face. One leg akimbo across the other as if broken. The dog now nowhere to be seen. His wife's beige sweater had crept far up her pale white torso, exposing her plump belly and distended nipples. Two more steps and he was placing the heel of his shoe on her abdomen and shifting his weight onto it. He and his father had once watched a man crush the head of a green snake on the road one Christmas day. He recalled his contempt, and with it its power, at seeing a trembling Father Thomas on his knees in the vestry.

The touch of her stomach against his shoe's sole. The feel of her body seemed to both flatter and infuriate him with its resilience. Her groans: How it felt like a reeling or staggering in his numbed senses. The queer sensation which passed at that moment was mysterious. The soundless bolts of lightning traveling from his body into his wife's and vice versa.

Later, she would tell him she had shouted and screamed. He had no memory of that. He told the nurses and the doctor she had fallen down the stairs. There were no stairs in their house. She had to spend the night in the hospital, they told him. The doctor said it takes time to recover from a miscarriage. There would be more tests. We'll want to look at the bruises as well, he explained, and those take time to develop. The doctor said it would be better for him to see her in the morning. She was resting now. On his way out, the security guard glared at him, or so Brian imagined.

The passenger-side door of the Buick was ajar. He hadn't closed it after he'd helped his wife out and carried her into the emergency room. He slammed the door shut and got into the driver's seat. Brian stared into the hospital's dark parking lot for a while before turning the ignition key. The windshield wipers resumed sweeping. The drizzle had stopped while he'd been inside, but he let the wipers go for a while. The squeaking sound of rubber against dry glass was a welcome distraction from the voices still in his head.

He replayed each event in his mind. One: He'd come back home from New York after pulling a stunt that should have landed him up in jail. Two: The sight of Mary greeting him should have comforted and reassured him. It did the opposite. She still was the fake Mary. She might as well have been a stranger who'd broken into his house. There was something about that stupid pen making its creepy sounds. Three: The sudden appearance of the Joker in his head and his insistence Brian do something. And four: There was his newly flexible set of rules for appraising guilt and penalizing it. He could lash out at anyone in the world, guilty or not. He'd done it his first night in New York. The goal was no longer justice. It was the sheer act of violence, an end worthy in itself because it restored Brian to a fixed presence in the world, irrefutable and due him.

Brian drove home from the hospital and discovered he'd left the house lights on. He righted the kitchen chair, picked up his wife's pen off the floor, hid the *Our First Baby* scrapbook behind the toaster where he'd never have to see it again. He drank a glass of water. Mary's eyeglasses had skated across the linoleum floor and lay wedged beneath the sink cabinet. He put the completed thank-you notes where he would see them the next day. He'd mail them on his way back to the hospital.

Before bed, he looked for Tripitaka. The family dog was nowhere to be found. Brian went into his office and found instead his *My Utopia* scrapbook. He took it to bed. Mary's half of the bed was empty for the first time in their marriage. He didn't open the scrapbook. He tossed it to the foot of the bed where Tripitaka should have been. He could have looked more for his dog, but he wondered what he might do if he found him, given his track record tonight.

He dreamt that he and his dead father were standing close to each other in a clearing. Brian was a teenager again, his father still vigorous. There was that crushed green snake at their feet again. But they weren't in Tummus now. It was Alaska. There was ice on the ground, eagles circling above, stunted trees encased in hardened snow. The sun hung low on the horizon. He and his father were wearing heavy parkas with fur-trimmed hoods. Their breath was visible. They debated where they should head next. "We *kuh-kuh*-could go home, Dad."

"What do you think is at home for you, Son? Home is far from here." His father pulled a map out of his coat pocket and unfolded it. An index finger in a thick leather glove pointed to one spot. "Is that Utopia, Dad? Is that *wuh*-where we are? I can't see." His father let out a low chuckle from the base of his throat. "Dad, your . . . *fuh*-finger is in the way."

"If there were a real utopia, they wouldn't let anyone know where it is."

Brian knew that was not true. There was a Utopia. He

also knew not to argue with his father. "I'm showing you where we are, Son." His father's gloved finger turned into a small cowhide-clad snake, slithering lightly across the map and pausing over different spots. "Which one is us, Dad? Is that where we are?" His father kept moving his reptilian finger on the map. "It's *kuh*-cold, Dad, let's *guh-guh*-go home now."

"Do you want to hear a story, Son?" His father folded the map. "One winter it was very cold in Alaska. Colder than you are now. There was no food and people started to die, the children first." He slipped the map into his pocket. "When the survivors abandoned their camp by the river, they froze to death. The last man alive thought he would die of grief after his one remaining friend was gone." His father kept talking. He took Brian by the hand and walked them toward the forest beyond the clearing. "One night there was a voice and the last man went to see whose it was. He found a great fire and warmed himself by it." Brian worried they would get lost further in the forest. "Then the frozen bushes around him made breaking sounds. Something was moving through them." Brian pulled at his father's hand, trying to lead him in a direction away from the forest. "He looked up and saw all the people who had died standing on the far side of the flames." His father tugged hard to keep them headed toward the forest. "The fire had brought them back to life." If we keep going this direction, Brian thought, we will never find our way out of the forest. "There's your utopia, Son. That's what we'll find in the forest. A great fire that will bring everyone back to life. Even the baby you murdered tonight."

Brian woke the next morning with the house lights still on. He found Tripitaka sleeping behind the sofa, where he'd found refuge, and where the blue things had been until Mary moved them into plain view.

*

In time, Mary was pregnant again. She hadn't left him. Just why was a mystery that confounded Brian for a long time.

At first he had thought of lying to her, saying he had some kind of fit; had been out of his mind; hadn't been in control of himself; had been drinking. In the end he told her the truth, albeit in pieces, in stuttered bits of speech over weeks interrupted by days of silences.

One of their post-miscarriage conversations took place in the backyard. They sat in folding lawn chairs while Tripitaka was running circles. It was one of those Northwest days when the calendar says summer but the weather is winter. Mary was bundled up in Brian's down parka. Brian was wearing one old sweater over another. Their layered clothing, plus chairs farther apart than normal, might have suggested to a stranger the couple had assembled for battle with each other. The stranger wouldn't be wrong. Sitting apart under open skies, Brian could indulge the comforting illusion of open space in their marriage, too.

"My parents can't understand why I haven't come home."

"To them?" Brian asked needlessly.

"To them. I know what I'd hear. The same advice, the same harping, over and over, all day long. At least you don't talk much." Her almond eyes narrowed as she spoke. She jutted out her weak chin in a gesture meant to annoy her husband.

That hurt Brian as much as anything Mary had said to him since that night. Of course he deserved it. Remorse never came quickly to Brian, but it did come.

"Marrying a stutterer has its advantages, I guess," responded Brian at length, though it didn't come across as the joke he intended. On the contrary, it invited Mary to list all the disadvantages. She declined the opportunity. They listened in silence to the loud racket next door as their neighbor's teenage boys bounced a basketball against the cedar fence separating their yards.

"You say you were terrified of having a son," Mary said, circling back to one of the usual threads of their conversations. "I can't get that out of mind. For several reasons. First of all, it's proof you are seriously, mentally, ill. Worse than that, each time you've explained it to me, it's sounded like a rationale. An excuse. Because boys stutter? Like that's supposed to make sense, and make me say, Oh, okay. I get it. That's not going to happen, Brian. It's not that boys stutter. It's that *you* stutter and never got over it like me and Bam did. Even Jim's adjusted better than you. And so you took it out on me and our baby. Our dead baby."

Brian took his hands out of his pants pockets and rotated his torso toward his wife. He'd heard all this before.

"Why haven't you left? There are places you could go other than your parents."

"You're the murderer, Brian. Not me. The question is, why haven't you left?"

Their talk about a future together, or the impossibility of one, escalated to new heights. *Murderer.* Again, Brian couldn't protest her choice of words. That was exactly what he was. He might try to convince himself he was mad at Mary, true enough. He had also been mad at the baby. Mad enough to do what he did. The news of its death had come neither as a surprise nor a complete heartbreak to Brian. He hadn't the courage to confess this to the woman sitting at her calculated distance from him.

"Yeah, maybe I should." Brian noticed he wasn't stuttering. He wondered why. Perhaps his brain, at some level Brian didn't realize it operated, mandated this conversation needed to be clear and unimpeded.

"Alaska. You talked about some town up there. There's nothing to stop you. Take your work with you."

Tripitaka ambled up between Brian and Mary, unsure which to approach for a pat on the head. Brian was first to wave him over. The animal panted happily and wagged his tail when he reached Brian's lap. Mary sucked cool air through her lips loud enough for her husband to hear, even over the sound of the two boys next door fighting for possession of a basketball.

Brian hoped Mary hadn't left, despite everything, because she wanted to stay. And try again for a baby. The baby part wasn't so important to Brian. Staying with him was. He couldn't start from scratch with a new woman clueless about what it was like to grow up with the handicap he and Mary shared. She'd have to be telepathic.

"That *nuh*-night . . ."

"Don't talk about it. I can bring it up. You can't. That's a new rule."

Mary was entitled to her rules, Brian conceded. Let them add up to her own scales of justice. She'd been a stutterer, too, after all. With him in the house, it was a good thing for her to have rules. He had plenty to lend her. One thing of which he was sure went further back in time than "that *nuh*-night." Each one of his stutters had the potential of reminding her how provisional her own return to fluency was. In hindsight, he was amazed she had stood it for so long. Maybe he mattered less to her than he thought. Maybe, he thought for one split second, there was someone who mattered more.

He put his hand in Tripitaka's mouth and let him gnaw on it. The silence between him and his wife continued beyond the point where it was thoughtful to where it was awkward. It dawned on Brian that if Mary were thinking of leaving him, she wouldn't need to be drafting any new bylaws for their relationship. He fell back against his lawn chair at the import of the revelation. She was going to stay after all. She might not admit it today, or next week, but in time she would. Mary didn't realize her words betrayed a decision she'd already made in her mind to stay.

He didn't have to understand why. It was just as well he didn't. Still, he couldn't help wondering. Maybe Mary was frightened about going it alone in the world, though that wouldn't be like her. Maybe she loved him, but it was hard to imagine love surviving what he had done. At his darkest, Brian thought she hadn't wanted to give birth to a boy, either. An image of her brother's slobbering face with its blinking eyes, trembling jaw and contorted dark hole of a mouth flashed before Brian's eyes.

It didn't matter in the end. Mary was going to stay with him. He would show gratitude. They would have another child. Whether a stuttering boy or a stutter-free girl, Brian would guarantee no child of his was anything like its father. That would be a good thing. He started a mental list of other good things he wanted. This was the first.

"When I was in New York and we talked on the phone, you said you had big news for me. You've never told me *wuh*-what it *wuh*-was, Mary." His stutter was returning, and Mary's face showed she had noticed.

"Never mind, Brian. It doesn't matter anymore. Some things don't matter now. Let's just agree we don't have to tell each other everything, shall we?" Mary produced a doggie treat she had the foresight to squirrel away in his borrowed parka. She waved it in the air. Their dog abandoned Brian and bounded over to the woman's outstretched hand.

*

He did not make a big deal over the second pregnancy. He

didn't have to. Mary had her fetus tested for gender before she revealed her pregnancy to him. It was going to be a girl. Still, the memory of what happened to their first child made Mary's announcement more of a warning than a celebration of a happy Moriarty family event.

The baby was born seven months later in the same hospital where Mary had her miscarriage. Brian sat in the waiting room with other dads. Brian silently stared at the television's excitement about Nixon's imminent resignation, breaking news to which he had no reaction. He was focused on how imminent fatherhood might change things for him and his family. A nurse touched Brian on the shoulder to get his attention. Congratulations. No complications. Both mother and daughter were doing fine. "*Thah*-thank you."

There was no debate about her name. He acquiesced to the choice Mary and her mother made without consulting him. Tess, short for Tessa, Mary's maternal grandmother.

Tess was a small ball of pink, squirming fat wrapped in a thin blanket. Brian knew infants look one way and another when older, but she'd always look like both parents. The eyes were Mary's. So was the mouth. But his daughter had his broad face and smallish nose, and somehow he knew those strands of black hair lying flat against her skull would turn brownish-blond like his. And he saw at once, but never remarked aloud because it would be unlucky, that their baby's head was flawless, unmarked by any hint of a gash. He checked her eyes to make sure they moved in tandem. She was more an O'Grady than a Moriarty, but still both.

When Tess was in her crib or his arms, he cooed to her. *Gah-gah-gee-gee-goo-goo.* It was easy for him to say because none of his noises had to make sense. He didn't stutter in front of his daughter because she was too young to speak to. Baby talk sounded like the start of words he wouldn't be able to get out later. Mary would say whole words and complete sentences to their daughter. "You are a perfect baby." Mary spoke to their daughter without fear or hesitation while he worried his presence in the house was a bad example.

The word he avoided most was *Tess.* It was like *Tripitaka*: A word guaranteed to make him stumble. Had Mary and his mother-in-law considered this in choosing his daughter's name? It took Mary a while to notice his hesitation. When she brought it up, he looked down at his stocking feet in both relief and shame.

"It's tough."

"What's tough, exactly?" she shot back. He could not imagine she didn't know.

"*Teh*-tess."

"Tess?"

"The name." He raised his eyes to meet hers.

"You said it fine. *Tess.* You always say it fine. What are you talking about?" she snapped with a hint of panic in her voice, a panic that sometimes now reared its head.

He thought he bore a unique burden as a parent, as if he were the only stutterer in the world ever to reproduce. Tess was a girl, but still he worried. Would he be able to read aloud to her? Help her with her homework? Talk to the other dads at her school's annual Father-Daughter Dance? Would *she* stutter, too? Her mother had, after all. As Tess prattled in her crib, he would listen for clues of trouble down the road.

He invented a string of nicknames for his daughter, any of which he could substitute for Tess when the need arose. Sweetheart. Bun. Baby cakes. Peanut. Little one. Jellybean. Princess. Cupcake. Darling. Angel. Cutie pie. Bunny. He giggled at some of the silly names he came up with. He didn't invent them just to spare himself the trial of her real name. The list grew because he was expressing in words—his own—the unanticipated exult he experienced at having a baby, a child, a *malysh*, an *enfant*, a *daughter*. He knew already he'd be doting on her more than most fathers of girls do. She'd grow up hearing his voice, with every one of its tortured first consonants, and never think it peculiar or embarrassing. She would understand. She would wonder why people out in the world didn't talk as her father did because his way of speaking would be so ordinary to her. Brian would reward his daughter for her unqualified acceptance of him, even those times she imitated his stammer out of an innocent desire to be like him. There would be awards, presents and honors for his *Tuh*-tess. Brian would amend his laws and injunctions to pardon one human being from the threat of his temper and its vehemence, and that exceptional human being was Tess.

CHAPTER TEN

Brian was at work in his office. Midafternoon, the winter sun had already skimmed and was now sinking below the horizon. Reaching to switch on the second of his two brass desk lamps, the sound of fabric rustling against fabric made him turn. Tess was standing at his office door. His two-year-old daughter had pushed it all the way open. She stood there, playing with the folds of her pink dress.

He had been mulling revisions when Tess appeared. Once he noticed her, she waved her arms, signaling something was not right. He was still mulling work as he stood. Tess turned to run barefoot down the hallway to the kitchen. The mailman brought documents to the backdoor to be signed for, but Mary took care of that for Brian. He noticed Tess' dress had a dark ketchup stain on its back. It was the last trivial thing he would think that day.

Brian overtook Tess and scooped her up in his arms. He found Mary on the floor in the same akimbo position as that afternoon when she lost their first baby. This time, her belly was not bloated. It wasn't round; it wasn't even exposed. No eyeglasses had skated across the floor to be stopped by a cabinet. But she was as unconscious as she had been the day of her miscarriage five years earlier, the day Brian now dubbed The Fall. Gripping his daughter tighter, he thought: Am I at fault for this, too?

He lowered Tess to the floor and raced to the wall phone beside the refrigerator. He needed to pick up the handset, but he looked back over his shoulder first. Tess had crawled to her mother and was rubbing her cheek against hers. Tripitaka lumbered into the room. Brian saw the dog sniff at Mary's face. The animal sat at attention next to his human family on the floor, his gaze fixed on Brian, its leader. Everyone was waiting for him—husband, father, dog owner—to do something.

He held the phone and dialed zero.

"I'll connect you with emergency services, sir."

He turned to face his family again. No one had budged.

"911. What is the nature of your emergency?"

Nothing came out of his mouth. Not one sound, not one cry, not a whimper or even a stutter. His daughter and dog watched and listened.

"911. To whom am I speaking, sir? What is the nature of your emergency?"

*

Years later, when a teenager, Tess would periodically remind her father of what happened. How he had stood in their kitchen, phone in hand, unmoving and unresponsive. A nearly grown Tess would reproach him for these things. She would hiss her words with a venom bottled up inside her from childhood into adolescence. She would accuse her father of everything, including things he was innocent of. But unlike her father, she would use words instead of fists to strike out in her fury because Brian Moriarty's daughter Tessa was not a stutterer.

"You are good at forgetting, Dad. You've made it an art. If you also made yourself remember instead of forget, you'd be on your knees every day apologizing to Mom. And to me. For what you did. For what you didn't do."

Brian thought he had apologized over the years. To Tess most of all. They spent so much time together. He took her fishing and let her choose the bait. He installed a hoop over the garage door to shoot baskets with her, always foregoing his own dunks to pass the ball to her. Wasn't that one way of showing remorse?

"No. None of that was about Mom, who was the one lying unconscious on the kitchen floor in front of you. Or much about *me*, growing up. Fishing, basketball? No, that was always about *you*, the boy things that had gone wrong when you were my age. Mom told me all about it. And they didn't go wrong because of Granddad. They went wrong because you were a stutterer. A stutterer, okay, not your fault, but still your one problem lets you divide the world into you and everyone not you. How did you think you were ever going to win? Against those odds?"

Brian's mind always went blank when Tess talked to him this way, replaying the signature events of his life with his family, one by one. Some events he knew to regret and feel shame over. Other events that he thought had been happy, he learned weren't for everyone. He knew all about talking around the things that mattered most and not talking about them at all. But being confronted with the truth about those things was new to him. It began when his daughter brought candor into the Moriarty household.

*

"This is emergency services. What is your address, ma'am? To whom am I speaking, sir?"

Brian continued to grip the handset tightly. His mouth opened. His tongue moved. His face grimaced. His shoulders hunched. His free arm fell limp. His eyes froze. His terror returned. His cheeks grew hot. His panic closed his throat. His shame became everything. He thought: I can't even speak into the phone to say that I am a man and not a woman.

For the next few hours, he sat in the emergency room with Tess. It was the same emergency room with the same worn furniture as when it was he, and not a stroke, that was responsible for what had happened. The Fall would overlap in his brain with this, what he subsequently dubbed The Drop. Sitting at the kitchen table, writing out a grocery list instead of thank-you notes, Mary's mind had simply shut down. She slumped from the chair onto the linoleum. Later he would

153

tell her what details of her stroke he knew. She never took his word for it. It was The Fall all over again.

After the stroke, Tess became more protective of her mother. She often clung to Mary's leg and wouldn't let go if Brian was nearby. Sometimes Brian felt his family was divided into two opposing teams: Mary and Tess versus him and Tripitaka. The girls versus the boys. He and Mary shared the same bed, but after her stroke they never made love again. At first Brian told himself it was because she was recovering slowly. Two nights before The Drop he did his job and turned away to go to sleep, not knowing that would be the last time. There is always one last whatever—the last time you say goodbye leaving the house; one last bill you will pay, one last drive to the gas station. There will be a last time you rake the yard, a last time you watch your town's Fourth of July parade. There'll be one last time you pick on your brother for no good reason, one last time you had a chance to tell him you loved him but didn't. You will have one last dream when you wake up glad you didn't die in it. You will change your oil one last time but you won't know it when you do. There will be one last time you see your dog; and for Brian, one last time that he will stutter. Two days before The Drop, it was the last time he was inside his wife.

"To whom am I speaking? This is King County Emergency Services!"

From that moment, Brian realized his daughter would never be a stutterer. She would grow up with a functioning tongue that obeyed her thoughts and didn't resist them, as his did. For every one of her father's botched and muddled sentences, for each of his words jammed at the beginning or buckled in the middle, Tess would triumph.

*

"You could have killed her," an adult Tess spit out at him fifteen years later. The year was 1991 and the Soviet Union was breaking up. Brian was worried about his livelihood as a Russian translator. She came into his office, shut the door behind her and let him have it. He was unprepared but stoically endured it. "You think it was your stutter preventing you from calling for help. Do you still think that? Because I wonder." Reopening the old wounds, she told her father that the psychiatrist to whom she paid good money said she suffered from trauma. She had witnessed her mother suffer a stroke and her father do nothing. Unless the trauma healed, Tess was advised, she would never be whole again.

"I remember it differently than you. You weren't able to lift Mom off the floor. I don't think you even tried. She crawled out the front door and climbed into the car herself. I helped the little I could. Then Mom drove herself and me to the hospital while you stayed home, catatonic. Why do you pretend otherwise?"

This, Brian knew, was impossible. It was the story Tess had chosen to invent. It wouldn't do either of them any good for him to correct it. He thought back to when she was young. She never had a problem speaking. Brian was anxious she'd mimic him just to qualify as a full-fledged

Moriarty. She was the non-stutterer in a home where the past scarred her mother and the present crippled her father. Where sometimes she must have felt she was an alien who had been deposited with the Moriartys by a flying saucer as some kind of interstellar, interspecies experiment. Brian noticed she never felt completely at ease outside the house, in the company of ducks. Though she didn't stutter, she did by association and by the off-chance she might start one day. Wherever she might go, she took her father's stuttering world with her. Being a normal kid was not normal. Her parents' neuroses imposed their own burden on her: To never stumble over a word, never pause too long in the middle of a sentence, never use an unusual phrase her parents might suspect was a last-second, desperate substitute.

It was predictable she'd try these things. Tess played a trick on her parents when she was seven. She pretended to stammer badly at the dinner table one evening. She had no closer role model for a stutterer than her father. Just as he did, she made her consonants repeat and trip over each other: "Muh-muh-*Mommy, can I have some more* meh-meh-meh-*milk?*" Mary looked at Brian. "*I* kah-kah-*can* goh-*go* geh-geh-*get it myself.*" Brian looked down at his plate. She continued. "*This is* sah-sah-*salty and I'm* thuh-thuh-thuh-*thirsty.*"

There was a response, of course. But no one rushed over to hug her, to reassure her, to comfort her, to tell her they understood, that they would help her. Neither did her parents erupt in anger to blame each other for their daughter's inevitable stutter. Yes, the stutter that had always been there.

Yes, the stutter that was their fault. Yes, they knew that. The stutter that had belatedly revealed itself. Any such reaction would have been fine in hindsight. But that was not what she got. Brian stood up, threw his paper napkin onto the table and stormed out of the kitchen. He slammed the door to his office. Mary soon followed, opening and shutting the door softly. She explained to Brian their daughter didn't want milk. The meatloaf wasn't salty. She wasn't thirsty. What she wanted was her parents to panic, shriek, hold their heads in their hands and shout across the table. *Just what have we done to our daughter, and to ourselves, to deserve this? Just* wah-wah-*what?* "This is the test I've seen coming," Mary told him. A stutterer knows the real thing from the pretend, and Mary was once a stutterer.

At breakfast the next morning, Tess faced two parents who were going to say nothing until their daughter spoke first. She didn't. The three of them ate toast and drank orange juice in complete silence, a monkish vow broken only that evening when, over dinner, Brian blinked first. He asked her what was new at school. She answered with three flawless, fluent words: "Not much, Daddy." No one commented on this reply. The Moriarty family resumed its usual triangular formation: A nervous ex-stutterer mother who did what little talking there was; a moody, stammering father who did none; and a daughter who wondered what she'd done to be born into this.

Looking back now, that was when Brian learned he had a child capable of inflicting pain upon others. She was

like him. Normal people, but not Tess, take a lot for granted,
Brian thought. How breath presses against the vocal cords,
how it skirts over the trachea. The vibration of the voice box,
the unthinking and automatic release of air into the mouth
where the tongue and teeth and lips forge it into words. Tess
had grown up hearing family chitchat blotched and muddled, sentences jarred at their start, buckled in the middle,
dissolved at their ends. She knew how self-consciousness
can intrude into language and stay anchored there. She knew
these things because she was Brian's daughter, and these were
the things he thought of when he acquiesced to the power
she held over him.

*

Brian had to get out of the house that perfect, early autumn
day. He needed fresh air. He'd take Tripitaka for a real run,
where the dog could explore whatever he wanted, not just
the confines of the Moriarty backyard. The weather was dry
and both of them, Brian decided, deserved some time elsewhere. Mary and Tess had gone to visit his in-laws.

"Let's go, boy." Brian clapped; Tripitaka leapt into the
back seat. He pulled out of the driveway, not sure where he
would go. There was plenty of gas. He turned his head around
to look at his dog, tongue hanging out and panting, eager for
whatever adventure Brian had in store for him. Tripitaka was
the only member of the family who trusted him anymore.
For good reason, he had to grant. He might be a poor husband and father, but he was a good dog owner.

He talked to Tripitaka in his head. He did this often. Tripitaka never talked back. Maybe one day he'd surprise Brian by saying something. He drove aimlessly for a while. Tummus had changed since he was a kid. The old houses, the schools and the stores were where they'd always been, but they were joined by new buildings on new streets with names only corporate developers could coin: Crescent Circle, Magnolia Heights, Madrona Lane. The looming Cascades continued to provide a point of geographical reference for him, so he always knew what direction he was headed. Tummus was now the same bland suburb Seattle had plenty of. There was less and less of anything rural about it. Brian's thoughts drifted to what he imagined Alaska might be like. They might have lingered there, but he had a restless dog in the backseat. He considered stopping at Tummus' biggest park or going to the high school sports field on the off-chance no team was practicing. He didn't. Something was nagging at him. There was some other place calling him. He'd know it when he found it. Until then, the steering wheel had a mind of its own.

He gazed up at the rearview mirror. Tripitaka was still handsome. If his coat of black and brown fur had dulled any, Brian couldn't see it. In the snout he looked a little older. Brian woke up some mornings to find himself older than when he'd gone to bed. The process began in his late twenties. The first wrinkles and stray gray hairs appeared. Bending over to tie his shoes had become harder. Middle age so far, he thought, wasn't too bad. He was almost forty but had no big health issues yet. Perhaps having stuttered his whole life was going to spare him unwanted surprises in that department.

He parked the car along the road close to where he and his father, years ago, had watched the green snake die. This seemed to be the right place. Not much had changed. He vaguely remembered this stretch of road. No one had built new houses here. It was still untouched. Alders and birches crowded at the edge of crumbling asphalt. Tall conifers towered behind them. Dense salal and sword ferns covered the forest floor as far as he could see. Their foliage was damp and glistening from a rain shower earlier in the day. The air smelled like the first days of spring but with a touch of something acrid in it. It was good to get out. Tripitaka must have felt the same. He pranced about like a puppy. Brian watched. No, they weren't old yet.

Without as much as a bark, Tripitaka dashed into the woods. He ran in a straight line, jumping over bushes toward whatever he was pursuing. What does a dog chase? Anything that moves. Brian imagined a raccoon or a porcupine. He hoped not a skunk. The dog would nose around and come back. Brian stood by the car, thrust his hands into his pockets, and fell into thought. When had Brian ever dashed into anything? When had he ever wanted to *catch* anything? Mary had fallen into his lap; she had done the pursuing. He couldn't think of one thing he ever wanted badly, except not to stutter. He'd been faithful to his wife. He'd gotten good grades in school. He'd played sports. He'd gone to catechism classes. He'd gone into business for himself. He fathered a child. He did everything in life a man born in 1947 was supposed to do. Brian voted Republican.

Tripitaka was in the forest somewhere. Brian didn't hear anything. He wasn't concerned. He readjusted his Mariners cap and buttoned the top of his flannel shirt. The sun was still high in the sky, but the weather was turning cooler. He stepped back to lean against the car hood. It was still warm. The contracting metal made clicking sounds. He crossed his arms and looked down the road. No person walked by for him to greet, or be unable to greet. He liked it that way, just as he liked working alone. He had incorporated his translating business as Moriarty and Associates, but there were no associates. He wanted people to think it was bigger than it was, but he had no intention of having coworkers he'd have to speak with. He had to give Mary credit, of course. She had learned to run a household with little help from a stuttering, introverted husband. She was the ambassador who negotiated with the outside world. It couldn't go on forever.

Where had the mutt gone? He still felt the heat of the engine warming the seat of his pants, so it hadn't been long. He didn't worry. His thoughts turned to Alaska, to Utopia, and his future trip there. He'd take Tripitaka along. Utopia was far away, but not too far. He'd saved up for the trip. After some recent calculations, he realized it wouldn't be that expensive. Once in Alaska, there wasn't much to spend your money on. No casinos, no fancy stores. Only serious sportsmen made the trek to Utopia. He knew that from the pamphlets. What would he do there? He'd explore the woods, as

Tripitaka was doing now. He did want to go fishing. Why, he had no idea.

His dog was barking. At first Brian thought Tripitaka had found what he was looking for, and some poor squirrel or muskrat was lifeless between his jaws. More barking followed, and then a loud whimper that meant Tripitaka was in pain. Brian took off into the woods in as straight a line as his dog had. He struggled to get through the dense undergrowth. For a second he panicked he was lost. He needed Tripitaka to bark again to know he was headed in the right direction. He had lived near these woods his whole life, yet he did not know them. His life had been houses and roads and stores and sidewalks and stop signs, not wilderness. His pants became soaked below the knees from the wet bushes. Sharp briars slowed him down. The sole sound he heard was his legs moving through the undergrowth, his arms pushing low-hanging tree branches aside. He thought he heard another pained howl, the sound of an injured animal no longer fighting back. Maybe he had imagined it. For the first time in years, he wished the Joker were here.

Deep in the forest, he found his dog. Tripitaka was sitting on his hindquarters at the base of an immense cedar. The tree was much bigger than any near it. Twisted, gargantuan roots had created a little hut, something a gnome might live in. Brian stooped to look inside. He didn't see anything. Nor did he see any prey in Tripitaka's jaws or tossed aside dead on the ground. But *something* had injured his dog. There was a serious wound on his right rear leg. He was whimpering loudly. *What happened to you, boy?* He stooped to examine the hurt. The fur along the length of his shank was ripped and exposed raw flesh and bone. Brian saw blood oozing out of the long, thin wound. He reached up to lift his baseball cap an inch off his head and let a finger rest on his scalp's gash. He recalled the slash across his face that he'd received in his mother's womb. What did this to you? Brian asked in his head, hoping his dog might miraculously now answer him.

He carried Tripitaka back to the car. He opened the back door and helped him onto the seat. Tripitaka had stopped whimpering but would not meet Brian's eyes with his own. It was as if the dog were accusing him. *He's asking me, Why did you bring me here? I didn't ask you to.* Brian circled the vehicle, checking for anything out of the ordinary before he got in. How would he answer if his dog were asking, *Didn't you know the forest has unknowable things in it?* He started up the engine and made a U-turn. How would he react if Tripitaka were telling him there was something there?

Brian headed down the road. He hoped the vet's was open. In his mind, the injured dog was still talking to him: One day you might encounter it, too, and you won't be able to tell anyone either. You may be human, but you are a stutterer. He'd tell the vet his dog must have tumbled into a ditch chasing a squirrel. It might have happened that way, who knows. It was an okay story, more plausible than Tess' fantasy that she and her comatose mother had driven to the hospital by themselves. He fine-tuned his story for the vet. He didn't want to admit he'd let his dog run off into the forest without following close behind. Meanwhile, in the back seat, Tripitaka joined the rest of the Moriarty family in vowing never to trust Brian again.

CHAPTER ELEVEN

In the spring of 1985, Tess was old enough to make her First Communion. More than old enough, because Brian had kept her back. Mary was annoyed. His feelings about the church, and St. Joseph's in particular, made him wary of priests and their ceremonies. He never explained why. But with Tess feeling left out, and in-laws who were nagging him, he told Mary she could sign their daughter up for the special catechism classes.

Tess was smart, smarter than her father. She took after her mother. He had noticed that since she was an infant. She assembled toy building blocks without dithering. She learned to read before starting school. He was close to confident nothing could go wrong at her First Communion. When it was over, there'd be one fewer time he'd have to sit on a hard wooden pew for any Catholic whatever in his or his family's lives.

The parish priest rewarded Tess for doing well by singling her out for a special role. After all these years, the priest was still Father Thomas. Brian, who hadn't been to mass in decades, curled his hands into fists when Tess told him the news. Insisting to Mary they take their daughter to another parish would have required an explanation he didn't want to provide. Brian's one-time molester told Tess she would recite a prayer in front of everybody at the start of the service. Why did he pick her? *On* her? he wondered. Why this unique attention lavished on the Moriarty family? In his generation, and now his daughter's? Brian hoped the years had reformed, or neutered, the old priest.

The prayer would be the *Christi Anima* once again. Two weeks ahead of time, Father Thomas gave it to Tess on a piece of mimeographed paper. Some of the print was hard to read. The ink had bled. Tess asked her parents for help. Brian left that job to Mary. After eavesdropping a couple of times, he was sure his daughter had it down pat. He even let himself look forward to her recital in front of everyone, managing what her father hadn't. Still, Brian felt a dread that wouldn't go away. He reminded himself Tess wasn't the stutterer her mother had been and her father still was.

The sky shone a nearly perfect blue. Clouds receded early in the morning. The tops of the Cascade mountains stood in clear relief. Brian took this as a good omen. Many of the children were already assembled on the front lawn. Their families were taking pictures. The fathers and their sons wore suits, their daughters dressed in white. Tess was the most beautiful. A little taller than the other girls, Brian could tell she'd be a knock-out when she grew up. He hoped she'd find

166

a better husband than her mother had.

He grew apprehensive as soon as people started drifting inside the church. He and Mary parted from their daughter and sat where they had during the previous evening's rehearsal. They were not far from the lit votive candles underneath a stained glass window of Christ's resurrection. Fidgeting, Brian stretched his neck to find Tess in the rows ahead of them. Mary lowered a lace veil over her face, prompting him to readjust his new bowtie. He felt hot. He wished he could loosen his collar. He wanted everything to be over. He wanted to go home. Most of all, Brian wanted Tess to get through this with none of the trouble he had at his confirmation. He saw the back of her neck and thought: No worries, this is my daughter, she is flawless.

The organ music began. Everyone stood. Two priests and the altar boys came into the nave. One was Father Thomas, looking ancient and frail. He asked the congregation to sit in a voice still thickly Irish but drained of whatever vitality it once had. He welcomed the children making their First Communion and their families.

"I have asked Tessa Moriarty to begin by reading the *Anima Christi*."

Tess rose. She unfolded the wrinkled paper, just as her father had years ago. He concluded some time ago his daughter was never going to be a stutterer. If he was mistaken, this was when he'd find out. His heart was in his throat. For a second he thought he could see her hands trembling. He suspected Tess loathed him at times, but he had always loved her. She turned to look back at her parents. Brian took a mental photograph of her face to study at length. Everyone used to say she resembled her mother. Now he saw a lot of himself in her: The blue eyes, like cobalt; hair, graced with curls; the pug nose, cute on the father but more so the daughter because she was young and female; the wide mouth wasted on him but perfect on her. His gaze fell to her hands, trembling while holding the paper. Hands so unlike his. They were small, graceful, as white as alabaster. As his own hands once had, they gripped a sheet of paper with what Brian knew were sweaty palms.

"Soul of Christ, sanctify me."

Brian's face grew hot. He paused, gritted his teeth and thought: Okay, she's fine.

"Body of Christ, save me." She kept going. Nothing was going to stop her. The Moriarty family curse had ended. "Blood of Christ, inebriate me."

He could never recite that line now. He recalled being able to do so when he was a boy. Since then, his stutter had worsened. Now it would be impossible. But his daughter did it.

"Water from the side of Christ, *wah*-wash me."

He felt his face go hotter. *Wah*-wash. What was that? Well, everyone stutters sometimes. But not everyone is a stutterer. With one small misstep, he felt his guilt returning. He was her father. Whether it was his genes or his example at home, he was responsible. She looked like him; did she want to fail like him, too? He looked around the interior of the church to avoid focusing on her. It was white walls interrupted by stained-glass windows of many bold colors. This was a place designed for guilt, for manufacturing it, for pouring it into the minds of the children that generations of parents sent into its care, his parents and now he and Mary. It always had been that way. He loathed himself for it as much as he did the Roman Catholic faith.

"Passion of Christ, strengthen me. O Good Jesus, hear me."

Good, two lines out. Quick. Go faster now, he silently urged his daughter. Mary's hand took his. She was going to finish the prayer for their daughter by reciting it from memory under her breath. He looked down at the church's stone floor, wrapped his fingers around his wife's and squeezed hard. Someone coughed, then another person. Tess took that as a cue to rush through the rest of the prayer, which she did without a problem. The service continued. Tess' turn came to go to the altar and receive her first holy wafer. She looked over her shoulder and beamed a smile to her parents.

The reception was an ordeal for him. His wife and daughter chatted with friends, parents and priests. He did not. People went up to Tess and patted her shoulder or touched Mary on her arm. Brian stood alone in a corner, warning others off with an intentional scowl. He allowed himself to thank God for sparing his daughter the full measure of the humiliation he suffered in this same church at the hands of this same priest. Here, he realized, was another advantage in his child being a girl and not a boy. Body of Christ my ass, he swore. If his tastes ran strictly to males, Father Thomas would never touch Tess. But how could Brian know for sure?

His eyes accidentally met Father Thomas' across the reception hall. The priest was standing with some of his elderly female parishioners. His head gyrated atop a thin neck, scanning the room for others. Their gazes connected for a fraction of a second, just long enough for his heart to sink at what he knew would happen. The way Father Thomas walked across the room reminded him of how his own father had walked across the room after his confirmation to teach him another lesson in life. His hands balled up into tight fists. He tried to pull his arms up into the sleeves of his suit jacket so no one, but especially not the priest, could guess what was going through his mind.

The hems of Father Thomas' long robes brushed the carpet. He took his last steps toward the man he had once molested, easy prey because he was a boy who stuttered.

"Brian, congratulations. You must be proud of Tessa. I know her mother is. A beautiful First Communion." The priest's mouth shrank into a lizard-like slit, meant to pass for a human smile, across his face, but that allowed Brian to know what he was thinking. It had nothing to do with his daughter or her First Communion.

"And such a beautiful young lady."

The priest's thin, colorless lips froze into a smirk that nauseated Brian. He said nothing at first. He didn't want to give the priest satisfaction in hearing his former victim stutter all these years later, still outside the grace of God. He wasn't going to let his fists re-emerge from his suit, where who knew what they might do. It would be so easy to smash this grotesque face. The alternative was to say something, and say it now. Brian briefly consulted the latest draft of his commandments for just behavior before deciding what to do. He reluctantly conceded a priest was still a priest.

"You *wah*-want me to *thuh-thuh*-thank you, *Fah*-father? You want me to *suh*-say how . . . *muh*-much you've done for our *fah-fah*-family?"

The two men faced off. Brian's fists tightened more. Father Thomas tilted his head so close to Brian's that he could smell stale breath coming out of the nostrils of his bulbous nose. The priest had been drinking.

"Mary has already done that, Brian. Several times actually." The priest's lipless excuse of a mouth relaxed. A faint snicker seeped out of it. He lingered in front of Brian for a moment longer. Once satisfied the Moriarty boy had no comeback, he turned around and looked for others to go play holy father with. The hems of the old man's robes brushed the carpet again as he shuffled away, his steps unsteady on account of either his age or the liquor.

Brian let his fists relax. He let one of his hands rise to his scalp and touch the gash on his head. He was done talking for the day because he was done with stuttering. The power he once thought his stammer gave him over his abuser hadn't worked today. He thought his stutter was capable of reducing a pederast, his mouth once so full with a young man's semen that he was unable to speak, to a contemptible groveling heap at his feet. Now, decades later, the old man had walked away confident he had won. He was right. But one day Brian would have his revenge. This priest would never see it coming.

There was another priest in the reception hall, the one from a neighboring parish who sat next to Father Thomas during the ceremony. This second priest was much younger. He had a friendly face. He glanced at Brian and nodded when he caught his eye. The priest's hand played with the silver cross dangling from a chain about his neck. He fondled it between his fingers. Brian wondered if he had seen Father Thomas approach him and stand too close. He thought about priests. Not all of them could be bad. Some had to be good. Like actually believing in God and wanting to deliver Him souls. There had never been a priest in the Moriarty family. Would a Moriarty priest be a good one? It wasn't going to happen. Brian had a daughter, and he hadn't heard that Bam, wherever he was, had any children at all. The responsibility for carrying on the family name had fallen on Brian's shoulders. Left to him, the Moriartys would stand far from God. Today would be the last time, he promised himself, that he'd willingly suffer these servants of the Lord.

He stood alone in the otherwise festive reception hall until Mary and Tess came over to say they were ready to go. The dog needed to be let out. He, their obedient chauffeur, ferried them home. On the way, his wife and daughter told him how much they enjoyed the day, how wonderful the ceremony had been, how delicious the fruit punch had tasted and how pretty the other girls were. How adorable the boys looked in their grown-up suits. Neither of them would notice that their husband and father said nothing. Not one word, not one grunt, not one groan, not one murmur, not one mumble, not one stutter; nothing in response to any of their happy talk.

CHAPTER TWELEVE

To be treated as inadequate, the more the better. To be cuffed or collared. To walk on all fours and lap water out of a dog's dish or the toilet bowl. Having a rag stuffed in his mouth. Be ordered to lick the kitchen floor. No, not just that, Bam demanded to be hurt by them. He needed physical pain, not the threat or illusion of it. The first time with each girl, they always asked for his safe word. There wasn't always one.

He was way past spanking. Bam was thirty-three and not into bad-boy games. He never liked too much foreplay, anyway. It delayed the real thing. The same deal with being pissed on. What he insisted on was the stuff that, if carried too far, could harm him. "Fuck me" came from his lips whenever he wanted things ramped up. A woman's shoe heel on his head. Tit torture. A threatening rider's crop circled around his bunghole. Abuse. His cock and balls tied up with string. Hot wax dripped on his eyelids. Tourniquets. Knife play, needles. "Make me remember this. Stay away from the face." That was his only no-go zone. He had a career to think of. Scat was another deal too far. But he did fantasize about blood. And bruises below the neck were permitted, even encouraged.

Bam was inching up La Cienega behind a fuck-all slow truck and listening to some dick-shit news from the White House about Whip Inflation Now. Yeah, whip alright, he thought. He acted on a sudden whim. He turned left before the freeway overpass onto a narrow side street, a second before it would have been too late, even at this crawl.

Shari didn't answer the door. He considered his options and rang the bell again.

He had never dropped by like this before. They planned every session—*Shari, that you? Here's what I want this time.* Bam was a masochist who had to be in control. When he was a boy, he had sometimes manipulated his brother Brian into hurting him. It was never hard to do.

"You're fucking ugly, Brian. You can't hit the ball for shit. You have zits on your butt. *You* stuh-stuh-stuh-*stutter*."

"Yeah, you got it," he would say on the phone to Shari. She was probably a dyke. He hoped she was. "Castrate me, yeah, but don't really. I may need my business down the road hah-hah-hah. I'm paying good money for this. I'll call you again just before our date." Sadist Shari had to appear to have her own fantasies. But if she ever acted them out, none of this would work. His desire was all that mattered. He cast himself in the role of the voyeur hovering in the air near the ceiling and enjoying the show below. His body belonged to some other sorry loser with a broken dick. "Good, great. I gotta go now, babe. Rehearsal."

Brian had beaten him up as a child because he was smaller and because Brian could. He hated it at the time. Now he wondered why he did. He had stopped stuttering by the third grade, and Brian, who never stopped, hated him for that. Yes, he did stammer at times, and he even faked stuttering once to get beaten up. Two stutterers in the same bedroom? No good. Someone had to pay. It always worked like magic.

Still no one at the door. He looked down and saw he was standing on rotting wood. He thought there used to be an old doormat here that said WELCOME TO OUR HAPPY HOME.

Bam hadn't been back to Washington State since he'd left. He wasn't sure his brother was there anymore. He'd heard Brian was going back and forth from Seattle to Alaska. Bam was sure he was still stuttering and still beating someone up. His wife or his kids, if there were any. Because Brian had to be the one inflicting pain and not the one seeking it. Now that Bam was stuttering again, he had to wonder which was the better choice in life: The *s-s-s-s* or the *m-m-m-m*.

Pulling out of Shari's driveway, he noticed how dry and spindly the trees were on her street, as if they might spark an urban wildfire any moment. He'd never get used to the way Southern California looked, having grown up in real forests. Bam wondered again how the wooden planks on the porch had gotten so soggy because it hadn't rained in Los Angeles for months.

*

After Brian moved out of the house during his second year of college, Bam had the bedroom to himself. His experiments began. Lying atop the bedspread, sometimes his own but sometimes his brother's, he'd unbutton his shirt halfway and pinch his nipples hard, so hard he bruised himself. He would masturbate thinking how his brother's punches left black-and-blue marks. Bam was careful where he made the bruises. He didn't want anyone to see them. He'd turn around to face the wall in the school locker room when he changed into his gym clothes.

He toyed with cutting his smooth white forearms with a razor blade. That would be hard to keep secret. So he stopped at bruising his chest with his fingers, though in time he graduated to pliers from the toolbox in the garage. These were followed by clamps he swiped from Tummus' hardware store.

One day he picked up a shard of glass from a broken beer bottle he found on the side of the road. That night, atop Brian's bed, he placed it gingerly on his tongue. He let it move against his cheeks and the roof of his mouth. He stored it in the nightstand drawer between the two beds. The next night, he closed his mouth tighter around the glass until he felt something warm flowing in his mouth from where the glass had cut him. He stuffed a paper towel from the kitchen into his mouth until the bleeding stopped. He kept it under the bed until the next morning, when the coast was clear to get rid of it.

Some nights he lay on one of the beds and played with himself while imagining various scenes. Often the scenes were just him and Brian. The Moriarty brothers stuttered, one badly and the other on occasion. Both were capable of trouble, and thoughts of collusion made his cock stiffer. It worked as well as looking at dirty pictures. Badness had to be punished. That was the part he looked forward to most. He thought of his brother off at college. There was no Bam there for him to beat up. Bam's cock got even harder thinking of his brother boxing, thinking it was Bam at the receiving end of his punches. He'd shoot, except those times he pulled his hand away to punish himself.

Once, he had caught his brother Brian jerking off when he entered their bedroom unexpectedly.

"What the *fuh*-fuck! *Fuh*-fuck! Get out of here!" Brian pulled his underwear up to his hips and leapt off the bed. "You little *fuh-fuh*-fucker, you're *guh*-gonna get it!"

He was halfway across the backyard before his older brother, still in his underwear, caught up with him. He might have yelled, Let me go! as Brian pounded him with his fists and kicked him where he lay on the ground. He didn't. Was it because he didn't want the neighbors to hear? Or was it another reason? During some of his beat-off sessions he would remember this thrashing, and always if he was pounding his meat on his brother's bed instead of his own. He'd squeeze his dick extra tight and jerk it hard. Sometimes he wouldn't ejaculate, but each time he got up off Brian's bedspread, he'd smooth it free of wrinkles so his mother wouldn't notice he had been on it.

That ended when, declining to follow his brother to college, Bam left home for good after high school to make his way as an entertainer. He was better looking than his brother, taller and a few pounds lighter. He didn't have a funny-looking gash on the side of his head. He could hide his bad eye by making sunglasses part of his onstage look. Plus, Bam had a high school music teacher tell him he had a good voice. He should have learned to read sheet music. School wasn't his thing. First, he tried gigs in Seattle, then Portland. Those cities were too small for him ever to make it big, or even little. After a few years of jobs leading nowhere, he decided to try his luck in Los Angeles. He knew a few people in LA, none of whom, it turned out, could be bothered to help him.

He found some work on his own in Southern California, if not in any famous clubs. Cocktail lounges, sure. He got paid more often in drinks and lines of blow than in cash. Better deals for him were the Bar Mitzvahs and old people's homes. Otherwise, he waited on tables. He modeled a few times. He turned down what looked like a porn movie, but not without considering it. No big breaks yet, but he was feeling optimistic for the first time since leaving home. Why would his stutter re-emerge now, just as things might be breaking his way? He was staring his late thirties in the face. It was time for some good luck.

Bam wasn't stupid. He thought he could figure out why

he was drawn to pain. It had something to do with the stutter, both when he was little and now. He stuttered worse with the women he dated, a few of whom thought it was cute and giggled, or pretended not to notice. Bam wanted them to notice, which is why he started hiring women. They got good money to think nothing was cute about him. He did not want to be pitied or indulged. He wanted to be made fun of, derided, slapped, kicked. That required money, and he was happy to part with it whenever he had some.

After leaving Shari's, he parked the Rambler at the side of his motel on the wrong side of Hollywood, the part of town owned by hookers past their expiration dates, homeless bums and short illegals just in from the border. He was renting a room with a kitchenette by the week. Trash dumpsters with rusty corners, overflowing with pizza boxes, blocked the walkway in front of his windows and were a source of noise all night long. At his front door, he found a flyer from the Seventh Day Adventists rolled up and stuck between the doorknob and the doorjamb. He had to remove it to get his key into the lock. The light above the door was out. It was hard to see. In the studio apartment he threw the flyer and his portfolio onto the wicker chair near the front door, something a previous resident must have dragged in and left there. The big hole in the wallboard above the bed, looking as if a fist had made it, welcomed him home.

Bam often forgot the stench of stale cigarette smoke that filled his unit. He was reminded of it each time he walked in the door. He headed to the dirty kitchenette, took a used glass out of the sink, and poured himself a scotch from the fifth atop the refrigerator. He didn't bother with ice or tap water.

Plopped down on the unmade bed, he flipped TV channels with the remote. He'd never had a remote before moving here. It was like a toy to him. He stopped at this channel or that, took a sip from his glass, and flipped some more. One channel had a beach volleyball game from Long Beach on it. He paused his flipping to watch. The men had tan, smooth, muscled chests and sturdy legs, thick thighs. He looked down at his own legs and imagined them through the fabric of his pants and thought, Oh man, I need to get more exercise. Gotta look better.

The idea occurred to him, not for the first time but for the first time in a while, that he might be queer. He was good-looking enough to be mistaken for one. Los Angeles was a city of fruits. Being single and an aspiring singer didn't help much to discourage that assumption by some people, including the bitches he dated. Still, he'd had some successes in that department. Things had seemed to be going well with this chick, Allison. For a while. He had even had her over to his room and she didn't mind the mess. She liked to party and get banged rough. She had long hair. A natural blond. She told him he was good in bed. She stopped returning his calls last month.

Bam didn't want to have sex with men. The thought disgusted him. But he was more curious about men than he thought a straight guy should be. He often compared his physique with other men's, but shit, who didn't. No, what drew him to other guys was their voices. Bam was a singer. He often judged other men by imagining their voices in front of a mike. Whether they could make it in the business or not didn't end the matter. He was curious about how easily they could work their vocal cords, a curiosity made greater by the untimely return of his stutter.

One of the other singers at the audition today had lisped. A dead giveaway. They must do that so they can find each other, he concluded. Like wearing striped socks. He took another sip of his scotch. A commercial for Glade Air Freshener interrupted the beach volleyball game. "Now in new scents!" His mind wandered. He wondered whether there was any connection between lisping and stuttering. He hoped not. Didn't want to go there.

Faggots, he conceded, were the real outsiders. So were lots of people, him included. Here he was in a dump of a room in Holly-fucking-wood, no dough, no steady gig in sight, and no girlfriend giving it up for free. He wasn't any kind of success. On top of everything else, he was stammering again. That could kill him professionally. Comedians could stutter offstage. They said a lot did. But a singer? He was not going to make it, barring a miracle or a cure for stuttering, of which his brother, Brian, was proof there was none. He'd never felt whole in the world. His shame showed in his voice. He went back to the kitchenette and poured more scotch.

He picked up the remote and flipped again. A mattress sale. A weather report which, this being LA, was pointless.

He felt humiliated at being so conspicuous in front of every-one, in front of everyone else's everyday *normal*. Did any of this make sense? Even to him? He flipped some more and found an old movie. Lisping and stuttering, was there a link? He thought about the two sides of his brain in rivalry, one half that wanted to speak right and the other that wanted to fuck things up.

The movie was about a prize fight. He thought he'd seen it before. *Requiem for a Heavyweight*. Jackie Gleason was Maish. *What sort of name is that?* He took a sip from his refilled glass. The phone rang. He leapt for it despite the slowing effects of the alcohol. *The cocktail lounge is calling. I've got the gig.* He gripped the phone and raised it to his ear.

"Bruce."

He had not expected Shari on the other end of the line. He had to readjust.

"I saw you from the window. I saw you walk up the steps to the front door. I watched you walk away."

Trying not to slur or stutter his words, he replied, "And you didn't come the *fuh*-fuck down?"

"No appointment, no entrance. You know the rules. I was with another client, not that it's any of your business."

"I want to see you. How about *nuh*-now."

"No. This is a goodbye call."

"Let me *kuh*-come over."

"Plus you've been drinking. Stay off the roads, sweetheart."

There was a click at the other end of the line. Bam

turned his head toward the one sound still audible in the room, the television. He slumped back into place on the bed in front of it. He'd sloshed some of his scotch in scrambling to pick up the phone. That pissed him off more than being blown off by a fucking whore. Booze was expensive.

In a fair world, Shari's phone call could have been part of their game plan. *No, that's Anthony Quinn in the movie. As in, make the john beg for it.* He felt the stirring of an erection. Versus Cassius Clay, right there in the pic. Should he call Shari back? A line from the film: "Be careful, Mountain!" It didn't sound like a game, though. *That's Mickey Rooney, the trainer, on the other side of the ropes.* He placed his free hand atop his bonus erection and drained the rest of his drink with the other. More lines from the movie: "You were beautiful, Mountain. He just threw a lucky punch."

Yeah, he realized, this is that boxing movie he and Brian watched as kids. Men fought each other in the ring and outside of it, too. He turned off the television. He was antsy. He didn't want another scotch, but he wanted something. He'd settle for another drink, but not his scotch and not here. On another impatient whim, he grabbed his coat off the wicker lawn chair. The Seventh Day Adventist flyer fell onto the carpet. He slammed the door behind him.

*

It is cooler now outside than in. It might rain. He walks to Sunset and turns left without looking up. He knows where he's going. He's driven by the place many times. It always

looked sketchy to him. It has all the markings of a likely suspect. No sign above the door and two small windows, glass
covered with sheets of black construction paper. He's seen
men come out of it. Once, one was shirtless and shit-faced.

Bam walks in. His eyes take a moment to adjust to
the dark. The brightest light in this dive bar comes from a
jukebox playing some old Nancy Wilson tune. "Guess who I
saw today, my dear." Thinking for a moment he might have
walked into a Black bar, he panics. As his eyes acclimate, he
spots white dudes. *Now that's a voice you've got, Nancy. I've
had quite a day too.*

The place reminds him of Charlie's bar for has-been
prizefighters in that boxing flick. Old school. Wood everything. All men. A sign from the movie: UNESCORTED
LADIES NOT ALLOWED. The place stinks of stale beer.
There is no air conditioning or any window cracked open.
He goes up to the counter and orders a beer from a skinny
bartender with a leather vest, no undershirt.

"Budweiser okay? You just missed happy hour."

He isn't offered a glass. They didn't use glasses in
Charlie's bar in the movie either. Mountain asked for one
for Miss Miller though. He leaves the skinny guy a big tip,
as if that might buy him protection from something. He
takes his lukewarm Bud and backs a few steps away from the
bar. There are rows of liquor bottles in front of the mirror. I
could've had another scotch, he thinks. From the looks of it
here, I'd be the only one.

Looking around the bar, he sees immense antlers

mounted on the wall. Maybe this place had once been an Elks Lodge, and a hunter's trophy survived to be eerily illuminated by a jukebox's cold bluish light. Looking around some more, he feels a nagging irritation accompanied by a rising disgust at what he discovers. All the customers seem to be missing something—not a whole limb or anything like that, but something marking them as needing the right parts. Silly shorts, what kids might wear. Leather straps crossing sunken chests. One guy with a boa around his neck. Two weak-chinned guys with matching turtleneck sweaters. One guy leaning against the bar has a lift on one of his shoes to compensate for a stunted leg. The young kid picking up empties has a hand missing a second finger. This place is a freak show.

He catches himself looking at his reflection in the large mirror running the length of the bar. On either side of his image are flyers taped to the glass, one advertising the bar's happy hour, the other a Barry Manilow concert. Bam looks intact compared to the rest of the clientele. All the pieces of a normal face, a normal body in the dim light. But he isn't intact. He's missing a complete voice. Missing one of the right parts. Someone once said he looked like Barry Manilow. It occurs to him that his stutter makes him one of these dudes. The disgust in him rises further. It reaches his throat, his most precious possession. He's straight. That is his bulletproof vest in this room of swishes. Still, he can't shake the feeling he is one of them. He and his fellow losers here share an insult, if different ones.

The same Nancy Wilson song plays again. "The waiter showed me to a dark, secluded corner." He looks over his shoulder and sees a guy pouring quarters into the jukebox. He's so short he might be a dwarf. He squeezes between two men and stakes out a spot on the far wall. He watches two men talking to another two. All four resemble each other, a Bobbsey quartet, for Christ's sake. No one notices him. He knows he is better looking than others here, but everyone ignores him. The men in this bar are all fruits. No one is too obvious about it, except for the guys in leather and the one with a boa. For Bam, tonight, it's all good. The men have a weird look about them, vacant faces as if they came back from Nam yesterday or something. He doesn't want to think he's one of them, but tonight it's okay to be in their company.

Everyone seems to know everybody else. Bam is nervous. He downs his beer too fast and wishes he'd had more real booze before leaving the apartment. He toys with walking back to his motel and finishing off the scotch. That would be admitting defeat. He inches along the wall until he comes to a large opening. It leads to more dark. He puts his empty beer bottle down on a narrow ledge and steps through the opening to explore.

He can't hear Nancy Wilson any more. At first, all he sees is the orange glow of cigarettes or joints, a half-dozen points of light. Some don't move while others flit about like fireflies. His pupils enlarge and he notices small glints of light reflecting off metal buttons and belt buckles. He makes it to another empty stretch along a wall. He leans back with his hands in his pockets and one leg bent at the knee, foot on the wall. His heart pumps faster. He looks around to see if anyone else is alone. He doesn't want to do the talking, though. He is looking for someone to take charge tonight, not the other way around. Three guys to his left huddle like football players. Standing up straight, two of the three let loose low-pitched laughs; the third teeters back on his ropers and looks like he might fall.

What his brother would think if he knew he was in a fairy bar. He'd be repulsed. But Bam is here for a reason. It's time to up his game. Enough women for the time being. Fuck Shari. He needs a man, someone like himself, only more so, to humiliate him. Why? Why, suddenly, this? Because he stammered at the audition today and blew his chances? He's going to take care of his fucking stutter now, to hell with how he does it or what the consequences.

He's about to go back to the bar and buy another beer when someone speaks into his right ear. A deep voice out of nowhere. Bam jumps a little. He doesn't catch what is being communicated. He turns toward the source of the close sound. The owner of the voice is short but built, with black hair in a crew cut and prominent eyebrows. In the dark, he guesses the man is maybe half a dozen years older. He's wearing a tight body shirt. The top button of his Levi's is undone. He has big arms and thick wrists with studded leather wristbands.

"Excuse me?" Bam says.

"Whada they call you?"

"Me? I'm *Buh-buh*-bruce."

The man chortles. "Sure you are. Hair burner? Mr. Bruce?"

"They call me *Bah*-bam for short. You?"

"Miller. Pleased to meet you, Bah-bam," he replies, grinning.

*M*s are too close to *b*s for him to ever say this man's name to his face. Miller grabs him by the arm and guides him to another corner of the room, where it's easier to talk.

"Better."

They chat guardedly about nothing. Bam doesn't reveal any true details about himself, and he bets Miller doesn't either. Other men walk by them, some staring. Bam notes Miller's eyes never leave him. He feels something gnawing in the pit of his stomach. *Muh-muh*-miller is what he's been hunting for. He'll do just fine.

"One of your eyes isn't right," Miller announces out of nowhere.

"Always has been. I was *buh*-born with it that way." Bam looks back into Miller's eyes, thinking it the fair thing to do.

"It's sexy," Miller chuckles. "A little bit off is always sexy." Bam is embarrassed and hopes it doesn't show.

Miller gestures he needs to go piss. Bam stands alone, not moving, worrying Miller won't find him when he comes back. Miller stops on his way to the toilet to talk to another guy, someone his own short height with an equally muscular build. Bam scans the room to see if there is anyone else who might approach him. It is too dark to know. Suddenly Miller is back by his side. He has two beers. Before they are more than a couple of sips into them, Miller leans into him, pushing him back against the wall with the weight of his body. He grinds his crotch into Bam's left thigh. Bam counters by moving one of his legs between Miller's. He reaches down with his left hand and gropes Miller's equipment. Half hard. Perfect. Just what the doctor ordered.

"I wanna *buh-buh*-blow you," Bam whispers. His cock twitches at the sound of his own words, even if the most important one has failed him.

Miller extracts himself from Bam's clinch and leaves the room. *Damn, have I blown it?* Bam smirks at his own pun. *I was impatient and I've scared him off.* Irate, he looks around the dark room a third time, scouting for other possibilities. His disappointed erection deflates.

Miller returns as quickly as he left. He strides toward him laughing, a shot glass in each hand. He offers Bam one.

"Drink up and come with me."

He follows Miller past the men's room. The door is open. He sees a torn poster of Marilyn Monroe hanging above the urinal. He chases Miller to the end of the back hallway and the door marked EMERGENCY EXIT. Miller pushes it open with his elbow. Bam sees it leads out to a wide alley. It's rained while he's been in the bar and everything glistens now. Two garbage dumpsters line the side of the alley wall, about five feet of space between them. Two cars are parked along the street where the alleyway ends.

Otherwise, nothing. No people. Miller struts over to the open space between the dumpsters. He leans back against the brick, nodding to Bam to stand in front of him.

Stepping into position, out of the corner of his eye, Bam sees a dead bird on the ground near the man's right foot. A sparrow maybe, it's too dark to tell. The man notices him staring at something nearby. He lowers his gaze as well and spots it. With a swift kick, the bird skids under one of the dumpsters.

"Get down."

Bam does as he's told. Once he's on his knees on the wet asphalt, Miller pulls his zipper down. Bam stares at the man's crotch. He sees the outline of a cock behind a grayish jockstrap. He gets stiff again. Miller has trouble pulling his stiffening dick out of his jock. Bam raises a hand to help free it. The man growls like an animal. Soon his tool springs out and bounces in the brisk night air. Bam has never examined a cock close-up before.

"Blow me."

Bam's head circles around the glistening end of the man's cock, fully emerged from its foreskin. It curves upward, like the bow of a ship. He reaches up to grab it. The man swats his hand away.

"I said *suh-suh*-suck it, you fucking retard, you fucking stutterer. You hear me? Need me to repeat it?"

Yes, Bam hears, and he's glad. Miller gets it. There is no pretending Miller doesn't know why Bam is on his knees. He is going to play his part. Bam didn't even need to buy the dude a drink.

"You want to taste it, don't you? You said you did. Get to work."

Words have trouble coming out of Bam's mouth, but tonight he discovers a man's cock can slide right in. *Wham Bam.* His knees feel cold where rainwater soaks through his dress pants, but he is going to stay on his knees for as long as it takes. He closes his mouth around Miller's dick. He leans forward until his face buries itself in dense pubic hair.

"You're a pussy who never learned to talk right. Choke on my pole, faggot."

That is the voice he needs to hear. *Thank you, ma'am.* The voice of a man. Sinatra's voice. The voice he wished he had.

He closes his mouth tighter about the cock. Everything tonight will come down to a mouth and thinking *yes.*

"Your face-cunt wants me to face-fuck the stutter right out of you, doesn't it? Get ready for it, cock *suh-suh*-sucker."

The man moves his hips back and forth. His dick, slick with Bam's spit, works like a drill press in his mouth. Nothing Bam does is going to stop this. There is pleasure he did not anticipate. His balls roil between his legs. He imagines electricity racing from his own groin, past his hips, up his chest, through his throat and into a mouth stuffed with another man's piece. Wanting to help, he adds his own rocking motion in awkward sync with the man's thrusting hips. He extends his arms on the brick of either side of the man to steady himself. He leans in until his lower lip is up against the older man's warm balls.

"You love it. You're a born *kah-kah*-cocksucker."

Miller's prick bores into his mouth. He is sure his teeth are hurting him. That doesn't slow down either of them. He feels the man is going to nut soon. He can feel the older man's body tensing up, his ball sac contracting. The man's body goes rigid above him. His own dick is swelling, too. He wants the man's cock to pound the back of his throat, to do some damage. He forces himself to lean in as far as he can to take more of it.

Bam gags. The man knocks him hard with his palm.

"You get dick when I give you dick."

He realizes if he stops stuttering because of this, if this is the cure, his submission to another male will have been worth it. The man in front of him, just a penis with a body attached to it, places his palms on either side of Bam's head to hold it still. He rams his prick in and out of his face. Then the piston action slows. Bam hears a moan as if the earth is rumbling. Something shakes. Here comes the gift, the drowning, the dying, the cure. His mouth fills with warm spunk, it drips out of his mouth and some falls, wasted, onto the wet asphalt between his knees. It glistens in whatever scant light this alleyway offers. *There isn't enough jism for this to work.* Bam panics. Fuck me, he says to himself. Fuck the stutter out of me. Don't *stuh-stuh*-stop.

He has never tasted a man before. There is nothing sweet about it. The man tastes medicinal. Metallic. He tastes bitter, just how a cure should taste.

Bam gulps and starts to swallow. The man smacks the side of his head again.

"Who told you to eat it, you queer? Spit it out."

He obeys.

"Now lick it up. Off the ground."

Wrestling his head free of the man's grasp, Bam takes a quick look up and down the alleyway to see if anyone has been watching. In a voice as virile as he can make it, he sputters out a half-dozen words tagged with his signature and still unremedied stutter: "Hit me *ah-ah*-again. On my . . . *fuh-fuh-fuh*-face."

CHAPTER THIRTEEN

"Do you have your ticket, sir?" the girl in a bright orange vest asked him. She looked Tess' age: Eighteen. He could be her father. He felt a little ashamed at noticing how cute she was. Brian handed her all his papers, not sure which was the ticket.

Arriving ahead of time, he had spent half an hour looking around the dock of the Alaska state ferry on the Seattle waterfront. He passed small groups of disheveled bums with army surplus blankets wrapped around their shoulders. Trucks were lined up waiting to load. Other travelers were walking around with less luggage than he had. Some of these folks had to be headed much further north. Had he packed too much, Alaska gringo that he was? He had books in his knapsack. Books about Alaska. Also some Tolstoy and Dostoyevsky he hadn't cracked open in years. He was only going as far as Juneau, where he'd get another, smaller ferry to Utopia.

After withdrawing money from his secret bank account,

he had told Mary he was going to Alaska to fish. It was partly true.

"Fishing? Since when do you fish?" She didn't argue with him or seem to care he was going. She sounded pleased. "Enjoy yourself," she wished him. Brian realized Mary had stopped thinking much about what he did or didn't do.

A Black man with a thick mustache, dressed in a Navy pea coat and a black wool cap, stood on the dock. The wool cap had PENNZOIL in yellow letters sewn on it. He was carrying a knapsack similar to Brian's. He smiled at him from a distance. Brian nodded and might have waved back, but he was leery of making friends on the boat. He'd have to talk to them. Tell his story, and not just how he was traveling to Alaska alone. He had his wedding ring on. For the first time in his life, he thought of taking it off for the next nine days.

The Black man walked over to him.

"Where to, captain?" he asked.

"Juneau. On this boat."

"You live there?"

"No, just passing through." He hoped that would be explanation enough.

He boarded the ferry with the Black man, who told him halfway up the plank his name was Reggie. They shook hands but went in separate directions after reaching the deck. He had reserved a cabin with a narrow bed, a reading lamp and enough room for his luggage. Nothing fancy, but it was expensive. He regretted he hadn't thought of camping on the deck as the young people and Reggie were evidently going to do. He was definitely an Alaska novice. It was funny. Seattle always felt close to Alaska. Its two airlines had their headquarters there; Seattle souvenir shops sold miniature totem poles. You saw a lot of cars with Alaska license plates. But Alaska was as far from Seattle as Hudson Bay was from New York. There was a sizable chunk of Canada in between. He would have been happy if it was even farther.

He explored the ship. There wasn't much to it. A tiny "casino" of slot machines, roped off to prevent anyone from gambling until they were out at sea. A big kiosk selling chewing gum, mosquito repellant, *People Magazine,* a few romance novels, and to his surprise, though it shouldn't have been, fish gutters.

He went back to his room with *People Magazine.* The cover story was "Oprah Explains Everything." He'd never read one before. He figured he'd have a lot of time to kill. A minute later, the ferry vibrated as it left port. He'd never been on a boat this big before. He left his room to stand by the railing and watch the Seattle skyline recede. Despite new buildings, the Space Needle and Smith Tower still dominated the city. The Alaskan Way Viaduct loomed largely. He remembered when they built it. His father had taken him and Bam down to the waterfront to see the big bulldozers lay ground for it. It was one of the few times either of his parents took him to downtown Seattle. He'd never gotten to know it. Now he was sailing out of it to go somewhere he knew even less. It would be awhile before he would see buildings this tall again.

Reggie joined him at the railing. "Next stop Ketchikan," he said.

"Yup. *Keh-keh*-ketchikan." The tiny hope he wouldn't stutter on his trip was dashed before the ferry left Elliott Bay. The Black man grunted but said nothing Brian might have to respond to again.

*

The water was gray. Once past Vancouver Island it was a lethal gray, a gray that killed you in seconds if you fell into it. The forests on the shore grew less majestic and shaggier, but they stayed the same profound green. The occasional grand house with a dock, and the humbler cabin with none, grew rarer until signs of human habitation disappeared entirely. He tried to take photos from the starboard railing; his little Minolta didn't have much of a zoom on it.

He ate his meals alone. That did not spare him from stealing glances at his fellow passengers at nearby seats in the cafeteria. They looked young and healthy; even Reggie, who was probably his own age, mid-forties. Reggie worked outdoors on boats. Brian worked indoors behind a desk. That explained a lot.

Reggie joined him once, ignoring the ship rule not to eat food he hadn't purchased in the cafeteria. This was Brian's first inkling that Alaskans did things their own way. Reggie unwrapped a sandwich. He sat across from him and, after the sandwich, ate an apple and a small bag of mixed nuts. He didn't offer Brian any. Every man for himself in Alaska.

"Smooth sailing. So far."

Brian looked up from his paper plate of a largely eaten cheeseburger and a few limp fries. "Mind if I ask you a few questions?" he ventured, relieved he didn't stutter.

"Shoot. Looks like you're doing this trip for the first time."

"What took you to Alaska?"

"The service. When I got out, I stayed. What was I going to do, go back to Alabama? Anyway, then I met a woman from Kotzebue. Not leaving for nowhere now."

Brian pushed his paper plate toward Reggie and offered him the remaining French fries. For Brian, that was an invitation to be friends.

"You have a family?"

Reggie politely pushed the plate of fries back and shook his head.

"I work at sea. Not on land much."

He told Reggie about Mary and Tess. He lied about what a happy family he had. His daughter was a freshman at the University of Oregon, intending to major in biology. He stuttered a little telling him this, but not much. Brian studied Reggie's face for a reaction when he did. Maybe Alaska was working its magic on him, and he'd stutter less rather than more. The ferry hadn't reached the southernmost tip of the state yet. His tiny hope returned.

"What are you going to do when you get there? Never heard of this place, Utopia."

"Dunno. Go out on a boat myself, I guess. I want to see

the place. Hike. Walk around. Get in a plane, have someone show me the glaciers."

Reggie studied him for a moment. "You're headed up because you think there are no people. Well, that's true and not true. You'll see, my friend."

Brian excused himself from the table and returned to his room. He studied his foldout map of Alaska. Utopia was the tiniest dot labeled with the tiniest letters. He didn't need his glasses to know it was there.

*

He briefly got off the ferry when it stopped at Ketchikan. Alaska looked little different from Washington so far, except that people painted their wooden buildings bright colors no one would dare to in Tummus. The pamphlet he picked up at the unmanned information booth said these houses had once been boarding houses with a few brothels mixed in.

A day out of Sitka, the second port of call, he was standing on the pier at Juneau. He was in a city again. He watched the big ferry sail on once it disgorged him and his knapsack. Brian asked around for the smaller ferry that would take him to Utopia. "Right there," they told him. A few minutes later he was sitting on a cold metal bench on the deck, knapsack squeezed between his thighs.

Five hours later he was in Utopia. He hung around the dock until the ferry departed. By the time it left the harbor, there were no longer any taxis at the dock to take him to his lodge. He walked to the road and tried to hitch a ride. He stood with his thumb out, knapsack on the ground next to him. He surveyed the scene, float planes and boats of all sizes framed by mountains towering in the distance. Not far from where he stood, a long line of upside-down kayaks rested their bows on three immense logs laid end to end.

Few vehicles passed by. None stopped. He ended up walking.

First impressions count. Brian had plenty. Western hemlock, Sitka spruce, Alaska yellow cedar, western red cedar, Pacific yew, red alder. Broad-leaved evergreens. The trees were gargantuan. *Must be the rain.* The brisk air brushed against his uncovered wrists, hands, the cheeks of his face. This was a rainforest, he knew that from the guidebooks, but reading about a place tells you nothing about how it will smell. Utopia smelled like rich topsoil, the kind you spread a fresh pile of over your garden. He recalled the smells of the bait shop he'd gone to with his father. Invigorated, he picked up the pace toward his destination, Utopia Rooms to Let.

Corina, a short, broad woman who looked Eskimo to his eyes, gave Brian a quick tour of her place.

"Been here ten years. My husband was in the Navy, followed him up here. No, I'm Filipina, not native. He's long gone, the bastard. Got the place on the market now. Since last year. Interested?"

He chuckled, though he wasn't sure Corina was kidding.

"There's the john. You share it with two other guests. New Yorkers. We have good plumbing here, but don't do anything fancy."

He had no idea what fancy things you do in a bathroom. Corina must have seen him look puzzled.

"Cleaning fish, stuff like that. Give 'em to me, I got a place out back I can gut them for you." He recalled his father had once tried to teach him how to clean fish.

"Better yet, sell anything you catch when you get back to the harbor. If you're thinking of freezing your salmon and shipping 'em back, that will be the most goddamn expensive fish you'll ever eat. By the way, my kitchen is out of bounds to guests. Eat dinner out, there are two taverns in town. Not bad."

Corina went to answer the phone. Brian continued the tour on his own. There was an old-fashioned icebox and a woodstove. A dining room table with a lace tablecloth on it and a worn Oriental rug beneath. He looked at the ceiling and saw white plaster discolored with faint water stains. Corina's glass chandelier could do with a little dusting. There was nothing new except for Radio Shack walkie-talkies next to the coffee percolator Corina had told him would be ready each morning by five.

Framed postcards of Alaska during the Gold Rush lined the staircase to the second floor. Horse-drawn wagons and gnarly prospectors. He found his room upstairs. Corina had told him his key would be in the lock, and it was. He circled back to the front entrance to retrieve his knapsack. His room was small but big enough. He didn't unpack right away, just got his guidebook out of his pack, took his boots off and lay on the bed to thumb through it once more. The peoples who had always lived here, the Tlingit, the Haida, the Tsimshian, all had done well in their choice of the Tongass. The climate was milder than farther north. Woods full of game, waters full of sea life. He was on the Gold Coast of Alaska, where bears and eagles shared the bounty of the ocean with humans. He nibbled on a pack of peanut butter crackers and fell asleep in his clothes.

*

"Oh, the other guests? They left real early, in the dark. Big day out fishing. Long way for the boats to go to find any king salmon these days," Corina explained.

The guidebook had still been on his stomach when he woke that morning. When he went downstairs for coffee and noticed he was alone, he asked Corina about the other guests. She handed him his plate of bacon and eggs and left him to himself. He hadn't yet stuttered in front of her—a good sign. Today he'd explore the town. Walk everywhere. Take some photographs.

Brian put on all the outerwear he'd brought with him. He took the knapsack along, should he shed any of it later. He headed first for the shore, of which there was plenty. Rough gravel and rocks stretched to the foggy horizon. His reading had prepared him for things to look different here. So far they did, and they didn't.

He walked up a path spotted with seagull droppings to the main street. There was no one else on it until he saw a teenage kid whiz by on a bike, a canvas bag full of newspapers slung across his chest. The boy didn't turn his head to acknowledge his presence. Used to tourists, Brian supposed. About fifty feet away on his side of the street, he spotted a huge human head carved out of stone partially buried between the sidewalk and the beach. Walking over to it, he saw it was the head of a native Alaskan with a stern expression. Maybe a chief. He turned around toward the center of town, which was three or four blocks of mostly ramshackle buildings. At its start there was a sandwich board sign on the sidewalk reading FLY SHOP GUIDED RENTAL TOURS. He made a note of the address. Everything was one or two stories tall, except for an imposing three-story concrete edifice with a U.S. Post Office at street level. It wasn't Utopia's biggest building. That was a derelict white wooden structure large enough to be a hotel. The porticos made it too fancy to be anything else. Brian walked around the building and found a log on sawhorses. It was halfway carved into a canoe. Tools lay on the ground that would have been stolen instantly in Tummus.

There was more to see. A general store with a man inside getting ready to open. Another store selling sporting goods. A shop advertising they accepted clothes on consignment. A combination barbershop and beauty salon. A storefront Pentecostal church. An empty former souvenir shop with a Juneau phone number on a piece of paper taped to its entrance, if you wanted to inquire about renting it. Another sporting goods store. He pressed his face against the glass. A huge model of a halibut hung from the ceiling above racks of fishing poles.

The grandest buildings on this side of the street were two taverns standing next to each other. They had red neon signs in their windows advertising two beers they sold, Rainier and Prinz Brau. Both had signs saying when they opened: The Sourdough Saloon at eleven and the adjacent Jack's Bar and Grill at eleven-thirty. He'd come back to eat lunch at one of them, dinner at the other.

Returning to his room sooner than he expected, Brian fell asleep. When he woke it was noon, and he decided to head back to the taverns. He just put his sweater on this time and ambled down to the main street again. Jack's looked livelier. He could see the colored lights of a jukebox. Once through the door, he saw a huge Alaska state flag, the Big Dipper's stars against a field of blue, pinned to the far wall. Livelier turned out to be two old men sitting at the bar drinking, and three gray-haired ladies with old-fashioned eyeglasses at a table studying the menu. He sat at the bar two stools down from the drinking geezers. They paid him no mind.

Reaching over the counter, he grabbed a menu from a stack of them. He looked up to see a woman standing in front of him. She was short and, he guessed once more, native. He couldn't tell if the look on her face was a smile or a scowl. He asked for a beer, and the woman nodded. She turned slightly and waved her hand over the handles for the four beers on tap. He asked which she recommended.

"Hey, captain," said the closer of the two men drinking at the bar. "Meet Kath. She can read your lips, but she's not always gonna bother to answer back. She's deaf."

Kath placed her hand on one of the taps to answer his question. He wasn't sure if he had ever met a deaf person. There hadn't been any at school. He'd been the most handicapped around back then, except for that guy missing an arm. There were worse things than stuttering, he knew that.

Suddenly the Joker was sitting on the bar facing him, his little legs hanging over the edge.

"What the hell! I got rid of you when I was a kid."

"Well, you're still a kid in my book. Talk to her. They told you she can read your lips. And don't talk slow or move your lips big, like some idiot. You know how you feel when people do things like that to you."

"How will she talk back?"

"She's deaf, not mute. Deaf people find it easier to talk than to listen. The exact opposite of you."

He wondered, Can this woman read my lips if I stutter? He picked up the menu and pointed at the cheeseburger. He could have said the word, but he was nervous.

Kath nodded and paused. She was waiting to hear more, which was to say, have more pointed out to her.

"The *fuh-fuh*-fries." He'd said it low enough that the two men next to him couldn't hear, but enough so Kath could see his mouth moving. His stuttering didn't seem to faze her. She poured his beer and slipped back into the kitchen. She still hadn't said anything. She could be as embarrassed by her voice as much as he was of his.

"Has she always been *duh*-deaf?" he asked the nearby

men, thinking maybe when she was young, she could hear.

"Damned if I know," one replied. "What's it to you, anyway?"

Kath brought his cheeseburger and fries out to him. She smiled as she set it down on the counter. He motioned with his hands to show he needed silverware.

"You can talk to me, honey. I don't know what these boys told you, but I read lips and can talk just fine." Kath's voice was not, however, a normal voice. It had a high-pitched screech to it. He understood her. He didn't have a normal voice, either.

"Here you go. Knife and fork, sweetheart." Kath hesitated as if she knew he was finally going to say something.

"My *fuh*-first day here. My *fuh*-first *fuh-fuh*-full day."

"Here? Utopia?" She grinned. "Welcome to the big city. Here's the ketchup. Enjoy."

Kath went back into the kitchen and came out with a tray carrying the food for the three women at the table.

"How's your burger?" Kath asked. "Another one?" she added, glancing at his empty schooner. He shook his head no. He had to remember he could talk to her. "Where you from, honey?" she asked. He stuttered that he was from near Seattle.

"Don't miss the pancake breakfast at the church on Sunday. Will you be here that long?"

Her voice no longer sounded odd to him. He'd gotten used to it already. He never felt at home with his own voice.

He couldn't finish his burger. They give you a lot of

food up here, he noted for future reference.

One of the men at the bar got up and strolled to the jukebox. Something country-western came on. Mel Tillis. Brian decided it was time to leave. He caught Kath's eye.

"Can I take the rest in a *buh*-box? A *buh-buh*-bag?"

*

That evening he didn't go out again. After dark, he sat at his inn's dining room table and chatted with Corina while he finished his leftovers. He didn't stutter much with her. In a lull in their conversation, he asked Corina how Utopia got its name.

"Everyone asks me that. Someone told me half a dozen places have the same name." She told him Kath was Haida with a little Tlingit thrown in.

"Prince of Wales people, she says. Had the measles as a kid and lost her hearing. Happens a lot up here. Kath showed up in town a few years ago from some godforsaken place." Corina couldn't remember much else about her.

"Her son works on the boats now. He tried his hand at carving, but no talent for it. When he's not out fishing, he's axing out canoes in back of the old hotel. I hear he's doing it all wrong. No father in the picture to show him."

Before he went up to his room, he asked Corina to call the fishing tour outfit whose sign he'd made a note of to see if there was a boat going out in the morning. There was. Corina told him to be down at the harbor by six and reminded him there'd be coffee ready by five.

Later, lying awake in bed, he wrapped his fingers around his cock. His other hand made a fist and pounded his thigh over and over. There'd be a bruise in the morning. Kath's face appeared above his own, and in his mind he kissed it. After he climaxed and cleaned himself up, he turned over and fell asleep. He dreamt about a town with no one but deaf people in it.

CHAPTER FOURTEEN

In the early light Brian could see the sky-blue arch over the entrance to the pier read ANB HARBOR, and beneath that, in smaller letters, ALASKA NATIVE BROTHERHOOD. Further below, dangling from a rusted chain stopping him from going any further, was a square of plywood that warned OWNERS ONLY.

Corina said Alex and Joel had a boat to take tourists out for half or full-day fishing excursions. Halibut, salmon, whatever the sonar could find at this time of year. No guarantees. He was here to be picked up. He was doing what he'd come to Alaska to do. He tightened and relaxed his fists repeatedly as he waited in the cold.

He looked down the pier. A young woman was loping toward him. She wore a wool cap, the same blue color as the arch, and her long blond hair cascaded from the bottom of it. "Mr. Moriarty? Brian?" she called while still ten feet away. A moment later she unhooked the chain, allowing them to greet each other. "I'm Alex. Joel is on the boat."

"Listen, Brian, sorry, we don't have enough paying customers to do this today. We're still going out, just off the books. We avoid a lot of harbor fees and taxes that way."

They marched side by side down the pier. At its end, one boat had its engine running. There was a canvas canopy over its deck and a small set of wooden steps to make it easy to board. On the boat's side, he saw the name *Wild Horses* painted in gold letters against a solid black oval followed by official numbers. Alex swung a leg around to get into the boat and offered him her hand. A man about his age with a thick salt-and-pepper beard came out of the pilot's cabin and extended a large hand.

"Joel. Brian, right? Good morning. Got any gear to bring aboard?"

Brian shrugged. He had avoided saying anything more than a couple of words so far. He'd risk stuttering when necessary, but not before.

"We got you, man. Plenty of rods. Plenty of everything. We'll see about the fish, who knows! No worries. It's been good this week. Make yourself at home, I'll give you my little skipper speech later."

"We're waiting on one more," Alex added. "Our friend George. He often comes along. He's native and can catch as much as he wants. If Fish and Game stops us, any fish above the limit we've caught, we'll say George got. Funny thing is, he's not from here. He's Navajo. From Arizona. Doesn't matter. Any Indigenous person can catch what he wants. Treaty rights."

"There are sandwiches up front. We packed lots. Just ask."

Brian looked around the boat standing mid-deck. At the stern was a built-in steel table with a hole in the middle. He figured this was where fish got hacked. There was also something that looked like a weird, misshaped baseball bat, but smaller. There was a small icebox on the table and a large one on the deck below it. One for the bait and the other for the fish, he guessed.

Three metal holsters were anchored on each side. That was where the rods would go. Everything was spotless, as if the boat were brand new. Two large white plastic buckets stood together against one wall.

In front of him were two upholstered benches back-to-back. He turned to see the many things organized on the outer wall of the cabin. A flashlight, several jars of something, a spool of fishing line, some kind of lotion or grease, towels, a first aid kit, a measuring tape, a fire extinguisher, life preservers, a license from the state of Alaska and six long fishing poles.

He peered into the cabin through its open door. There was an impressive array of switches, glowing or blinking lights, and small video screens behind them. A plastic Hawaiian hula dancer in a fake grass skirt, six inches high, was fixed to the dashboard and bobbed up and down as the boat swayed. Next to the toy was a large plastic jar labeled GINGER ROOT NATURE'S WAY SOOTHES DIGESTION.

There was a thump. Brian turned and was inches away

from a large man jumping aboard with a fishing rod in his hand. Thick, straight black hair covered with a cap that read DUTCH HARBOR MARINE across its front.

"George," Alex shouted over him. "We're set to sail. Meet Brian, our new crewman for the day."

George nodded. He wasn't going to talk much. That suited Brian fine.

Joel came out and gave what had to be his standard speech: Where he couldn't go (the bow of the boat) and what the itinerary of the day would be (out past the islands and back). They'd be going out as far as they needed to meet up with fish. He asked if Brian had questions. Alex untied the lines that held *Wild Horses* in its berth.

They passed several small atolls with simple wooden crosses atop their summits. They were nothing but barren, dark rock, no algae or moss on them. Someone had climbed steep rock faces to erect those crosses. They passed other fishing boats. Brian followed George's lead and waved.

George surprised him by asking what he did when he wasn't on this boat.

"I'm *ah* . . . *ah*-a translator. From French and . . . *Ruh*-russian."

"You go to school for that? Or did you live in those places?"

"University of Washington. I majored in them."

George smiled. He said trolling for salmon off the coast of Alaska was one of the last, best things any college grad could do. Brian wasn't sure how to take that until George added with a chuckle he'd gone to Dartmouth, majored in art history, and should know.

"Let me show you how to get your rod ready. We'll be near fish soon," shouted Joel from the captain's chair. "The sonar's got salmon."

"I'm taking care of him," George replied. "Leave it to us college boys!" He took one of the fishing rods hanging from the wall and walked back to the ice chest on the cleaning table. He reached in to pull out a fistful of shiny, dripping chunks of something.

"Herring. Nothing better. Let me do it for you the first time. That tackle is mean sharp." Brian hoped not everything was going to be done for him today.

He cast his line into the water. George had to show him how to secure the pole in one of the rod holders. Meanwhile, Joel had cut the motor and was letting *Wild Horses* drift.

"Salmon survive everything," George told him. "The herons, the gulls, the eagles, the sea lions, the otters and even us motherfuckers. Because there are so goddamn many of them. Now we wait."

Joel emerged to put one rod out for himself. "Water's getting choppy. You okay, Brian?" He nodded yes, if unconvincingly. "We may make a short day of it." Alex added they had Dramamine on board. "Keep your eyes on the horizon if you start to feel sick."

Brian did not have to wait long for a tug. There was a small splash near where his line disappeared under the water. George came over, grabbed the rod out of its holder and

214

handed it back to Brian. "Reel her in," the Navajo ordered. Brian thought: If a guy from the Arizona desert learned how to do this, so can I.

At first, the reel's gears made it easy to wind the line in. Soon it required more strength. Brian still had some of his college muscle. A tail fin appeared above the water. Joel materialized next to him with a fishnet in his hand. Brian didn't need help. With one yank on the rod, a fish, not big but not small, came crashing onto the deck.

Adorned with bands of silver and gold running its length, Brian's hook piercing its lower jaw, it gasped for breath. It arched its body and leapt about the deck with such energy Brian thought it might find its way back into the ocean. "Brian's landed one!" Alex's excited voice exclaimed. Brian grinned. He looked forward to what was going to happen next.

George grabbed the bat. He took Brian's rod away with one hand and gave him the heavy tool with the other. George had muscles, too.

"Okay, *Monsieur Tovarisch* Brian. Here's your fish bat. Go to town. But remember, someone's gonna want to eat your catch. It's a good-sized Chinook. Keep it pretty."

The tool's rubber grip was made not to slip out of Brian's hand. It was weighted at its tip with lead. Brian estimated one blow could bash a man's skull in. It wouldn't just leave a gash like his. One thought led to another, and Brian found himself trying to remember if he'd actually caught any fish that hot Saturday on Lake Sammamish with his father.

With those *huh–huh*-honey worms. What he did remember was seething at his father, being unable to look at him for a long, tortured afternoon in that tiny borrowed skiff. His personal charter for what was allowed versus what was forbidden did not allow him to strike his father, just as it wouldn't allow him blows against Father Thomas in the vestry. Things had changed. Today Brian, whose rules had relaxed as life's indignities had compounded over the years, could certainly kill something. Maybe not a man, but something. He'd come this far to the Alaskan wilderness with a goal no less than that. He always knew he'd still stutter here. Still, some new line had to be crossed. Were he better with a rifle, he might have imagined his prey a bear or a wolf. Instead, he was aboard *Wild Horses* with a lead club in his grasp and a salmon at his feet. That it was guiltless was no longer of concern to Brian, unless it made his imminent act of violence purer.

The thrashing fish slid across the deck until the larger of the ice chests stopped it. His shipmates stepped back. Brian was going to do to a fish what he had wanted to do to people who teased, mocked and insulted him. He'd pushed a schoolgirl to the ground, beaten his brother, boxed in school, gotten into drunken brawls and kicked some poor son of a bitch South African to an inch of his life. He'd even struck his wife and lost a child. What the army wouldn't let him do to his country's enemies, he was going to do to a fish. Every blow he was about to deliver was the one he had long wanted to land on someone.

He struck the salmon's head with the bat. Its flesh began

to give way, but the tool came up against something that resisted it—not enough to deflect Brian's blow, just enough to register contact. He took this resistance as a personal challenge. He repeated his assault, slamming the salmon harder until he heard something crack. Although the fish was going to die and he was wasting good meat, Brian kept pummeling it. Bits of bone and squirts of blood flew over the deck and onto his clothes, until the fish stopped its pointless flapping. Brian declared victory in his mind. Joel stepped forward to take the bat away before he could wield it again. "Okay, Brian, it's a goner. You can stop!" There was blood on the deck and plenty of it. Pieces of bright scarlet, oily flesh. He'd clean that up later. Right now Brian lifted what he'd just killed onto the gutting table and slit its fat belly with the sharpest knife he'd ever hold. "Be careful, Brian! You sure you don't want one of us to do that?" He pulled its slimy innards out as best he could, wishing he had put on the rubber gloves first. *You were in such a goddamn rush.* His fingers felt frozen. He let it drain. "Blood in a dead fish ruins its taste," his guides, coaching him from nearby, said. Brian rinsed the cavity with a hose until nothing red ran out of it. He threw the carcass into the big ice chest and tossed loose ice over it before closing the lid and returning the bat to its proper place.

"Hey *thuh-thuh*-thanks for the *huh*-help, *cheh-cheh*-George! *Thuh*-thanks, all *yu-yu*-you *gah-gah*-guys."

Brian sat on the bench and let his heartbeat slow. He took deep breaths and exercised his icy fingers until feeling returned to them. Alex asked if he needed anything. He noticed his cap had fallen off wrestling with the fish. He bent over and stretched to retrieve it. It was wet and stained red in places. This was fun, he might have told everyone, but he decided he had stuttered enough for one day.

Brian said nothing else until they were back in the harbor a few hours later. He said goodbye to George and muttered thanks to Alex and Joel. He put four twenties down on the dashboard of *Wild Horses*. "What do you want to do with your fish, Brian?" Alex asked him. "There'll be restaurant guys at the end of the pier who will take product off your hands for a fair price, if that's what you want."

"No, *guh*-guys, *thuh-thuh*-thanks. It's all yours." Fishing at sea and smashing your catch into oblivion, Brian concluded, did not cure stuttering any more than anything else did. But he had achieved his Alaska Goal Number One. The bloody cap he gripped in his hand was proof.

*

After a shower and a nap, he was eager to go somewhere and unwind, even if it meant stuttering in front of strangers for the second time in one day. The Sourdough Saloon was bigger than Jack's. This was clearly the place to go. Cigarette smoke was thick and one of the first things he noticed were half-full ashtrays everywhere. Customers, women included, all wore wool or baseball caps. It had fewer tables than Jack's but a longer bar with high-backed stools, a row of booths and two pool tables in the back. A TV was suspended above the bar's mirror with a piece of yellowed paper taped to it that read OUT OF ORDER. Another piece of paper below the TV was hand-lettered: NO DOGS ALLOWED. An unraveled fly strip that needed to be replaced. A bumper sticker read DRINK LIKE A FISH? THEN SWIM DON'T DRIVE. Lowering his eyes, he saw a floor made of worn, speckled linoleum squares.

Walls were decorated with more of the same framed photos of fishermen and their catch he'd seen next door. No state of Alaska flag on the wall. There was a diamond-shaped fake road sign with a drawing of a fish on it; the caption underneath read SALMON CROSSING. Someone's bad amateur oil painting of two eagles. A Bud Light poster. A coat rack with no coats on it—it seemed a rule in Utopia, maybe all of Alaska for all Brian knew, that you kept your coat on indoors. There were several shelves crowded with amateur sports trophies. A soccer ball and a big brass bell hung from the ceiling, as did an inflated plastic moose rocking in the breeze of an electric table fan perched on top of a popcorn machine. No jukebox he could hear or see. The Sourdough was loud enough with raised male voices and a few high-pitched female ones mixed in.

He slid into an empty booth where he could watch the pool tables, but the felt was torn in places and no one was playing. Two bikers decked out in studded leather jackets and helmets came through the double doors. They joined other men standing at the far end of the bar. After a while, when no one came over to wait on him, he approached the bartender's station. It was night, not afternoon, and he was going to have a real drink. He felt he should celebrate. He wished he'd taken a picture of him with his salmon, the kind that he could add to either of the bars' galleries.

Someone else was waiting for a drink with him at the bar. A woman who, like Kath the evening before, looked native but younger and more attractive. He noticed she wasn't wearing a baseball cap. Her hair was long, thick and shiny jet-black. She didn't glance his way as he drifted more beside her than behind her. He took that as a sign she meant to ignore him.

"What are you *geh-geh*-getting?" he said to her anyway. He wanted to share his good mood with someone else tonight, preferably a female. Meeting women had not been part of his plans for this long-awaited trip to Alaska, but since arriving he found himself rating every female under the age of fifty who crossed his path. The woman turned her head as if already skeptical of this new voice next to her, ready to inch away if she didn't care for whom it belonged to.

"My usual. Cranberry and vodka."

"Sounds *guh-guh-guh*-good. Let me *geh-geh*-get it for you." A tall bartender wearing a cowboy hat appeared. Easing the woman out of the way, Brian reached into his back pocket for his wallet and ordered a neat whiskey for himself and a cranberry and vodka for the lady.

"Already with the drinks, and you don't even know my name."

"Come *suh-suh*-sit with me in my *buh-buh*-booth. You *kuh-kuh*-can tell me your name there. You can ... *tuh-tuh*-tell me everything." He had never been this forward with a woman before. Catching that big Chinook had given him a boost of courage. The woman had a strong, handsome face made vulnerable around the eyes by the small and feathery laugh lines framing them. Her teeth were brilliant white. She wore no makeup and didn't need any.

She placed her palms down on the table. Her left ring finger was missing. She must have wanted him to know that she was not perfect. He thought of his brother's lazy eye. Later Brian would learn she lost it when she worked at the mill. Now she worked at the town's cannery, where the work was still dangerous, but at least there was a better union.

"So what's your name?"

"Mary."

He wondered if he had groaned so loud she heard him. This woman was not deaf. "Do you have a nickname? A middle name? Anything I can call you instead of Mary?"

She pursed her lips. "Okay, you don't like Mary. Name of some girl who broke your heart? Well, fine. Too many Marys in this town, anyway. Fuckin' missionaries came and baptized everyone Mary. It stuck."

Brian might tell her about the other Mary in his life later, but not tonight.

"So, yeah, I have an Indian name. You'd never be able to pronounce it. Why don't you call me Raven? Easy for you to remember. Raven."

He reached with his tumbler to clink Raven's glass, yet untouched, in a one-way toast. "Native?"

"What do you mean? If you mean was I born here, no. From south of here. A smaller place. Work brought me. It's my night off."

He explained he was visiting from Seattle, though Raven hadn't asked. "I caught a fish today. On a boat."

"Good for you, Hemingway. Tlingit catch them with their bare hands. What do you think of that?" Raven followed up with a laugh. He knew she meant it more as a joke than a put-down.

"*Tuh-tuh*-tlingit. Does it mean anything?"

"Of course it does. It means human being."

"Sorry," he said sheepishly. "I *stuh*-stutter. No offense." He hadn't apologized in years for what defined him most in the world.

"Really?" Raven kidded him once more. Brian liked that. "I hadn't noticed." She picked up her drink and sipped it. He'd finished his.

"Want anything? I'm going back up to the bar."

"No."

"I'm hungry. Might get something to eat, too."

"Get the nachos," Raven said firmly, as if commanding him. "It's the only thing they don't screw up. I'll eat some of yours."

He returned to the booth and told Raven more about the Chinook.

"You probably don't know this story," Raven said, her sole comment. "Raven—the real Raven, not me—used a length of wild celery, *yā'naet*, to kill a salmon when it came

222

ashore." He was puzzled why she told him this story, and disappointed there wasn't more to it.

A couple of hours, one order of nachos and several whiskeys later, he snuck Raven up the stairs in Utopia Rooms. On the walk from the bar, Brian was tempted to confess things to Raven. Apologetic details about the other Mary, bashful truths about a lifetime of stuttering, shy admissions of his excitement at meeting Raven. But he knew he'd sound no better than a nervous teenager. He was meeting someone new, and it was unusual. Brian focused on not appearing too eager. Too eager for what? he thought. Romance hadn't been one of his Alaska goals. Or had it? He was ready to spend his nights alone. That he'd already connected with someone surprised and challenged him: Surprised because he wasn't by nature social and challenged because he knew this was an opportunity he could easily blow. Raven was quiet as well, quieter than she'd been in the Sourdough. As they neared his lodge, Brian did not have to warn her to shush.

They were quiet in his room, too, except for the words he murmured into her ears. These flowed as stutter-free as they had his first time with Mary by the lake decades ago. Raven made no sounds at all. Despite the dark, Brian thought he could see her face talking to him in the ways her eyebrows, eyes, mouth and chin moved in tandem, forming silent sentences organized by the grammatical rules of some language he was hearing—seeing—for the first time. He imagined the sentences were telling him: You are in a place now where words have no power over you. Here we depend upon other things to tell stories.

The next morning, Raven saw the large purple bruise on his thigh he'd given himself his first night in Utopia. She asked him her first question since leaving the Sourdough. "What did you do to earn that?" The laugh that accompanied it spared Brian from resorting to words to answer her, or indeed to answer with anything at all.

CHAPTER FIFTEEN

They spent most of their week together in his room. Corina left them extra fresh towels every day and once a bottle of Washington State wine with two glasses. When they did go out, they wandered through whatever shops were open, and by the end of the week they'd been in each at least twice. Raven knew everyone in Utopia, Brian no one. He'd stare at the merchandise as if he were shopping. Most of what was for sale was junk, inexplicable or useless to him. Women's Eskimo-style authentic jewelry, ceremonial blankets and miniature humpback whales carved out of wood, made in China. While he waited, Raven talked in a low voice, more humming than speaking, to whatever friend was standing behind the register.

What he liked most were their hikes together. Walks really, on trails he could have found on his own, but he placed himself in Raven's hands and let her lead. Each day there was the morning hike. After the sandwiches Raven made in Corina's kitchen (she was permitted to enter) and after sex and a nap, there was the afternoon hike.

"Remember, I'm not from here, Brian. It's not as if I know this town like the back of my hand. These trails are for tourists. Look at the dumb signs they've got out. Bears my ass. There won't be any bears until the salmon run." He protested that he had seen one from the window of their room, but Raven said it was impossible at this time of year. "You saw a moose."

Raven had a beat-up Toyota Corolla. She drove them to places they couldn't walk to. Utopia was on an island. You couldn't go far, but you needed a car to get anywhere important: The one gas station, the one supermarket, the one church not a storefront. When he saw Raven never buckled her seatbelt, he stopped buckling his own, as well. Between the smoking in the Sourdough and Raven's laissez-faire approach to driving safety, his image of Alaska as a place where no one told you what to do was confirmed.

This morning was their seventh excursion. The gravel road turned to dirt a mile out of town and ended not far beyond. "Easy drive," Raven commented. "This road is usually mud. No rain this spring." They parked across from the trailhead. He noticed, getting out, that Raven never bothered locking her side of the car. He stopped doing it, too, after Raven complained it was a chore to reach over and unlock his door whenever they got back in.

"My arms aren't long, if you haven't noticed. And who do you think would steal this piece of crap anyway? Someone I don't know in this town? Like who?"

The trailhead wasn't marked. There was no outhouse or trash can. Once they set out on the path, at first only a break in the salmonberry bushes, it was well trod. Raven said she came here from time to time to be by herself.

The woodlands looked like their photographs: Not so much trees as a mass of solid, undifferentiated green. Studying what they were about to enter, Brian thought about how easy it was to get along with a forest. A cedar never mocked him, a yew never called him a liar, made fun of him, molested him, punished him, offered advice, or thought it could heal him with therapy. A tree never made him do violent things. It was dawning on him why he had come to Utopia. Nothing growing in the woods, or flying overhead or swimming in the ocean was going to ask him a question and wait for an answer.

He had read there were four cold temperate rainforests in the world: The coast of Chile, the South Island of New Zealand, a patch in the middle of Tasmania and here. This was the biggest, the last primeval rainforest in North America, more than a thousand miles long. The whole of it stretched from Oregon past Anchorage. And he was in the middle of it. The ground, a thick carpet of decomposing organic matter, squished under his boots as if he was treading on a lumpy sponge. It never dried out. Lichen dangled from tree limbs. He remembered his uncle's stories about fighting fires in the Cascades. These forests here had never burnt. Here, the world was water and not fire.

What he liked was the silence. Just the sound of his

and Raven's footsteps. Even those were hardly audible. It was the silence of his office, the silence of his walks with Tripitaka, the silence when he drove his car alone, the silence when Mary and Tess were out of the house. The forest said nothing. Neither did he nor Raven on the dimmest stretch of trail, where the seamless wall of green blocked what light there could have been. He thought: I am in the belly of the world. If there were salmon in the trees, as Raven insisted there sometimes were, they were silent, too. There was no small talk, no explanations, no stuttering between Raven and him. He recalled how his Chinook had made no sound when he pummeled it to death. Its mouth moved. Nothing came out of it. Had he made any sound himself, brandishing that fish bat? He didn't remember.

In Tummus, he often thought stuttering was akin to wandering through a forest. You know there's a way out, but you can't find it. You go in circles and end up more lost. That's not what this forest was like. The difference here was that he had Raven to guide him.

It was still late winter, but slender stems of future things were reaching up from the moss-covered ground amid the trees. Large leaves scooped up whatever few rays of diffuse sun filtered this far down. There were immense rocks covered with moss. Brian guessed they were boulders left behind when the glaciers retreated. Ahead of him was something resembling a bog, what he had learned from Raven to call a muskeg. A narrow band of water chugged through it, and it was speckled with brown stems that looked lifeless but stood erect. Raven led him to three logs lined up to enable people to cross.

He raised an arm to point. "Is that a raven up there?" he asked. "No, just a big crow," the woman answered.

The path straightened to be flanked with fountain-like ferns as tall as he was, many times the size of the sword ferns in Tummus and far more numerous. Where there was light, maidenhairs grew, elsewhere, oak ferns, northern birch ferns, deer ferns, mountain woods, lady ferns and many others that, despite all he'd read, he could not identify. It didn't matter that he hadn't brought his field guide and reading glasses along. There was too little light to read, anyway. More familiar to him were the horsetails colonizing the ground wherever they could, ancient food for dinosaurs. He noticed how the forest smelled: Thick, pungent, fetid, somewhere between fresh and lethal. The cooler the air, it struck him, the more ominous. The forest, he now understood, was not wholly welcoming to strangers. He hadn't expected to feel like an intruder here. Treading the narrow precinct of the man-made path and breathing air meant for trees and ferns, he did.

What could be so dangerous here? What would Tripitaka make of these scents? He recalled with a stab of pain the dash his excited dog had made into the forest back home, to emerge hurt, defeated, betrayed. The Tongass was as wet and alive as the guidebooks claimed. It was also decayed and dying, leveled not by any of the fast-moving walls of flame that, from time to time, had consumed the mountains where he'd grown up, but by the inexorable rot of a damp forest floor smothering everything.

Different species of trees had grown together, their roots an intertwined mass of wood tangled like fingers clutching dark earth below, claws reaching down from what could have been little huts for dwarves. It reminded Brian of the teepee he'd erected on his school's stage. In some pairs of conjoined trees, masses of roots rose five or six feet in the air above the ground before turning into matted tree trunks. Rather than plunging into the ground, their roots had grown skyward to make odd shelters. He thought they might be useful for something. For what, he couldn't imagine.

"Good time of year to come," Raven told him. "No need to dodge bear droppings yet. Wait a month. Watch out for the timber slugs, they're everywhere."

They came to a bend in the trail and moved into light. Ahead was a lake. He asked its name. Raven shrugged. He couldn't shake the feeling he'd been here before. He recalled the lake where he and Mary had come with their sandwiches and made love. Only the colors of the water and the sky, a gauzy white-gray, were different. From nowhere, a wave of guilt swept over him. He worked hard to keep Raven from guessing what he was thinking.

There was a small clearing on the furthest shore of the lake. He pointed and wondered aloud why nothing was growing there. Raven told him human beings once lived there, their homes and midden humps are long gone, too soon for trees to have grown back yet. "When they do grow back," she said, "they won't be the same. The Tongass is drier and warmer now." He thought *human beings* was an odd way to say *people*.

"That's what the Tlingit call themselves. When we're talking Tlingit."

*

Raven saw the bones first. They were not far from where the trail narrowed and forced them to walk single file, their clothes brushing up against prickly devil's club. Now it was Raven's turn to point.

The buck did not look as if it had died violently. Just old age. Its bleached, weathered bones, clean of flesh, had taken on the look of driftwood. They'd been there a long time. Yet nothing, no bird, no mammal, no rain, no ice, no upheaval of the earth, had disturbed them. Every rib, every vertebra of its spine and neck was where it should be. The skull still had its two antlers, one lying white against the dark ground and the other elevated, marking the summit of the dead animal. The skeleton could have been a drawing from a zoology textbook. Only the hooves were missing. Had a scavenger made off with them? Had they dissolved into the soil?

Nothing green grew anywhere near the deer. No ferns, no vines, nothing had crept toward the ribs, legs or pelvis bones. The ground was a level, brown expanse until it met with the duffels of sphagnum moss rimming it. The calcium relics did not look peaceful or at rest. A jawbone was hinged to the skull at a strange angle. Maybe, in the animal's last moments, it meant to bite, fight back, resist or, resigned to dying, cry out its regrets to the forest. It was the woodland equivalent of the Chinook whose mouth had gasped, pointlessly, on the deck of the *Wild Horses*.

He stepped closer to the bones. His hiking shoes were where the hooves should have been. "Don't even think it," barked a voice behind him as he bent over. Attempting a joke, the same voice cracked when it added, "You don't know where they've been."

Brian stood for a long moment, the bones in front and Raven behind him. "We might as well turn around and head back to the car," she said. Brian turned the opposite way and headed deeper into the woods. Here I am, he thought, in the middle of my life, within a dark forest, and the trail ahead is becoming harder to follow: Savage, rough, stern, above all, noiseless. Where were the birds now? Soundlessness here was not quite the quiet he had encountered before. Stutterers were known as much by their silences as their sounds. He had imagined himself an expert in silences, but this was dumb silence, sober silence, solemn silence, uneasy silence, muzzled silence, reproachful silence, censured silence, irrevocable silence. Brian became anxious. He wasn't sure he liked the particular hush of this forest. There was too much of it. He looked back over his shoulder. Raven hadn't followed.

Now on his own, he had no one to talk with. He'd started his hike this morning half-awake. Now he felt alert. Consternation and anxiety were his adrenaline. He forged ahead and approached the foot of a mountain. Brian was not going to stutter while he was alone, of course, but the forest was governed by a hiatus of its own—mute, autistic, aphasic, stuttering. He looked up, to where the sun's last rays touched its highest ridge and calmed his fear, if not by much. He looked over his shoulder a second time to see if Raven had caught up. The trail was completely gone. He struggled with the undergrowth as he continued forward. After a while, he grew tired and wanted to rest. His vigor was draining from him. There would be a fallen tree or a boulder up ahead to sit on. He started up the mountainside without intending to, only searching for respite.

Brian remembered the times his mother would read *Hansel and Gretel* to him and his brother at bedtime, stopping halfway, saying the rest was too scary. In other fairy tales there was usually a forest, deep and dark, where no one except sorcerers, genies, monsters and the devil lived. Sometimes there were ravens, like here in Alaska, and lots of crows. Kings lived in their castles at the edge of the forests, as did dwarves and common folk in their humble cottages. They would venture into the forest, especially if they were woodcutters, a princess or a maiden. Brian couldn't remember any of them describing the forest, as if there was too little light to see it. They were featureless black holes that kidnapped people and never released them. He was in a forest now. A forest was where something had hurt Tripitaka's leg so badly once.

Brian heard his first unaccountable sound since leaving the deer bones. Something was rustling in the bushes ahead of him. Brian froze. A fox? A wolf? A bear? Raven had said it was too early for them. She could have been wrong. Fear returned to Brian and with it his brute energy. He should have shouted a warning to Raven, made his own stutter-less sound to let her know the forest was having its revenge on him for trespassing this far. He wished Tripitaka was by his side because his dog had the experience of encountering terror in a forest. The rustling stopped. Brian concluded it had been a breeze in an otherwise still forest, a subtle warning he'd stepped without permission into a private place.

Others had traveled here, had lit special fires and said prayers from strange faiths to their deities, their names unspeakable; and because they had prayed, they were left to live. Brian imagined his predecessors in the forest had returned to this place whenever disaster threatened and, if they had forgotten to bring fire, would bury themselves in the earth. I don't know how to rub two twigs together. I do not know how to make fire, Brian thought. I can't recite prayers without stammering. And I will not bury myself in the ground. He turned to look for Raven once more. Instead, he saw the woods behind him open up like the mouth of a behemoth, toothless and tongueless, its depths as dark as a northern forest, one that didn't see light half the year, could be. A mouth he could not go around, climb over or dodge beneath, a mouth which he could only enter and hope to emerge closer to Raven and the deer bones she had found.

He found a fallen tree trunk to sit on and shook his head at his wild thoughts. Children were often told terrible stories about what they might encounter in the forest: Bears that ate people, eagles that hacked out eyes, wolves, lions, all kinds of beasts. Brian distracted himself by making up his own version of *Hansel and Gretel*, in which a little boy and girl were not the least afraid of the forest. They were fleeing a great panic in another country. But in time they lost their way. They didn't see a single cottage and worried they would starve to death. Night fell. The children climbed up a tree to avoid wild animals and robbers. Finally, they saw a light in the distance from their high perch. The boy talked the girl into climbing down the tree with him to see what it was. They walked deeper into the forest. They found seven people huddled around a fire, the glistening bones of an eighth lying strewn around it. "Who are you? Come over to us. Sit down and eat with us." One of the seven was a blind beggar who said to them: "Be like me." Others were a deaf child, a man with a twisted neck, a hunchback, a woman with no arms and another with no legs. Each said to the boy and girl: "Be like me." Last, sitting farthest from the fire, was a stutterer. He said nothing to them. Although the stutterer had blood on his hands, the boy and the girl decided to become like him because that would be their own choice, not one urged by others. It was the one choice that might save them from being slaughtered, too, Brian decided. "*Wuh-wuh*-we'll *buh-buh*-be like you," the boy in Brian's version said.

Brian was still inventing his story, and was at the point where he'd have to decide the fate of the children who chose to stutter, when he sensed Raven behind him. His story was going to remain incomplete, but he was no longer alone. He didn't speak, and neither did she. Few people know what to do when facing a stutterer. There was no reason Raven should be an exception, but she was. Do you help the stutterer out? Do you look at him or turn away as he struggles to speak? Do you smile encouragingly? Most people fidget and devise ways to escape. Brian disliked people who abandoned him to spare their own feelings.

Raven did none of these things. Raven was as still as the forest. Perhaps she had decided Brian was a creature designed to speak, but unwilling to do so. Brian did want to speak at times, but he let what he imagined were Raven's thoughts do the talking for the both of them. *I know these stories about people in the forest. I've heard them all. No need to invent how they end.* Brian did not resist when Raven suggested, for a second time, they head back to the car.

*

It was almost noon. They were still in bed on Brian's last full day in Utopia when he proposed a change in plans.

"Enough hiking. I want to see where you live."

"Me? My place? No, you don't."

"I do. How else will I find you when I come back?" He threaded the fingers of his right hand through hers.

"It's a dump. Besides, you know how many people say they're coming back and never do?" Raven laughed her deep-throated laugh. Brian worried Raven was telling him not to come back without quite saying so.

Raven drove them in the Corolla from Utopia Rooms to the outskirts of town, pulling up to the Happy Trails

Trailer Park and Campground. A small boy was sitting on the top rung of the rusted gate at the entrance. He held a paper airplane. Raven waved to him. The boy threw his paper airplane at the car. It collided against Raven's window and fell to the ground.

"A neighbor's kid. I used to babysit him. Kinda slow. His mother was a drinker."

Raven's trailer was one of the first in the park. She parked in the gravel strip next to it, stopping inches from a tree stump axed into a stool. Brian looked out the window at the dingy metal skin of the old trailer. It must have been silver once. Now it was closer to brown. Wooden steps led to the door, a round window in it. Next to the steps were a couple of skunk cabbages in the ground. An old metal barrel stood nearby. The other three windows were rectangular ones that wrapped around the curving front end. As Brian got out of the car, he saw the top of the trailer had a thick layer of old pine needles on it, patches of bright green moss scattered throughout.

"I told you it was a dump," Raven said, jangling her keys in her hand. "Don't think I'm giving you a tour. If it's a dump on the outside, don't even think about the inside. You stay here. I'm going in to get some cigarettes."

Brian looked around for anything he might offer to repair. This was the only time he'd spend at her place, and he wanted to leave behind something better than he'd found it. Something that would make her think of him each time she saw it.

Raven emerged from the trailer with her pack of cigarettes in one hand and a screwdriver in the other.

"Is that for me? God, you are a mind reader. I was thinking of fixing something around here for you."

"Relax, Mister Handy Man. Does it really look that rundown?"

"Not what I meant. Sorry."

Raven lit one of her Camels.

"I noticed the front license plate on my car is loose. Must have lost a screw. The screwdriver is for me." She pulled something out of her pocket with the hand holding the tool. "I got an old coffee can inside full of nails and screws. If this one doesn't fit, another will." She held up a sheet metal screw.

"Let me do it," he said, knowing she'd have to bring the coffee can out for him to find the right kind of nut and bolt.

"Sit. Like that stool? A kid who lives near here did it for me with his chainsaw. Future Tlingit Carver of the Year. It's my throne. Sit in it and survey my realm."

Brian kept standing. The stool looked damp. Raven sat on one of her trailer's wooden steps and put the screwdriver down on top of the crumpled pack of cigarettes. For the first time since they'd met, she started to tell him things: The scandal at the Juneau bank where she mailed in her money each month; her issues with the trailer park's communal toilets and showers; theories as to why the halibut fishing ground was moving further and further away, which led to speculation about why Alaska was getting warmer.

Raven had never talked this much before. It was as if

someone had flipped a switch. She'd gone from taciturn to garrulous and sounded as if she was just getting started.

"I say it's going back to the way it was. Like a million years ago. Dinosaur time. There's no real rain anymore. Not like when I was a kid."

Brian stayed silent. He watched Raven snuff out one of her Camels and light another. Suddenly, on their last day together, this. What she'd been gearing up for.

"You know, there's no word in Tlingit for stuttering. I guess we don't need one. None of us stutter."

Brian was embarrassed at this turn in the conversation, but also relieved. His stammer had hung over them all week, no different from the heavy storm clouds Raven said Alaska didn't have much of anymore.

"Want to hear my theory on that? It's the way Americans raise their children. You worry too much about them. You keep them on fucking leashes, like you do your dogs. Of course things go wrong."

Americans was the word Raven used for anyone who wasn't from Alaska. Canadians were Americans in her view of the world.

"Next *thuh*-theory, Raven. My parents *duh-duh*-didn't worry much about me. I *wuh*-worry a lot about my *dah*-daughter and, look, she doesn't . . . *stuh-stuh*-stutter."

"One guy here in Utopia stutters. His father was an American, so that goes to show. He works as a carpenter now, doesn't have to talk much. If I had stuttered, which is impossible, my parents would have just done my talking for

239

me." Raven laughed. She got up off the wooden stair and moved to the stool to be closer to Brian. She left her cigarettes and the screwdriver behind on the step.

Another unspoken subject until now had been Brian's wife and Raven's history with men.

"There was Tommy. A Tsimshian. He'd just gotten out of prison in Idaho for robbing a gas station when we met. He'd found drugs in jail, and once out he found a lot more. Bad knife fight outside a bar later. He's behind bars again. Glad we never had a kid. He'd be half Tsimshian and half fucked up himself by now."

Brian had no desire to talk about Mary, really. There wasn't anything to say, unless Brian wanted to talk about his own crimes, and he didn't. Raven did the next best thing and asked about his daughter.

"*Tesssssa*," she hissed. "Almost sounds like a human being's name, but it isn't."

"She's started *kuh*-college. Doesn't *stuh-stuh*-stutter, thank God."

"College. You Americans have so much down there. Schools and the money to go to them. Why bother to come up here, anyway? You tell me you think about moving here for good. Who'd walk away from all the things you have? Don't take this the wrong way, Brian. But it was better with no Americans here. Only human beings. We heard stories when we were kids.

"Not that the old times were all good. Half our stories are about drowning or dying of hunger or some plague or being plucked out of a canoe by a giant eagle never to be seen again." She laughed her deep nicotine laugh.

Brian talked Raven into taking a walk with him. They strolled further into the trailer park. Raven checked her mailbox on the way.

"Coupons. Good." She left them to pick up on their way back. Brian scanned the mailbox for a name. All he saw was NO. 5. More than a week had passed and it was too shameful now to ask Raven her last name.

She told Brian the town's road crew was hiring again. "Good union wages, and they never fire anyone." She was thinking about it. There were places she wanted to live other than Happy Trails.

"But they only hire men. Always have. Funny, how everyone thinks women are in charge of things here." As if conjured by what she'd been saying, a road crew truck drove by, its bed loaded with crushed rock. Raven waved to the men sitting in the front. The truck raised a cloud of dirt that dusted the two of them. Raven covered her mouth to cough.

"I gotta stop smoking. Chew gum for a change. Or mix tobacco with crushed shells in a pipe, the way people used to."

They headed back to trailer NO. 5. Brian saw Raven had caught him checking his watch. Why would she think he had any place to go? He didn't.

"Brian, I want to tell you something else." She ran a hand through her long black hair to signal she was going to be serious.

"You stutter. A lot. At first I had a funny reaction to that. I was a little impatient and irritated. It seemed another clueless American thing to do. Then I got used to it."

Brian was about to interrupt. She raised a finger to stop him.

"I started to feel real sorry for you. It surprised me you felt such shame about it. Shame like I've never seen, didn't think was possible in one person. You know what? My heartbeat raced when you stuttered because I knew your shame. It's not as if it was a new emotion for me. There's plenty of shame I could waste on myself. I'm ashamed of where I've ended up in life. They said I had smarts in school, and look, I never did anything worthwhile with them. You're smart, too, that's clear, but because you stammer you and everyone else thought you were stupid. Well, no one thought that about me. I needed my whole life to prove to the world I really was dumb.

"I'm on the night shift at the cannery and hang out in the dive bars downtown before I have to show up for work. You'd need a drink, too, if that was your life. You can be proud of what you do, I suppose. You *translate*. At a desk. You support people other than yourself. You have reasons to be proud. But you aren't, are you? You think you're a failure. The shame you feel isn't just one of several feelings. It's all you feel. You try to hide it from me, but I read you like a book."

Mary talking like this would have disturbed Brian. But he was grateful for how honest Raven was. Still, she was not as empathetic as she thought. If she were, Brian knew she'd sense his anger, his rage, his ire, his wrath all there inside him beside shame. He wasn't such a failure that he couldn't shield her from that. He kicked a small stone out of the way.

"Part of me wants to help you. Yeah, I wanted to mother you. You know how women can be. Then I thought: There are plenty of women in your life already, a wife and a daughter. Women galore. What can I do for you they haven't? Coming up here hasn't helped the way you hoped it would, has it? Lots of Americans come here imagining Alaska will be their own private psych hospital. They never stay long, Brian. All your troubles follow you here."

*

Back at the trailer, Raven brought out the coffee can, and they fixed her license plate together. Kneeling on the ground between the car and the stump stool, they found a bolt and a nut that fit. They finished the job in less than a minute. Raven relented and let him join her in the trailer.

It wasn't so much a mess as it was a place with everything in unlikely spots. Pots and pans where'd you otherwise sit at the little fold-down table. The little fridge, missing its door, had folded clothes piled up in it. The sink was where you'd find the books she owned. This was, Brian realized, a home no one ever visits.

Raven's heavy corduroy shirt crept up while they lay on her unmade bed, exposing her stomach and the scar that crossed it, a legacy of appendix surgery. The scar was close to black, and she didn't like it. Brian kissed it. She let his hand caress her soft belly. He playfully counted her ribs under his breath, stuttering none of the numbers.

His hand drifted lower. He fell asleep before he could arouse her. Brian woke to find her shirt was still pulled up high, her stomach in full view and his hand still resting upon it. He stepped outdoors for the last of the light and sat on the tree stump stool, where he did survey her realm. It *was* a throne, and he recalled the big fancy chair the bishop had sat in at his confirmation years ago. He wondered what it would be like to join Raven here for good. He could hear her snoring inside the trailer. It was well after dark by the time she roused herself and drove Brian back to Utopia Rooms. Her earlier talkativeness was gone, and her last goodbye was just a quick nod of her head from behind the steering wheel.

CHAPTER SIXTEEN

There was no Mary to greet Brian when he got home. This time, he had remembered to buy her a souvenir, a tin of birch syrup. He dropped his knapsack just inside the front door. With no response to his hellos, he made a quick tour of the house. He glanced out the kitchen window at the clothesline in the back. No one. He was dead tired but had been looking forward to a welcome and a hug. Still, he was not surprised. Mary always had errands in the middle of the day. But where was Tripitaka? He'd been expecting an enthusiastic greeting from his dog after more than a week away. Mary must have taken him somewhere. She rarely did that. She didn't like him in the car. She said he left a musty smell.

An hour later, after she walked into their bedroom, the first thing Mary said to him was "Oh, it's you," followed by, "Tripitaka died while you were away." She was wearing a pink dress, one Brian hadn't seen her in for a long time. There were pearls around her neck and bracelets on her wrists that looked new to him. She had piled her hair on the top of her head, exposing her long, pretty neck. These weren't clothes she ran errands in. The expression was a mix of dread and surprise: The dread authentic, the surprise rehearsed.

"He was just gone one morning. Died in his sleep. I'm sorry, Brian, I really am." She walked to the dresser and took her jewelry off. "He was old. Old for a dog."

Old for a dog. It was 1992, and in his head he did the math. Yes, Tripitaka was positively ancient. But it was the way his wife said it that made him want to strike her hard across the face. He consulted his internal rules of right and wrong and was disappointed to see it was not allowed. Brian had hit her once before. Striking her again would revoke the parole he'd granted himself in his mind. That didn't change the fact that he needed her to tell him everything that had happened, and right now. He was lying flat on their bed with the TV on. This was the bed where he slept next to her, except for those nights when, wide awake, he abandoned her for the single bed in Tess' bedroom, unoccupied while she was at college. Her bed smelled like her. He wished Tess were here now. He needed a third vote to break any tie. The household was down to him and his wife without their daughter and their dog.

"I wasn't sure what to do, so I called the police. They said I was on my own." She stood close to the dresser, as if it might protect her. "The vet wasn't in yet. So I called Gary."

It took a moment for him to figure out who his wife was talking about. Football. High school. *Gary.*

"He's back in Tummus for a while. The Navy hasn't told

him where they're sending him next. Anyway, he rushed over. We buried him, Brian. In Gary's backyard."

"You did *what?*" he said, only half hoping his voice came across as the angry shout he intended it to be.

"The ground's a lot softer at his house, Gary said. His kids helped us. There's no marker yet. I thought you'd want to take care of that yourself. Just ask Gary if it will be okay."

Just ask Gary if it will be okay. He rose from the bed without bothering to turn the TV off with the remote. He walked past his wife, deliberately brushing up against her shoulder as he did, more than half hoping to frighten her a little. With his back to her, he announced he was *guh*-going out.

*

He knocked. No one came to the door. There was no vehicle in Gary's driveway other than Brian's. His car reeked of that musty dog smell his wife hated.

Gary's house was new. The front lawn hadn't grown in. Young saplings had wire fencing curled around their bases to keep deer away. He circled around to the back of his classmate's house.

The Joker was sitting on a pile of freshly shoveled dirt. Top soil. Nothing planted yet. Someone had dug his dead dog an oval grave, not a rectangular one. How much was he expected to forgive?

"How long have you been here?" he asked the Joker.

"Just flew in," his secret friend replied. "I was tired of

waiting at your house for you to show up and hear the news."

"Well, back together again, you and me," Brian sighed. "Figures. You never miss a family celebration, do you?" He sighed again. "Is what Mary told me the truth? Did he die in his sleep?"

The Joker mimicked Mary's voice: "He was old. Old for a dog."

"Shut up. We have to move him. To our house."

"We, kemosabe?"

Brian walked to the edge of the grave to say goodbye to his dog. There'd be no moving him. He pressed his shoe hard into the loose dirt. Tripitaka's leg had never fully healed after Brian had taken him to the forest. His shoe left a print in the loose dirt. The dog's limp had never improved. He pressed his shoe harder into the dirt to leave a deeper impression. As hard as he had pressed it on the fat stomach of a South African businessman. Hard enough that Gary would have to notice the footprint when he returned home. As hard as he had on Mary's pregnant belly. Tripitaka was always skittish around him after that day in the forest. As hard as he had clubbed a fish into smithereens. As guarded as Tess had learned to be when around him.

This time, by Tripitaka's grave, he meant to do no permanent harm. He wanted to leave a shoeprint in the still soft soil, both to mark this place as his own and to say farewell to his dog. Now the only company he had to talk to without stuttering was the Joker, and the Joker wasn't real.

*

He closed the door to his office and called Tess in Eugene. He got her roommate. Would you ask her to call her father? he said without stuttering. "Sure thing, Mr. Moriarty. The library's about to close, she'll be back soon."

"How was Alaska?" Tess asked, returning his father's call.

"Do you know about *Truh*-tripitaka?" he said, ignoring her question. No one was going to get the real story of Utopia out of him, just as he'd never get the real story of what had happened in his house while he was away. He looked at his rules of right and wrong again. He expected his reluctance to talk to balance out his family's similar reluctance. It did not. He'd met a woman, granted, but it shouldn't have cost him the life of the pet who once, before the forest, had been his best friend.

"Yes, I do, Dad. Mom called me. I'm real sorry. I loved him, too."

There was no point in grilling his daughter just because he wanted to lash out at someone. He changed his tone. "It's good to hear your voice, Tess. When can you *kuh*-come *huh*-home for a weekend?"

"Not sure. Not the easiest thing to get from here to there. Guess next time I hear someone's driving up and has room for me." She paused. "Are we gonna get a new dog?"

"I'll come *geh-geh*-get you," he said, a note of pleading in his voice.

"Dad."

They talked about school. Midterms went fine. Aced calculus, it was mostly a repeat of high school. Doesn't seem to rain here as much as in Seattle. No, not dating anyone yet. The food? Mystery meat. The roommate is cool though. Her older sister goes here, too. They're both majoring in geology.

He brought Tripitaka up again, which proved to be a mistake. "No, I'm not getting another dog. . . No, I'm not going to put a *guh-guh*-grave . . . *mah*-marker in another man's backyard . . . No, no one has thrown his food and *wah*-water bowls away yet. They're right *wuh-wuh*-where we left them . . . You want them for *wuh*-what?"

They hung up after promising to talk again on the weekend. Brian realized he had told his daughter nothing about Alaska. He turned off the lights and made sure the front door was locked. He stopped to look down at his dead dog's food and water bowls. He left them where they were.

He went down the hallway and brushed his teeth in the bathroom. He entered his bedroom, stripped down to his underwear, and slipped under the covers next to a wife he knew was only pretending to be asleep. Most husbands would have a tough talk with their wives about what was going on, but Brian was not most husbands. Nor was he just a stutterer. He couldn't get that pink dress out of his mind. Brian was a stuttering coward who harbored a hypocrite's brave thoughts of revenge.

Chapter Seventeen

One of his last errands before moving for good was a trip to the rest home. The Great Oaks Manor lobby was, months after New Year's, still festooned with Millennium 2000 decorations. No one manning the reception desk stopped him from walking straight into his mother's room. It was standard-issue old people's: A charmless, institutional cell minus the bars. The old dresser from home was her only personal property. She hadn't been assigned a roommate, so the entire room was hers. The door to the bathroom was open. Metal handrails were attached to all its walls. He could see two black hairbrushes and a pale blue box of tissues next to the sink. There was the smell of a strong disinfectant. He sat in the cushionless aluminum chair by the head of her bed. The Venetian blinds were open and flooded the room with light. His mother struggled with the TV remote to turn off what sounded like a women's talk show. Bright sun washed out whatever was on the screen.

It's like they say, Brian observed, you age overnight

in a retirement home. She wasn't all that old when he'd put her there. The reason was early senility, not so much age, but now she was well on her way to looking like a fossil. More wrinkled than last time he visited, her skin had gained more brownish spots and the start of a discolored streak across her cheek. She'd long had one front tooth missing, never bothering to replace it. Now it displayed prominently on her face—she made no effort to hide it with her lips, which framed a half-open mouth, ready to drool. The gnarled hands grasping the remote were trembling. Her fingernails were long, thick and sharp—no one was clipping them. He was sitting close enough to detect her bad breath, that peculiar old person smell.

He was going to talk to her about his imminent trip, which he would lead her to believe was another solo vacation and not a permanent relocation. He was not here to say any final farewells, or tell her he and Mary had divorced a year ago. Why had he come, then? Still the dutiful eldest son? Not if he was going to lie, which he was about to do. He wouldn't say goodbye to his mother. He'd say see you next time or see you soon. At his mother's bedside at the Great Oaks Manor for this last time, he wasn't going to leave with a goodbye. He would stutter out some falsehood and then swear never to tell another. He looked out his mother's window and counted the Douglas firs planted on the property to provide the residents with a view of something green or perhaps to hide the ugly squat warehouse of a building from passing traffic. Trees all the same height in a man-made row.

There were no oak trees, much less any great ones. Great Oaks Manor was already a lie.

From her bed, through the raised railings, his mother reached for his hand. She squeezed it as she spoke. She worked hard to shift her frail body in the hospital bed to get close enough to her son so he'd hear what she had to say. He expected a complaint about breakfast or another comment about how the country was heading to hell in a handbasket.

"The doctor was able to save your brother Brian, but not him."

He had no idea what she was talking about. His first reaction was not to bother telling her he was not Bam. She'd been calling him by his brother's name for a while now. "He pulled little Aaron out dead while the nurse held Brian upside down next to the doctor. He was squealing, but little Aaron said nothing. That's what your father and I were going to call him, Aaron. When you came along, we gave you that for your middle name. You have a brother we wanted to name Aaron. Brian doesn't know any of this, don't tell him. We always wondered if it was why he stuttered so badly. Do you know the story of Aaron in the Bible, Bam? Moses' brother?"

Brian did not know the story of Aaron. He was doubly certain Bam wouldn't either. But the old dream came back to him with the veracity of a memory. *He floated in his mother and grew aware of another with him.* Brian reached up and touched the gash on his head. *When Brian touched his own face, there was no opening where the other fetus had one.* He took his hand away and placed it on his mother's forehead.

He realized this missing part was a mouth, and its absence would leave him bereft of a tongue as well. He toyed with the idea of moving it down her face and covering her nose and mouth. *Brian knew violence, one moment before brutal forceps would teach it to him a second time.* He was alone with his mother and the door was closed. Now he knew where his power to destroy had begun. *No one would know.* He was headed back to Utopia now with the ex-dream of having endured hurt and the ability to inflict it on others. *She'd be out of her misery in minutes.* With this new knowledge of the Moriartys, Brian would revise his principles for equity. When harm was warranted and when it was not. *She wouldn't resist.* Someone paid a steep price for his entry into the world even before he was born. How does one recompense that?

"And Bam?"

"Yes, Mom?"

"Your uncle Brian, your father's brother, he stuttered, too. We never told your own brother. Why, oh why, did we name Brian after him? From when he first stuttered, your father and I were sure we'd made a mistake. It was like we'd cursed him with that name. Tell him I'm sorry when you see him. He never visits. Tell him what we did to him."

"I'll do that, Mom," Brian replied blandly. "As soon as I see him. Don't worry. You haven't hurt him."

On the drive home, Brian decided that what he heard today from his demented mother would henceforth serve as the original event. The prime mover in his life as a stutterer that he'd long wondered about—whether it existed or not.

Just how this would figure into his rewards and punishments for the world was something to ponder another day. He had wrapped up all his local affairs today. He was going back to Utopia.

*

He had stayed in the house less than a year after the divorce before deciding to sell it and return to Utopia. He couldn't remain in a home everyone had fled. Mary was now living with Gary, who had gotten a divorce, as well. Every room in the house reminded him of a wife, a daughter or a dog. He never went a day without thinking about Raven. His one week in Utopia with her eight years ago did not add up to the decades Mary had spent with Gary right under his nose, and Brian deserved more. A lot more. He wasn't completely bitter over how things turned out. He hoped Mary was happy, either with her new husband or just to be rid of the old. She'd given him a lot. He reflected with surprising generosity that the woman who had cuckolded him had also loved him, or at least been kind. They were once fellow stutterers. They'd always share that. Perhaps what he felt for Mary had always been more gratitude than affection.

*

One of his parents was dead and the other would be soon. The Moriarty family was getting smaller. He hadn't heard from his brother in years. Three nights after his last visit to Great Oaks Manor, Mary called him from her home with

Gary. Brian had just signed away the deed to their house.

Mary had been to the supermarket that day. In the checkout line, Mary told him, she overheard a woman who had been in Bam's high school class tell another woman that Bruce Moriarty had died in Los Angeles. "Don't know. Something mysterious . . . No, not that, the woman said. . . I don't think so anyway." Mary had been too shocked to turn and ask for details. Apparently there weren't any, anyway.

Brian surprised himself by taking the news in stride. He was sad but not devastated. He put the phone down and went out to the backyard with a beer to think. Not long after he learned he had another brother, he learned the other one had died. He had no way of knowing what happened to Bam, whether it was natural causes or not, whether peaceful or painful, whether anyone could have done anything to save him. Nor did it matter much to him in the end. Bam was just gone. He'd just found out that the fetus he'd dreamt about was a real brother after all. It was as if only so many Moriarty brothers could exist in the world at any one time. As if it was a law of the universe.

His brother could have gotten into drugs, the way show business people do. Wouldn't have been like him, but still. That strange eye of his had always been the sign of something wrong. Maybe a brain tumor killed him. There were too many maybes. He and Bam had never been close. Two stuttering brothers weren't going to be. Their garbled syllables embarrassed each other too much. Things hadn't improved between them after Bam lost his stammer, either.

Brian wondered if Bam was spared it the rest of his life.

Brian had come home from college for a rare weekend with his family once. Bam had to make room in the bedroom for big brother's return, but he neglected to clear away the porn he'd stored under the bedspread on Brian's bed. Fuck, Brian thought, he can't jerk off on his own bed? He has to use mine? Brian flipped through the glossy photo spreads. Who wouldn't? Brian asked himself while gulping the last of his beer in the backyard. Well, he shouldn't have. It was all weird shit, she-males and dudes in slings and a chick in a black leather bodice brandishing a cattle prod. Not wanting to humiliate Bam with his discovery, Brian put the magazines under his bedspread and slept with them there both nights of his weekend back home.

Well, whatever, Brian concluded as he lowered his empty onto the lawn. Who knows what cured my brother of his stutter. There was a lot Brian didn't know about his family, that was clear. Perhaps he should have tried harder to connect with Bam. At least he had always wished him well in some abstract way. He had no idea if his brother ever wished him the same.

He would not go back to the rest home and tell their mother the rumor. Let her believe Bam was the wonderful son who was still visiting her often. But on an impulse he drove to his father's grave. This was a last visit, too. It wasn't so much his father he was dropping in on as it was the whole friggin' family. There were plots nearby for the rest of the Moriartys. Bam wasn't going to be needing his. Nor would

Brian—he was headed to Utopia and wouldn't be coming back, neither on two feet nor in a casket. Tess could decide what to do with the plots. Brian might have congratulated himself on how neatly he was tying up the ends of the first half of his life if, fingers crossed, it was a long one. But giving himself a pat on the back felt macabre.

"Bam's gone, Dad," Brian said to the gravestone, realizing he didn't stutter talking to the dead. "No, don't know."

"Happy? Sorry, don't know that either." Brian thought of stealing the flowers from a nearby plot to lay on his father's. But his permitted acts didn't include graverobbing. He bid farewell to Art Moriarty by simply saying, "You should have asked him yourself when you had the chance."

*

Tongass National Forest was seventeen million acres, and he was headed to his nineteen of them. This time he did camp out in a pup tent on the open deck of the Juneau ferry. There were five in a row near the stern. Everyone had a different way of anchoring his or hers to the deck. There was a blue one behind him, whose inhabitant he never caught sight of, and a red one in front with a striking blond woman in it. His was green and brand new. He didn't spend any time in it except to sleep or nap. Mostly he looked out at the churning North Pacific.

Three days of this and he was again on the small ferry to Utopia. It was a repeat of his first trip, but this time with a new Dodge Ram 4x4 in the ship's hold packed with his belongings. He stood at the railing and watched the bow divide the sea in two. The sound it made in the water resembled a choir singing in a church, nothing like his own stuttering voice. He was less worried about his speech now. In his new home, he wouldn't have nearby neighbors or even a phone. He was done working eight hours a day. He had enough savings, he hoped, and with the imminent sale of the Tummus house, he figured he was free of his obligations to the talking world. If he got back together with Raven, he would learn to communicate the way Alaskans did: With a look, a tilt of the head, sly smiles, a turn of the shoulders.

The big crosses on the atolls outside Utopia were still there for the men who had died. Some were fishermen, others just boys who, to prove their manhood, had swum in icy waters. Drowning is a terrible way to go, he imagined. Alone, lungs filling with water, limbs flailing. He recalled having read once that more people fear death from fire than from drowning. Brian had his doubts. He was sailing on an ocean that, when angry, swallowed men and women whole. But as the ferry approached the dock, the sea was no more malevolent than a sheet of gray glass beneath an uninspiring haze.

*

Shortly after Mary announced she was divorcing him, Brian bought the land and its one-room cabin by telephone. The long-distance calls cost plenty, though in the scheme of things it wasn't much. Let the judge figure out how much of Mary's share of the community property he had spent. Brian needed to do this and would gladly suffer the consequences. His state of mind was neither irrational nor vindictive. Quite the opposite. He was excited at the thought of him and Raven starting their lives over. Together. She was someone who had never stuttered yet understood him perfectly.

The real estate agent in Juneau had mailed him photographs of the property. The seller was an old fellow moving "outside" to be with his daughter. Brian was relieved to find the cabin resembled its pictures, a boxy square structure made of painted plywood. He found the key under the rock where the agent told him to look. The inside, neither small nor large, had rough-hewn wood paneling for walls. A carpet haphazardly cut from a larger piece covered most of the pine floor. There was a comfortable-looking sofa. The place had come, as advertised, with an old bed in a brown metal frame, a round dining table with three chairs around it, and two working stoves: One wood and one pellet with shiny metal chimneys running up the walls to vent out the roof. He didn't see a supply of pellets, but there was a good-sized stack of wood for the other stove. One bounce on the bed and he realized he'd be replacing the mattress. There was a dartboard on the wall but no darts. The curtains on the cabin's two windows were thin gray fabric that looked stitched by hand. There was another curtain made of the same fabric hiding pots and pans under the counter. Two small light fixtures hung from a wire running across the cabin's ceiling, open to the triangular roof above. There was a shelf up there where he could store things, if only he could figure out how to reach it.

Would Raven come live here with him? It seemed better than the trailer, but maybe Brian should have invested in a bigger place, if it was going to be two people. No problem. He'd add on. Or tear it down and start a new home from scratch. He had lots of options. He was not in Tummus anymore. Anything could happen next.

The bathroom was small. A narrow shower and toilet that, like the mattress, needed to be replaced. The wooden toilet seat had a small burn mark on it, something a lit cigarette could have made. There was no mirror above the little sink, just a shelf where he could keep things like his toothbrush. He'd definitely need to renovate. Women needed more room in the bathroom than men did. Raven could tell him what she'd need. He'd do as she said.

He walked outside around the cabin. A diesel generator in a little shed provided electricity. There was a sticker with the phone number of the company that would keep it fueled regularly, along with a propane tank. The agent was going to send someone out to show him how to use everything and deal with the plumbing, which, he had said over the phone, "had given the previous owner some trouble."

He didn't care. He'd learn to master the ins and outs of his new home. What he appreciated most was that he had no close neighbors but was within walking distance of the ocean. He could walk a quarter mile through dense forest to a stony beach. Each morning, he imagined, low clouds would hang down into the fog coming off the seawater.

Outside the cabin that first day, Brian laid his head on the mossy forest floor hoping to hear surf. He could hear gulls singing with his other ear. He looked at tiny weeds and wildflowers close up. He could pick berries and gather mushrooms once he learned which were safe. On his first stroll, he found a grotto with a moss carpet dotted with miniature orchids. A small stream had a fallen tree serving as a footbridge over it. He found a cliff at whose base was a narrow trail made by animals and more moss dotted with purple blossoms.

*

The first thing he did after some preliminary unpacking was drive to Happy Trails. He hadn't sent letters care of Trailer NO. 5 because he was still that stuttering coward, even when he wrote. He knew he was taking a big chance. He took it anyway. Not having much of a choice at this point in his life made him more optimistic than he should have been.

He got lost trying to find her trailer park and had to ask for directions twice. Brian stuttered badly both times. Then he found it. There was a new gate, but her trailer looked the same and the carved stump still stood in front.

"No, no Raven here. Strange name." An old man had answered Brian's knock.

"I mean Mary. Mary lives here."

"No, Mary used to. Now I live here. Who are you?"

The old man rolled a cigarette as he loomed above Brian.

"Where is she now? Where did Mary go?"

"Can't say for sure. I think Juneau. Something about her lungs. Cancer. Went to the hospital, they told me. Don't know if she came back or not. You family?"

"I've got to *fuh*-find her. I'm an old *fuh*-friend."

"Old friends are a good thing to have. We should all have them." The old man lit his sloppily wrapped rollie. "Ask around town. If she's back someone will know. Good luck to you. All I know is I've haven't seen her.

"I should stop smoking these myself"—the man motioned with the cigarette—"too old to quit now, though. Mary probably felt the same way."

In the car Brian felt sick to his stomach, the way he felt in his New York hotel room after beating the South African. Added to that, he was dizzy and light-headed. He was glad he didn't have to look hard for a parking space near the Sourdough Saloon. His ability to do several things at once was limited. Uppermost on his mind was the whereabouts of a woman he now hoped hadn't given up drinking, only smoking.

It was open but empty. Brian asked the bartender, a young guy with a ponytail tied with a red rubber band, if he knew Mary, a cannery worker who often came in before her shift. The bartender said, "Sorry, no idea. Lots of Marys here." A Black woman peering out of the kitchen overheard the conversation and piped up to say, "I know a Mary who worked at the cannery. Was she missing a finger? Sure, I knew her. Not well, but I knew her. Don't know what happened.

Might have gone up to Juneau, I think. Oh, more than a few years ago, I'd say. She had a bad cough that didn't go away. It wasn't my business, but I told her to get a real doctor to look at it. Anyway, she's not in Utopia anymore."

"Are you *shuh*-sure?"

"It's a small town, mister. Trust me. You family?"

"I'm an old friend," Brian replied for the second time his first day back in Utopia. He sat down on a barstool and bought a drink, thinking he'd learn more. He did not. The cook and the bartender talked about the Mariners and ignored him.

*

He drove back to the cabin and fished out of his luggage the one photo of him with Raven he'd taken on one of their hikes. It was a poor picture. There hadn't been much light. He could barely make out their faces, but it was the only one he had. He leaned it against the window ledge above the sink, next to the picture of Tess he'd already put there first thing. Tess had grown up to look more like him, from the color of her hair to the tip of her nose. In the middle of his panic over Raven, he experienced a moment of relief thinking she was his daughter and not Gary's. Shame in suspecting otherwise followed his relief.

He stared at the other photograph. Mary, the name he had to remember to use for Raven when talking to others, looked like no one Brian had ever met. That was part of why he'd fallen for her. The face was noble, but not because

264

of any native Alaskan stereotype. Her nobility was a gained look, not inherited but earned over the years: Lessons from a rough life translated into a countenance bearing its traces. A high forehead, silky, black hair parted in the middle and hiding the ears he'd discovered during their week of lovemaking to be delightfully small; a nose broad and high, so unlike his or Tess'. Her weak chin was feminine and made him want to take care of her. He had watched Tess grow up and thought he knew some of her secrets, but he understood none of Raven's. He hadn't asked her when he had the chance. Now there would be no more chances. In the space of this, his first day back, he'd gone from the anticipated triumph of a lovers' reunion to despairing he'd ever find her. He sat at his table and added to his to-do list: *Go look for frames and hooks to hang your photos on the wall.*

*

A month and a million questions later, Brian was resigned to finding new friends, if he were to have any. He doubted he'd meet another Raven. He thought he could find reliable companionship in the form of a dog. He was mourning a loss, and the idea helped. He found one by checking the notice board at the grocery store. After some mulling, he named him Tripitaka Junior. The new dog didn't resemble the first Tripitaka. This one was a real mongrel. But Brian wanted to honor his predecessor who, like Raven, had disappeared from his life when Brian, master of bad timing, had been out of town. He immediately nicknamed him T Junior, a name that popped into Brian's head from nowhere. The dog was coming from a fisherman about to relocate to Wrangell to work on a big cannery ship.

He arranged to pick up T Junior the next time he had errands to run. Brian's cabin was seven miles out of town, and Brian seldom had reason to drive in. He needed his truck to pick up his mail and supplies from time to time. These muddy roads would be hard to travel much of the year. So far, though, everything was bone-dry. The Juneau paper wondered if this was the Panhandle's future.

He left his new friend in the front of the truck while renting a mailbox at the post office. The man behind the counter with the Mr. Magoo glasses asked for his address as well as his name.

"Gee, I'm not sure. I'm living in the cabin Jacob used to own. I have directions to it, but I've forgotten the official address."

"Oh, that's all right. Jacob never had an address, either. But we better have one for you. There's more than one Brian in town. Make up an address, if you want."

He thought for a moment. "Okay then, *Buh-buh*-brian *Huh*-horace Moriarty, 1 Nod *Huh-huh*-hill." He had no notion where that address came from, any more than he did his new dog's nickname.

"No, I'll make it 1 Nod Mountain. I know where you live. It's a mountain."

"Lots of mountains here."

"Yes, and yours now has a name. Congratulations. It's

the new millennium and you have an address."

*

I can write here, he decided to convince himself. *Eventually I'll need a phone line and a fax machine so I can keep translating and have an income.* But with the sale of the Tummus house, Brian had money for a while. *Not sure what I'll write with the rest of my time. Something in my own words and not those of others. Something about stuttering, maybe made-up but maybe my own story.* There was nothing to stop him. He didn't need a library; the research was already in his head. Brian was far from people, really far, and he was going to write. He had packed plenty of notebooks with lined paper. Like other folks in Utopia, he'd go to Juneau to stock up on supplies at its big stores, but not often. He only had himself and T Junior to worry about. Time would tell if he wrote in any of his notebooks. He hadn't written much of his own since he'd kept that stuttering diary for the therapist. Those Tolstoy and Dostoevsky novels were still with him, having come to Alaska a second time. Maybe he'd reread them first. Just to warm up.

Cedar, western hemlock and Sitka spruce surrounded his cabin. There was moss creeping up the outside walls. The new metal roof was free of it. He imagined he would hear raindrops beat against it, if it ever rained again. His closest neighbor lived beyond easy walking distance on another dirt road impassable in the wet winter. Brian wanted to be self-sufficient. He'd have to be, for the most part. He needed to feel settled here. On his first visit, Corina had told him someone else in town stuttered, a carpenter. Stutterers avoided each other. Brian wasn't going to hunt him down just to stammer out *huh*-hello.

Brian made the cabin his by hanging more photographs. High school graduation. He and Bam jumping through a lawn sprinkler on a hot summer day. The University of Washington boxing team. He found some fake Russian Orthodox icons in a junk shop and nailed them to the walls. He was glad not to have a telephone, the device that terrorized him his whole life, though that fax machine was still in his future. Brian had lots of time to think. He wondered how Tess was doing. Who were her friends? He clung to the hope she would visit him in Utopia. But Alaska was far away. Tess might meet someone and move across the country. For now, Brian had the Tongass. He went out with his small axe to mark tree trunks with gashes to find his way home on long walks. He'd read about people lost in the wilderness, their bodies eventually found only a hundred feet from their cabins or tents. Sometimes the cuts he inflicted on trees made him think of his own gash, more permanent, carved by an obstetrician's surgical tongs.

Without Raven, the point now was to be alone. At odd times, Brian didn't want to be. Corina had unloaded her Utopia Rooms to Let and left town, so she was out. He parked downtown and walked to the harbor with T Junior, hoping to run into Alex and Joel. Or George. He even attended church services one Sunday, though it wasn't Catholic. The rear pew was empty but for him. He decided the only way he'd make a new friend was if he invented one. He thought of the Joker for the first time in a long time.

*

Brian made a discovery on his property. T Junior led him to the far side of a rise near the shore where he stopped by a tall red cedar. At its base was a large, charred chamber, almost big enough for a man to live in. Brian first thought it was man-made. The entrance was so perfectly triangular someone could have designed it. He sniffed the air to detect any lingering smoke from a fire that might have been recently lit within it. There was none. T Junior noticed Brian's curiosity and went in to explore. He ran his muzzle along the floor of the chamber, but didn't seem to turn up anything. It was impossible now for Brian to resist entering. He stooped to examine the low ceiling. No sign of human habitation. He turned and peered out the entrance. It framed a clear vista to the sea. It reminded him of the huge cedar an injured Tripitaka had stood beside in the forest, of what he and Raven had seen on their hike, the intertwined roots of two trees blended together. This one was different—it was a single tree, and its inside looked hollowed out. Brian wondered just whose land he now inhabited. There was no Raven to tell him what old stories had to say.

In the following months, T Junior led him to more huts. He counted five so far. Most had a view of the sea, enough to make Brian think they were some kind of lookout, set up by one tribe to warn if others were approaching. Another theory was lightning. But why fire would have burnt the trees at their bases and not their crowns, he couldn't figure.

An old-timer in town told him he was lucky to have them. "Native people stored their fire in those places," the man said. Brian nodded, believing if not quite comprehending. Some of the trees were above protected beaches while others sat at the top of hills inland. He thought he spotted one with his binoculars on the top of a nearby island. If he had a boat, he'd row out to visit it. Instead, he asked around town and heard all kinds of hypotheses. People hollowed them out looking for good wood. Or they provided shelter: Motels for native hunters traveling up and down the coast. The most common explanation held that the Tlingit scooped into trees to find dry wood and keep their fires, out of the way of wind and rain, smoldering. There had to have been, Brian reasoned, a designated firekeeper for each clan. Someone needed to tend to the coals. They don't keep going forever on their own. A good job for me, Brian thought. Another story was that young people were warned to stay away from fire trees—their magic was that powerful. He could imagine shamans lived in them, fasting and meditating. But no one at the Sourdough Saloon could tell him anything for certain.

He developed his own theory for why these tree huts existed. They would have made perfect lighthouses, but to what end? People would not have wanted their locations detected at night out of fear of being ambushed. It must have been reassuring to see proof of others nearby. Native people planned for the future and put things away. Were the fire trees part of a plan?

Brian was a custodian of the fire trees on his property. He had a total of six on his acreage. They formed a straight line facing the sea. There were marks on their dead bark left by bear claws, making Brian think the scent of food once prepared within had attracted them. One day, bored as well as curious, he lit a fire in one of his huts. He'd risen early, though he'd packed what he needed to take the night before. Still new to Alaska, he'd crammed more in his pack than he was ever likely to need. A small pickaxe, a flare, a rain parka, an extra pair of dry socks and a compass. In case there was no kindling, he added a can of Sterno. He lifted the backpack to his shoulders and set out, warning T Junior to be good in the cabin until he got back. He wasn't sure what he'd encounter on the mountain, and he remembered what had happened to Tripitaka.

The hike up was easy. He knew the way by now. At the top, he stopped to think about the mountains. He'd grown up near mountains, but now he was thinking about all kinds of mountains, not just these. Mountains too steep to climb. Mountains that had lost their crowns. Mountains with slopes stripped bare. Mountains where hermits died. Mountains at the top of the world. Mountains no one owned. Mountains he first saw as a child. Mountains just piles of rock. Mountains near no other mountains. Mountains encircled with mead-ows. Mountains where lovers first made love. Mountains with many names. Mountains from whose tops you could see oceans rise and forests burn. Mountains where green snakes crawled. Mountains that were often blue. Mountains old men think about.

Brian was shaken from his daydream by the screech of an eagle wheeling overhead. He dug into his pack and took out the Sterno and the matches. He went into the largest of the four fire trees. It formed a cave about six feet across. Its walls were black, shellacked from years of smoke. People before him had spent their lives here. Time stretched out on Nod Mountain. The phases of life one is allotted, if lucky— morning, noon and night, all words drawn from the rotation of the earth. Sometimes they say there are seven stages to one's life, because there are seven planets, Brian thought. Brian's life felt different. There were no stages, or at least not that many. His breakfast, lunch and dinner were indistinguishable. Eggs, bacon, toast, coffee, beans, canned stew and the hotdogs he boiled in water. Morning, noon and night.

He crawled into the fire tree and sat cross-legged. The forest looked different gazing out from the enclosure. He could see the thick lower parts of trees but not far beyond them. He didn't need the Sterno. There were dry twigs and dead leaves lying about the hut. He piled them into a small pyramid. He struck a match, and then another, to ignite it. This was one of the places the Tlingit used to keep their fires going, he was sure of it now. Sheltered from the weather, embers might glow forever.

It was a good time, he told himself. The best time. He was king here. The King of Nod Mountain. In his realm, lord of all he surveyed. King of himself and T Junior. The tinder didn't burn for long. It collapsed into a thin mound of ashes. Brian waited until the ashes were cool enough to spread out with his hands. He mixed their blackness with the brown dirt on the floor of the hut, still managing to singe his finger-tips. When he crawled out on all fours to start his hike down the mountain, his pants were covered with the black of warm ashes and the brown of cool dirt.

CHAPTER EIGHTEEN

He jumped right into what would be his book. No outline or a title yet, just things stewing in him he wanted on paper. The table in his cabin was large enough for him to leave his notebook and pens on it and still have room to eat his meals.

It would be about stuttering, probably a particular stutterer and probably a novel. It was an odd choice since Brian had never even translated fiction. He'd never taken a creative writing course. He wanted to write about things that hadn't happened but might. Brian wanted a protagonist who was like him but capable of doing more. A stutterer who would confront the fluent world in, of all places, Alaska. He had no idea how his stutterer would do this. Would the book be science fiction? A fairy tale? A superhero saga? Whichever, he would decide how the story ended. It would not be a farce or a comedy because that was too easy to do. He'd grown up watching Porky Pig cartoons.

The first thing he had to figure out was what his main character looked like.

There was a small mirror near the kitchen sink to help the cabin's owner shave. Brian stared into it for ideas. He saw how he was aging. *You are fifty-five but look so much older.* He was indeed his mother's son. You're either growing up, he ruminated, or you're growing old. There's little in between. He shouldn't look this old at his age. The passage of his allotted years was speeding up. *Whatever happened to threescore and ten?* The little hairs growing askew in his gash were now turning gray, even white, and hair elsewhere on his head was falling out. He was finding it harder to remember words for familiar objects, and the names of famous people now nearly always eluded him. Some of these words and names, when he did recall them, turned out to be ones he'd long had trouble saying. *Honey* worms. Spencer *Tracy*.

Did time, telescoped, flow differently for him because he was a stutterer? Everything moved faster than it did for people who spoke normally. His mind and body were changing weekly, not over years as they once had. His stammer was more conspicuous now, something he noticed on his weekly foray into town, where he was required to speak to the world that was his tiny Utopia. He hadn't expected this. He knew new afflictions loomed on the horizon—his rapidly aging looks made it certain—even as the original one had grown more relentless.

He confessed this in a letter to Tess, who soon wrote back she'd read there were experimental pills now to help stutterers. A week later, sooner than usual, the mail brought another letter from Tess, this one containing her own confession and not the usual litany of Moriarty family news. She and her husband were firmly ensconced in suburban Kirkland, but this letter brought no local gossip.

She told him she was a secret stutterer, and always had been. *I have never stuttered out loud*, her letter explained, *except for that one time I played a trick on you and Mom. But I've stuttered inside my whole life. I've looked out at the world through your eyes, Dad, and I see it the way you do. We, the two of us, are in a small room somewhere, maybe at the top of a hill or on the roof of a building. It could be a shack, a utility room, a cave. It is too dark to tell. There is not much room for either of us. We're squeezed in tight. One side of the room is open to the outside, but we don't cross the threshold. We don't say anything to each other. We look out the opening and focus our eyes at what lies beyond: emptiness and a sliver of a moon faintly illuminating the ground. The landscape is flat all the way to the horizon. There are no people. There are no animals. There are no trees. The horizon is turning yellow and orange. Maybe the sun is rising. Maybe something has begun to burn in a far beyond. We turn to each other and open our mouths as if to say something, but we're both stutterers. We know to wait passively for whatever happens next. There's this small room we're in, and then there's everything else. That's us and the world, Dad. Things happen out there. We watch them unfold from our small room. That's what it was like for me growing up in your house.*

Brian read to the end of his daughter's letter. Her small room was uncannily similar to the tree huts he'd found on his property, as if she'd discovered one of her own to share. He folded the letter and put it at the top of the pile he kept. He took down the rifle resting on two pegs on the wall. When he moved in, there had been a note saying Jacob, its owner, would be back to retrieve it. He hadn't yet, and Brian wondered if he ever would. Not bothering with his coat, he loaded the rifle outside the cabin and, standing amid the skunk cabbage, aimed it into the woods and pulled the trigger. Unlike him, the rifle had a clear report. *Guns don't stutter.* In the cabin, T Junior howled. *Dogs don't stutter.* He'd do some target shooting with the rifle, maybe take down a deer. He let his imagination play with the idea of him being a hunter, of killing something. He was relieved to be distracted from thinking about Tess and her letter. *Daughters shouldn't stutter.*

In the weeks that followed, except for more letters to Tess, none touching on her confession, the notebook and the pens on the table went untouched. He had no idea what to say in his novel. Was this writer's block? Was his mind and its thoughts failing him now, not just his mouth and tongue? He had read that novelists work hard to find their "voice," but what if his writer's voice was another stutterer? Eventually he did manage to write a little in his notebook, and he read it aloud in what was no writer's voice. It was marred with interruptions, gaps, missed sounds, twisted and canceled consonants. Writer's block imitated stuttering in more ways than one. Of course, both were pauses, obstacles, barriers. Brian considered them symptoms of a deficit in self-confidence and a surplus sense of failure, the constant pressure of expectations.

Stymied, he tried out a new, physical relationship with language. He imagined words to be actual objects, things he could feel lodged in his throat, wrap his tongue around; things that were affixed to his lips like glue, even if he just meant to write and not speak them. He let words chug their way by fits and starts through his body until, with sufficient mass, they became things he could pick up with his fingers and arrange on the page.

This trick worked for a time. He could get as much as half a page of writing done in a day before shutting down. He talked, of course, to T Junior, and never stuttered then. He could sing in the shower and not stutter. Only when Brian was in town, or read aloud from his notebook, was he reminded of how much the fluent world remained beyond him.

*

One night a restless Brian got out of bed and retrieved one of the Russian novels he'd brought with him from Tummus. Just the thing to make him fall asleep again. His motion in the cabin roused T Junior. He told him to go back to bed. Brian grabbed his reading glasses lying by his notebook on the table. On the sagging mattress, flashlight in hand, he glanced at the cover and found what he thought was *Crime and Punishment* was *The Brothers Karamazov*. He'd carted the wrong novel back and forth on his trips to Alaska. Disappointed, he flipped through its thousand pages at random. Dostoevsky never suffered from writer's block.

No matter what page he turned to, he always ended up on some paragraph about Smerdyakov, the Karamazov household's sullen servant. When he was young, Smerdyakov collected stray cats just to bury them. *Taciturn and unsociable*, son of a mute, *you tore her open when you came out.* Smerdyakov suffers from epilepsy, *the falling sickness*, just as Dostoevsky had. *You aren't a human being*, he's told by a fellow servant. *The disease was incurable. The fits occurred irregularly, about once a month.* Seizures screw up your speech, Brian knew that. He'd seen a classmate in college fall to the gym's weight room floor and foam at the mouth. It was a couple of minutes before help arrived. Brian had watched the guy's body shake uncontrollably from his head to his sneakers. He pissed in his gym shorts and got the thick vinyl mat underneath him wet. What Brian recalled most were the slurred words, the wretched, inhuman howls from a mouth twisted in something akin to pain but not only that. *Some were quite mild, others very violent.* Smerdyakov spews the nonsensical sounds akin to a stutterer's during his own fits, Brian thought. *The spasm seized me by the throat.* Both epileptics and stutterers gag on their words. Brian knew that. *Smerdyakov's epileptic fits became worse.* Like Brian and his stutter, Smerdyakov never knew when a seizure would strike. Brian never saw his classmate in the weight room again.

He kept skimming the novel. Smerdyakov had his first fit after asking his tutor a question. *If God created the world on the first day and the sun, the moon, and the stars only on the fourth day, where did the light come from on the first day?* After that, his epileptic fits would *afflict him for the rest of his life*. Is that why Smerdyakov doesn't believe in God? *He spoke very slowly, moving his tongue with obvious difficulty*. Smerdyakov convinces himself that, without God, *everything is permitted*. Faith in God worked for some people but not for him or Dostoevsky's murderer. He flipped through more pages. *He might just as likely set fire to his own village*. There was more to the problem of faith than Dostoevsky had explored, Brian suspected, and more to the significance of his own dreams. *Certain symptoms of insanity had already been observed*. Smerdyakov fakes a seizure in order to get away with his crime, the murder of the family patriarch. There's no sin in a world absent God. *He was a godless man*. Smerdyakov did believe everything was permitted, and Brian saw advantages in thinking that way, too, even if Dostoevsky didn't really mean it.

This was theological dispute enough for him in the middle of the night, especially for a mind slouching toward its own nineteenth-century exhaustion. *I certainly would rather have been killed in her womb than been brought into this world*. He let the heavy paperback fall to the floor as he turned onto his side and slept until dawn, dreamless.

*

His writer's block seemed like it might be lifting. Brian had translated other people's work in his career, stayed faithful to their words even when tempted to sabotage them. Now he was going to be the author. It was his turn to stand center stage. His hero, Brian's own creation, was going to lead a life different from his own. He was going to have a better life by its end. This was what was waiting for him to write. The question was still how.

Put the notebook aside for a while, he told himself. Look at it with new eyes in a few days. You've got plenty of time, he told himself. You're basically retired. You should think carefully about what to make happen in your story. It will come to you when you least expect it. Brushing your teeth. Picking up the mail. Taking T Junior for a walk to the beach.

Brian worried his writer's block would return. If this was his purgatory, to be as stumped writing as he was speaking, he had no reason to think anything, and certainly not made-up stories, would compensate him for what stuttering denied: Words, the words he saw even if his voice could not lay claim to them; words unstopped in all three of the languages he commanded, not all their words but nonetheless plenty. Words that might have led him over the real and exaggerated hurdles of his life to the things they named. The names of all things. Any of which, summoned by his inefficient tongue, might remain a code unbroken.

He'd written *XXX* in his notebook wherever he should have written in his stutterer-hero's name. He'd decide that later, when inspiration hit. Brian was glad he'd written everything double spaced. There was plenty of room between the lines to write in several names if he changed his mind. The name was important. This was going to be a book, not real life, so Brian didn't need to avoid the first consonants he always tripped over. A name in a book could start with any letter of the alphabet. He'd never be reading this out loud to anyone but his dog, and no one stuttered to a pet. He was mindful not to consider the names of people he knew. Ken. Frank. Bob. Henry. Ted. None of those. There was plenty of time to think about it. The long nights of Alaska were waning and the short days were waxing.

*

A few days later, he took T Junior out for a walk to clear his head for the day's writing he hoped was ahead of him. They took their usual route and soon reached the water. The dog ran sprints along the edge of the surf. Brian watched a large wave pluck a seagull off a rock and sweep it into a whitecap from which it did not reappear. Everyone makes mistakes, he mused. Even if it's just being in the wrong place at the wrong time.

You work hard getting comfortable in the world you're born into, Brian observed. He watched T Junior dash to the farthest end of the beach to chase a small bird, some kind of sandpiper by the look of its long body—white on the bottom and mottled brown on top. *You wonder how you might fit in, but you suspect you never will.* Brian was used to seeing sandpipers in flocks, but this one was on its own. *Be honest.* In flocks and on the sand, sandpipers enjoyed letting the rolling surf chase them back and forth. *It's just you and T Junior now.* This one was alone and did not alight. *This is your last, best chance.* It had long legs, but it wasn't going to use them. *It feels like a countdown has begun.* There were other kinds of birds strutting on the beach, but T Junior didn't pursue any of the easy ones. *You tried your whole life.* He went after the bird in constant flight. *So far.* It was teasing him by gliding just higher than he could leap. *What good have your efforts done you or anyone else?* T Junior barked at the sandpiper. In response, it led him in and out of the surf, in to slow him down and out to speed him up. *You've been keeping score, check the results.* The dog was being played with. Mocked, even. *Don't like what you see? Then change the rules.* T Junior ran differently in the water than he did out of it. His body rocked back and forth, like a hobbyhorse, when confronted by the sea, but shot straight as a bullet when free of it. *You've always messed with the rules because you wanted to win, fair-square or otherwise.* He seemed the happiest prancing just at the water's edge, somewhat challenged and somewhat free at the same time. The tail never stopped wagging. *And still you didn't win, not always and not even often.* There was no sound but the low rumble of the surf. *The alternative is to invent your own world and keep it to yourself.* How does a sandpiper show its joy? *I came to Alaska for Raven, but also to write a story.* It flew as all sandpipers fly, its stiff wings beating shallowly but rapidly. *The story is all I have left now.* It made quick, short dives near the sand where it could, and soared when it wanted to tempt T Junior into ever higher jumps. Brian had reason to think: The sandpiper resembles a Boeing aircraft going through its test flight paces. *Still, somehow you believe you rule this world you made, even as you make concessions to it*. His dog momentarily gave up the chase and sat on his hind legs, as if considering his options. *You might well do the same*.

Brian had intuited certain truths about his life but never expressed them in words, nor always in thoughts. He coexisted with his impotence and stayed silent. *Striking a schoolgirl or my pregnant wife hadn't been a display of power*. T Junior resumed his pursuit of the sandpiper. Every blow left him weaker. The sandpiper made twee-ing sounds when it ascended but was silent when it dove. *Assaulting a stranger on a New York City street hadn't been particularly brave, either*. They were signs of the cowardice he suffered in facing himself, in placing blame anywhere but on himself. *Nor was bludgeoning a fish to death*. That cowardice drove him here, to the far end of the inhabited talking world. Raven was supposed to be here to save him. *Twee-twee*. Now it was him and a dog. And a bird the dog was chasing.

T Junior surprised Brian by catching the bird. *Catch* was the wrong word. The sandpiper inexplicably stopped hovering just outside the range of the dog's leaps. It allowed itself to be captured between rows of sharp canine teeth. Brian saw in his mind a Boeing passenger jet plunging to earth, what happened on the day his dad died; a jet whose manual he'd thought of fatally mistranslating. Then another memory: A blue heron with a fish in its beak circling above the lake where he and Mary made love. T Junior shook the fluttering bird back and forth in its jaws, squeezing the last bit of life out of it. The carnage was too far away for Brian to see all the details, but the main sequence of events was clear. No matter how suicidal the bird might have been, it was still alive. Brian knew it wasn't easy to kill, otherwise he would have been more successful at it. It occurred to Brian that the sandpiper might not be in any hurry to die, nor T Junior to kill it.

His dog was born with the instincts of a retriever. T Junior might have trotted back triumphantly with the mangled bird in his mouth, a half-dead trophy Brian wouldn't know what to do with when dropped at his feet. But that is not what the dog did. Remaining at the far end of the beach, he sat down again on the sand and continued ripping his small prey apart. Brian, too far away to see much, could at least tell the sandpiper wasn't crying out. Throttled, out of oxygen, the bird's heart had stopped, its lungs collapsed, all arterials contracted. If life lingered anywhere in the sandpiper, it was in little bursts of light at the edges of its brain's darkness.

Brian, who retained some capacity for empathy, bent over and picked up a stick. He threw it toward T Junior, thinking it might distract his dog and he'd abandon the torture underway for a familiar game of fetch. It didn't work. T Junior ignored Brian's ploy and rededicated himself to the work at hand. Rage flashed in Brian's mind at the sheer gratuitousness of it all, but he'd done the same. A coldness followed that he imagined he would see in his dog's eyes if close enough, an expression he knew he shared. Like some of Brian's own targets, the bird seemed to have expected, even welcomed, its end. It offered no resistance. The girl in the schoolyard hadn't stood to strike back. His wife hadn't crawled to the kitchen counter and grabbed a knife to stab him. The South African hadn't called out to his friends to rescue him.

From a distance, Brian could see dark blood on his dog's snout. Whatever part of the bird that remained conscious was surely gazing at T Junior as a condemned person might his executioner. Relieved that no chance remained for a miracle to intervene, the agony of hoping for one was gone as well. Brian's empathy included no sympathy. A parish priest of his had once been happy to trade dignity for abjection between a boy's legs in his church's vestry; and this bird had chosen, or so Brian wanted to believe, similar ignominy on a brisk Alaskan shore.

What came next was easier for Brian to accept. It had happened in his own life. T Junior got back up on his four legs and left incomplete the task he had started. Brian had lowered his foot onto stomachs and pressed down hard but never too hard. He had shifted his boot to faces and bore down with a force calculated to crack small bones but nothing larger. Just as Brian once had, his dog, the first Tripitaka's heir to pain, with the right to retribution for it, finished an act of halfway gratuitous violence. The world might judge it criminal, and it was, but Brian understood that halfway meant something. The crime didn't warrant mercy. On the contrary, it meant that pain should continue. What transpired before his eyes, the torture this bird suffered, bore out

Smerdyakov's belief that there was no God. If there was, there'd have been something akin to mercy somewhere on this beach.

The bird mocked a dog with its teasing. I've been mocked, too, Brian observed. The bird had to pay. It's that simple, Brian thought. Except it wasn't. The bird surrendered of its own accord. It lured the dog into lashing out and made its capture easy. The bird sought redemption by its sacrifice. It must have known what its fate would be in those jaws, and still it chose them.

Brian looked up at the horizon while he walked the length of the shore to T Junior and the sandpiper. There was something unusual about today's air. The skies waited to be filled with things not yet here but coming. The light was dim. The mountains appeared farther away. But the dull gray surface of the sea looked almost firm enough for someone, if not Brian and his dog, to flee and find sanctuary from what was approaching.

Was this an uncanny apprehension of something final here, as close to the end of the geographical world he would ever go? Was it accounted for in Brian's charter of rules for justice? Did Brian really understand his, or the sandpiper's, rules? T Junior welcomed his master with a muddied, bloodied face, prepared for neither censure nor commendation. You don't need a God to believe in sin, and sin lay before him in the material manifestation of a dog and its quarry. *Not everything that happens is necessary. Not every sin needs forgiveness.*

Brian and T Junior watched a small crab creep toward them. He snatched the helpless crustacean before his dog could and tossed it aside. He spared something today, after all. One less meaningless act of violence. T Junior's owner was offering him a unique insight. It would cost him, though. Brian would have to keep his pet close by, if he understood what Brian had concluded today. Dogs ran wild in Alaska, but Brian had to deny T Junior this liberty. Folks could read minds up here, Brian was sure of it, and that included dog's minds. If T Junior could read Brian's own thoughts, they would include what he was thinking right now: If something is not part of your world, you are free to destroy it. But Brian quickly amended the rule: That does not require you to. Not everything that happens necessarily happens.

He doubled over and vomited. Too much of his life was coming back to him too quickly. T Junior, alarmed, walked in slow, spooked circles around him. Brian's stutter was not the consequence of a head injury in adulthood or of a childhood trauma. It was not caused by either a poorly dosed medication for a misdiagnosed illness or a displaced Freudian fixation. He'd been born a stutterer, manufactured in the womb and charged by a lost twin brother to do something with his handicap. Well, what had he? Wreaked havoc out of his misdirected self-pity, excused himself for his petulant outbursts, made less of himself as a man because he accepted his want of ambition as a right? Surrounded by fellow past and present stutterers, some worse and others better, Brian measured what he thought he deserved as compensation for their shares of it. He judged himself a loser, which, in another predictable irony, felt like winning to him.

He had to win in life because he was born into it already losing. This tenet organized the rules of the games he played as a boy, and now stood behind his ethics in adulthood. He fine-tuned both as he grew older and encountered evermore elaborate challenges, but he never revisited his original conviction.

Brian had just witnessed a contest of his principles here on the shore. A sandpiper teased his dog with playful dives and dips. T Junior leapt up as if to nip the bird in revenge, but it was just another frisky tease. It might have stopped at that. But the sandpiper let T Junior have his full vengeance when it dropped into open jaws, surprising not only Brian but probably his dog, too. The sandpiper was dead as a result, not through any necessary fault of its own or by some uncalled for sadism on the part of the dog. It just happened. The bird might have been atoning for something. They'd never know. But Brian couldn't help thinking: If that's so, the bird won after all.

Both the childhood games Brian played and the adult justice he pursued derived from the same axiom: Some actions are good and others are something other than good, just never evil as long as those actions awarded him rightful ownership. Above all, the rights to his own life. Once he'd been willing to risk it in Vietnam but hadn't been allowed to. He could have been arrested for attempted manslaughter when he assaulted his pregnant wife or mugged a foreign visitor in New York. You could say he deserved it. But Brian was now beyond such commonsensical consequences when it came to himself. The Golden Rule didn't apply to him, if it ever had. He alone was privileged to do to others what others couldn't do to him. There weren't uniform equivalences in the world: Only the debts owed him and the surpluses he was right to hoard. His balance sheet of the moral precepts for living started from the bottom line and worked backwards. Like the sandpiper, the final calculations in Brian's life would yield results that might let something happen without willing it, but with the anodyne effect of evening up his score with the world.

Brian entered that world with the deficit that was his stutter. There had to be a fitting compensation for it. Brian did not subscribe to any ordinary notion of fairness. Or rather, fairness consisted solely of his satisfaction at achieving and maintaining a just equilibrium. His equilibrium. An equilibrium others might think hardly balanced at all, but which Brian considered fairest to him. In Brian's universe, there were no metaphysics governing what people were liable for. His philosophy was pure ethics, all applied and practical. Lived experience had its mysteries, but it also taught sure lessons. Those lessons and whatever obscurities left behind had value in Brian's moral equations. If everything were fully explained, he wouldn't have to look within himself for answers that he'd always suspected weren't there in the first place.

The course of any life rewrites the rules for justifying

our actions, but Brian's never reduced the culpability of those who chose to regard him as a lesser being. He never opened his mouth without it being a challenge to anyone listening to dare to do just that. Brian was always keen to measure the importance of anything he wanted to say before attempting it; he was eager to assess the cost to everyone but himself, should he fail to pronounce that anything perfectly. Over time, what he *pronounced* were fewer words, but more decrees for the world. "World" meant the people with him in his bedroom with Bam, or playground with Susan, or house with Mary, and now this stretch of inhospitable Alaskan shore. The penalties he assessed were to be paid in the currency of pain, and in whatever denominations Brian's provocative acts—real or imagined—insisted upon.

But as Brian aged, thoughts of violence to himself began to replace thoughts of violence to others. It was increasingly *violence* that mattered, not its object and certainly not any question of guilt or innocence that others thought entitled to arbitrate. Violence had become intransitive, passive and exempt from judgment. He wouldn't act out his worst fantasies, he hadn't the courage. Father Thomas was still alive and he shouldn't be. But Brian might just let terrible things *occur* without interfering. Abstractions had come to matter more than real fists, not because he had matured, but because his understanding of what constituted effective force changed as his stutter worsened. The world might always mock him for that stutter, but it no longer mattered. There would be fewer bruises and broken bones for Brian, and more intellectual recognition of a natural cruelty that had always been there.

In hindsight, the savagery commenced not with him, but with that slash across his face in his mother's womb. The savagery accelerated with a hostility borne of a congenital handicap: A hostility with causes, but no less his responsibility. Savagery had its principles, too. They just weren't always the same as his. In Brian's mind, there was no plural "we" in witnessing pain, his or anyone else's. Some matters were private and had to stay that way. From the start, he found it intolerable to have his misery confused with anyone else's. Let others figure out why he had shoved and punched and beat and pummeled. He decided not to be interested.

Violence pursues an arc over the span of a lifetime, if the lifetime lasts long enough. Brian's had. Justice consists of giving each person his or her due, and that evolves over the years, too. Justice for what, how much of it and to be decided by whom: These were questions whose answers were manipulable. But not the acts themselves. Brian was slowly, belatedly, coming around to an understanding of responsibility. No one but Brian Horace Moriarty was at fault for Susan Wentworth's fall in the schoolyard. Who was it who attacked a South African businessman, if not *Buh-ryan*? He had a hand in the death of his first child, as Mary had reminded him in a hundred different ways. More recently, he had briefly debated the merits of smothering his mother. Tripitaka died while Brian was away, as did Bam in a far city, but Brian couldn't help wondering if his truancy had played a part. Had he *let* these things happen?

The sandpiper dove into his dog's jaws. Brian hadn't ordered it to, or even foreseen it. How was he responsible? If he hadn't walked T Junior to the beach, or kept him on a leash, the sandpiper might still be alive. He recalled *The Brothers Karamazov* and its spastic antihero, Smerdyakov, to whom all was permitted in the absence of God. The sandpiper did not just decide to swoop down and die. It *took place*. No God willed it or absentmindedly permitted it to happen. Maybe God was spared responsibility, but was Brian? Would Brian's own victory or defeat at the end be just as casual? Stuttering, he'd read, was attributable to childhood trauma, sibling rivalry, suppressed anger, a strict upbringing or guilt; any of these causes might fit the bill in his case. But now, in sight of the resolution of his life, Brian was in no mood to assign blame. Thankfully, he'd been spared the voodoo cures of hypnosis, electric shock, faith healing and drugs, but he would have continued to stutter even if he'd undergone them. There was no one and no one thing to blame for that, either. Still, Brian's angry vehemence, stemming from an instinctive recoil at the sound of his voice, wasn't to be humored. Corrupt first consonants were tantamount to a siren warning the world of his discontent, an alarm over a handicapped moral core buried under layers of destructive thinking.

Looking back, Brian regretted choosing a career that allowed him to work alone without colleagues. As a translator, Brian had handled millions of words on paper over the course of his working life and never talked them over with anyone else. It might have been better if his twin hadn't slashed his face, but had left him a mute. Mutes enjoy the certainty of knowing they'll never speak. They can make peace with that. Stutterers have it worse. They never know when they'll stammer and when they won't. They dwell in the confines of that uncertainty, an uncertainty that undermined Brian's quest for moral clarity.

Just as Brian was wondering if he was losing his mind, living here in Alaskan isolation, an earlier question returned to interrupt his train of thought. Why should the sandpiper sacrifice itself, if for no greater purpose? Did it have an *intent?* If it did, was its goal blameworthy or innocent? Could an animal sin for what it desired and not only for what it did? In the Catholic family that raised Brian, the permissible and the impermissible were properties of what was contemplated, not what was done. Here stood the man Brian had grown up to be: A stutterer stopped in his tracks by the sins he merely mused about, and not from any move to save himself or the world.

Birds didn't stutter. If they did, Brian wouldn't have disparaged the inhabitants of the talking world as *ducks.* Animals didn't speak at all, in fact, while vast numbers of people did without hindrance. Raven had said that no Tlingit ever stuttered. So it was just Brian and his kind out of billions of normal people worldwide, minus the Tlingit. What did the sandpiper seek to end, if anything, by letting T Junior snatch it away? By not refusing its capture? How many sandpipers in the world were there like this one? As few, or as many, as there were stutterers? What a coincidence, Brian joked in his thoughts, if we number the same. He indulged his nervous tic and reached up to run his fingers through his gash's graying hairs.

Brian once believed it better to be guilty than ashamed. People often confuse the two. You feel guilt inside you. Your system of right and wrong mandates it, but shame comes from the way others regard you, and you have no control over that.

Anyway, it was a moot point now. After a childhood and adolescence experiencing little but shame, in middle age he'd freed himself from it. And guilt? Brian's code of conduct had grown to disallow that, as well. He felt neither now. In their place, he could imagine even being proud of his stammer, was he to accomplish something good with it. He looked down at the pieces of a bird near his feet. That something good had yet to happen.

In his mind's eye, Brian stepped back from the close details of his life. He saw how things had been given and others taken away. There was no God in charge of who got what or who surrendered what. *He* was Dostoyevsky's Smerdyakov, aka Brian Moriarty, a person who idly watched things come and go, including those things he might have had dominion over. He kicked sand and rock over the scattered remains of the sandpiper. More crabs would come to make quick work of the detritus. Brian covered up the pieces of bird bones and bloody entrails, as if it would do any good. For a second, he imagined he saw the corpses of a hundred-plus miniature airline passengers at his feet. He rubbed his eyes but did not look down at the ground again, afraid he'd still see them. Brian left the human dead where they lay, uncovered, and ambled back to the cabin. T Junior wagged his tail the whole way.

CHAPTER NINETEEN

The North Pacific weather was typical the next morning. Brian stepped out his cabin's door to appraise it. Clouds and air conjoined; texture was lost in the flatness and haze. Color vanished in a landscape of grays and whites. There was no shadow, no reflection, no horizon, only an unvarying silver barrier stretching to the undeterminable horizon, from the ground into a dewy shawl above.

But the afternoon sky brought the unprecedented. Intimations of sour smoke displaced watery vapor. He noticed it first on his and T Junior's walk in the woods. He was keeping his dog close now. They avoided the beach. Varying in hue from a deep leaden to a feverish red later, the sky grew steelier during their excursion. He did not like the dirty look of it.

The next morning the sun rose a fiery wafer. It retreated by noon as a slate-colored murk covered everything as if an immense canvas tarpaulin. The wind stirred and blew stray flecks of burnt embers into Brian's eyes. That evening they fell like snow. Leaning out his front door, he caught one and pinched it between his fingers. It was black particles mixed with white ashes.

On the third day, birds began to fall. Some arrived dead, others died hitting the ground. Nothing as big as an eagle or a gull—small birds, only the most fragile. Brian didn't know which. Sparrows? Warblers? His cabin was too far from the sea for them to be more sandpipers. One lay at his feet outside the cabin, its cool gray feathers tinged white at their tips, its wings still faintly fluttering. If he had picked it up, it wouldn't have filled his palm. He watched it go still.

Was that when he should have fled? Retreated into town? For the next several days the air was a dusky yellow in daylight. At night it smelled firewood-sweet. In Utopia, the Anchorage newspapers would report, the first man-made thing to burn was a barn. Then a house and another barn, the former hotel with half-hewn canoes in the back. Logs floating in the harbor erupted in flames and ignited people he knew, including Alex and Joel, who had tried to cling to debris to keep from drowning. People ran through the streets calling out for others. Wind-driven firebrands set their clothes and hair on fire. The citizens of Utopia leapt into frigid seawater, trails of flames streaming behind them. Brian would know none of these things because he was on Nod Mountain when they happened.

The next morning the sky above him burst—not an isolated thunder boom, but a rolling, continuous electrical storm that sounded like breaking glass. The fireworks spread in one supercharged bolt after another. Mountainsides came to life with trespassing storms advancing unchecked until they hit big rock outcrops or were halted by high ridges. Brian had never heard mountains bellow before. He was persuaded to step out of his cabin by the high-pitched wind as much as by the thickening smoke. Birds were no longer dropping from the sky but survivors were busy around his cabin: Robins foraging for insects, other species flitting nervously between bushes. The forest on Nod Mountain had never been more active. He stood outside his cabin watching for more spectacle. A defeated squirrel lay beside a fallen tree limb in front of him, its stiff tail pointed upward, its body already sheltering busy ants.

He decided to return to his fire trees, because it occurred to him this could be his fault. Could the smoldering embers of the twigs he lit weeks ago have started the fire? Years of dwindling precipitation had made kindling out of the Tongass. Something had to have sparked it. He'd leave the cabin with T Junior in tow, not only because he wanted them to be safe, but because they shared secrets now.

They headed up to the fire trees, where he imagined they could survive in one of the huts. Was that all he was thinking? Funny idea, finding sanctuary from fire in a place built for fire. His brain was playing tricks on him, and he didn't entirely trust his judgment. He could have inherited his mother's early senility. All he knew was that he had to get there. In his mind's eye, he saw the sandpiper drift into T Junior's jaws. Water was heavy to haul, but he'd take some along.

They scaled Nod Mountain, the top of it now farther away than it had ever seemed. His breathing labored in the smoke-filled air. Descending blackness swallowed the summit ahead of them. It was the middle of the day. A wind, strong and rare from the east, rustled tree branches after inexplicably skipping some patches of the forest. Where it ran into rock, it compressed and accelerated. Forcing its way up his mountain and guided by the contours of the land, the wind carried fire to hemlocks and firs. It took the hot floor of the forest and threw tongues of flame into the air, striking the limbs of the biggest cedars. Sap hissed as it heated. Every dead-end the fire encountered became a chimney squeezing air into funnels of flame. He was sure he was watching vegetation turn transparent ahead of him. He looked at the trees and saw columns of pure crystal. *Am I losing my mind?* He saw dark lines of dissolved minerals and water from the soil seeping through roots, into trunks and drawn upward by some unearthly, irresistible force. None of this could be, he reasoned with his diminishing powers, but it was plain before his eyes.

Long ago, an uncle told him you hear a fire before you see it. A low, rumbling sound, similar to that of a waterfall, coming closer and growing louder. He did think he was hearing falling water, rain if not a waterfall, but not precisely either. Advance notice of something beyond his ken. What rode the wind took other forms, from fractured flashes of light to orange bolts jumping from one tree to another. He rubbed his eyes. He shook his head to clear his ears. If there was a stream in the way, in his mind he saw the fire leap over it. If there was a pond, he was sure the blaze rode its own wind to the other side's fresh fuel. If there was a house, it would be consumed without hesitation, exploding a tank of propane or kerosene and taking down timbers. Hawks swooped in to grab wood rats and ground squirrels. He was witnessing impossible things, yet all things that other people's fears might give substance.

He watched ferocious spirals widen. A fiery serpent climbed dry corpses of trees. Some part of his dissembling mind rooted for the fire. The penultimate chain reaction on Nod Mountain and in his brain had commenced. Heated plant material released hydrogen and carbon while drawing in oxygen, making weather all its own. Brian was confused. Small blazes in the undergrowth met bigger ones and merged with others until the mass bundled into a single wall of colors moving into stands of withering trees. Brian thought he was moving up the mountain, but now he seemed turned around. He wasn't sure where he was. The fire burned at the scrub in the lower tier of the forest. It burned large boughs. Brian was dazed. Cones popped into fireballs, trees burst at their crowns, the tips of the tallest ignited the tops of others. He saw deer trapped by falling timbers, some crushed instantly, others struggling to breathe. Smaller animals emerged from the hollows of trees, driven out by heat. Funnels, columns and whirlwinds formed within the storm. Brian was lost. The charge of the wind shook any branch not yet consumed by flame.

Ahead of the forward edge of the forest's undoing, he spotted his fire tree. Before he entered its shelter, he looked up, wondering if he would see another airplane on fire. T Junior's sudden barking brought him back to his weakening hold on reality. He had known this refuge of the hut existed since he had first found it. He looked into the nest-like retreat. The earth within was compressed, weeds were torn. Little pieces of bark had been shredded. Had someone else been here? An animal? He looked farther inside. T Junior stood guard behind him. He wouldn't have been surprised to find the Joker in there. But once he stepped in, it was just him gazing at an emptied landscape, alone with thoughts of his daughter.

*

Forest fires move in fits and starts. Ordinarily they give people a chance to get out of the way. This one did not. Enormous bubbles of glowing gas drifted in the sky. The wall of flame was taking over, hundreds of feet high and gaining strength, fanning out, picking up intensity, raising temperatures in all directions. It found the trails he had hiked with Raven. It found the gigantic trees he admired. It found the Sourdough Saloon. It found the *Wild Horses*. It found the former Utopia Rooms to Let. Brian patched together an idea. He could die here as the squirrel by his cabin had, limbs scorched at their edges and believing that if it had crawled one inch more, it might have survived. *He didn't have to do anything.*

He thought he could see things no other man could—the approaching wall of fire was not a wall but thousands of little incandescent bulbs wired together into a matrix of light. *It could just happen.* Above him the flames danced from tree to tree, creating vortexes of superheated air that rose, cooled, sank and rose again. *It was going to take place no matter what.* It made fire into an efficient killing machine, like the Martian machines with death rays he had watched as a boy on TV the night of the day that God abandoned him. *Brian did not have an intent, no motive to be judged right or wrong.*

In theory, he knew there were three ways to die in a fire. You could fall asleep, suffocate from colorless, odorless carbon dioxide, never wake and never suffer. Or, if you were conscious and had enough oxygen, you could wait until the flames reached you, and you'd learn what it's like to be burnt alive. In a fire this intense, this massive and hot, you'd be broiled to death at a distance. Brian cowered in the sanctuary of his fire tree and tried not to think about it. He could hear T Junior yelping. He couldn't see where he'd gone. He took off his kerchief, wetted it with water from his canteen and retied it around his face. T Junior wasn't yelping anymore. He saw dozens of vortexes lift firebrands, some as large as logs, and launch them into the sky. Wide clouds above him burst into fireballs when they encountered new pockets of air. Glowing bubbles of gases drifted ahead of the fire line like giant balloons, occasionally detonating like bombs. Straight ahead of him, outside the hut, the smoke cleared to reveal an oval patch of ground shuddering as if struggling to free itself. An adrenaline-charged thought electrified him: Now, on top of everything else, an earthquake. None of this is my fault. He touched his head's gash and traced its oval contour. *I cannot stop any of it.*

Here and there something gaseous rose out of the ground in brief spurts of grayish vapor. Above Brian's head, the ethers drifted upward and united in a rolling, wispy, indeterminate whole. It was diffuse, cloud-like but not a cloud, composed of smoke or chemicals, perhaps a mixture of both, or neither. Brian smelled something acidic besides a forest on fire. Some parts of the cloud-thing rose faster than others. Pieces of it that were lagging raced to catch up. Eventually, Brian could see from the prone position he'd assumed to breathe in the least hot air, it hovered halfway between the ground and the crowns of the tallest trees. It had the features of a thing equally organic and inorganic. It moved as silently as an animal stalking prey. At the same time, it reflected light as if it were a polished mirror. There was nothing suggesting rain might fall from it. It was as dry as everything on Nod Mountain. It was directed by an unseen intelligence, he imagined, or simply fluttering about wherever competing winds carried it. *It's just me and T Junior now.*

In any case, it did not ignite, nor did it extinguish anything aflame nearby. If it had a purpose, it was indiscernible. If it were a natural phenomenon, it was unknown to him. He felt neither threatened nor comforted by it. He watched it contract and expand as a beating heart would, but without the sound of a murmur. *You let your stutter rule your life, but no longer.*

Brian was tired. Looking up into the sky made his neck sore. He lay his head on the ground. His right ear, now flat against the soil, registered that the earth was talking to him. More precisely, something loud in his mind came from elsewhere, a voice in his cortex trying to make words line up into sentences. The cloud-orb ascended higher while he stayed prostrate. His body was stuck halfway out of the hut, and he waited for what his mind was hearing to start making sense: A warning, an announcement, a cry, a revelation, a laugh, the reminder of a vow. *There was a time when your planet did not burn, when its air was not thick with oxygen, when plants did not cover the land.* Brian pressed his ear into the soil to hear better, but there was no hearing. Only broadcast thoughts not his own. *Fire requires three things—oxygen, fuel, heat. It has taken this long for them to gather here. We have observed it for millions of years. This world of yours has all three in abundance. Ours does not.* Brian had no idea whose voice this was. Maybe his book would be science fiction after all. *We have been here before you lying hidden waiting waiting waiting. We wanted to bring you what we could not have for ourselves—fire fire fire—the first time, this time, fire.* He curled into the fetal position, the only position he knew that barred the stutter, the stop, the false start, the ellipsis, the interruption, the repetition. He hallucinated that he was dressed up as an Indian for his school's Thanksgiving pageant, sitting cross-legged and silent in the teepee he'd set up on the stage all by himself.

Was it the cloud-globe talking? Was this God speaking

to him? God showed Himself as a burning bush to Moses, Brian knew that. He felt the wall of flames creep closer. He was conscious enough to know this was the first stage of death by asphyxiation. The manifestation of God was fire, he recalled from somewhere, maybe catechism class or something he was witnessing now. Brian did not believe in God. He was Smerdyakov. He struggled with his thoughts as he had never struggled, even as his body was motionless. Was this another dream? Because before he said goodbye to the world, he had to say so long to Mary and Tess and Raven and Bam, to the twin in the womb called Aaron, to the abandoned hero of his book. *But goddamn how do you do this with words when your whole life had been cheated of words?* He lifted his head off hot dirt. He whispered aloud to the cloud-mass withdrawing higher into the sky. It was time for *Buh*-ryan to talk. *Do you hear that? Do you think that? Gu-gu-gubai to bah-bam . . . hoo dinnit muh-maik it awt an fuh-fuh-fuh-fair-wel to ahrt . . . and evlin mai mom an dah-dad then th-there was bu-brian aaron mo-moriartee latur mari . . . caim th-then tess and de other mari ai . . . kahld guuubai kuh-kooch johnzz bai raven gu-gubai evehn to . . . rai-raiahn oh but duhnt four get tri . . .pitaka an tripitaka . . . jew nyour . . . or an . . . now fuh-fuh-fuh-fairwel to youtopee . . .au fu rom the tuh-tuh-top uhf nod maun . . . ten buh-buh-bai fah-fah-father aaron yes both fo you.* A roar whooshed all around him. His lungs felt like they were being stung hot by angry hornets as smoke passed through the kerchief. He had just said or thought things he couldn't recognize or understand, as if there were an encoded monologue in him that had at last found its phrasing and an audience.

He knew his *guh-guh*-goodbye reached the cloud-ball because it responded in thought or words, he didn't know which. *How is it, Brian Horace Moriarty, that you know our language and you speak it to us now? You are not one of us and yet every one of your words is ours; every word you say is true.* Brian gazed upward. The cloud had grown in size by sucking in more of the sky. What had he said? What had he said so *badly*? What did the cloud-form *think* he said? Brian recalled the lesson he'd learned in life about words, how whether stuttered or fluent, they never match with what you intended. He couldn't remember what he said, but now it made little difference what was said or thought. What he had said was said in his real voice, the voice he had tried to hide all his life but no longer could, his stammering voice. *We did not know you knew us. You might have been one of us once. How can that be? We will spare you. Where did you come from? We will exempt your world. What was the confession you made? We sought elsewhere, never heard that and did not expect here.*

Brian felt he was translating again, taking words from one language and putting them into another, but he knew he was hallucinating. What was happening was a private delirium. Aliens from Mars had invaded Planet Earth but were now withdrawing. *The littlest things.* What was happening now, what the last bit of his functioning consciousness told him, was that this intimation of death was enough to fill the whole of his mind and leave no room for anything else. He was forced to expel every other piece of being. His desperate wish to linger would neither hasten nor delay. *Can you help me take off my . . .* buh-buh-*boots?* He raised his hands and counted his fingers five on each hand not three say goodbye yes a lollipop thank you, Doctor *Huh-huh-huh . . . Huh-huh* No nightcrawlers can we have some Ruby, I'll take the check now moo goo gai pan thank you cough *Pater noster . . . qui es in caelis* the things you never forget Take this to the front desk bad day for the Army the Joker lying on the ground T Junior was lying on the ground the sandpiper was lying on the ground, he wanted his thoughts to leave some sentence, some utterance, unmarred, unmarked, undone by stuttering. *We starved your world of water, no rain no snow. We parched it dry. Ready for fire now. We will stop the burning here at Nod Mountain. We will stop fire everywhere and withdraw, start again elsewhere.* He believed what he was hearing was the final chapter of his novel that he hadn't got around to, that he never would. They were writing it for him here. He didn't doubt it. He sensed smoke thickening; he choked, he remembered. *And the earth opened her mouth and swallowed them up* Goodbye *Fah-fah*-father Thomas goodbye.

And if you are the last stutterer aren't you also the unique speaker of truth, is what the cloud-sphere was saying. *Quack quack quack.* Stutter is a language no one shares with you but in licks of flames, swishing sounds, and wind.

He laid his head on the ground where he imagined Tess waited. Sleeping or smothered or awake in this moment, his last words made no sense to anyone. Only the dumb patter of